MURDER IN TRANQUILITY PARK

"So this is where you found Jonas's body?" Bruno asked, standing underneath the tree house. "Yes, on our way back from the other side of the park," Jinx replied.

"And when you found him did you see anyone nearby or running from the scene?" Bruno followed up.

"No, it was very early and the park was deserted that morning," Jinx replied. "But Gram did see something inside the tree house when we ran past it the first time."

Bruno's blue eyes lit up. "What did you see, Mrs. Scaglione?"

"First, call me Alberta," she replied. "Second, I'm not exactly sure what I saw. Vinny thinks it was a bird, but I believe it was a person, though I can't prove it."

"Let me set up one possible timeline," Bruno said. "Someone was in the tree house along with Jonas when you entered the park, you and Jinx jogged past, that person pushed Jonas to his death, then jumped out of the tree house himself, or herself for that matter, ran off, and was out of sight by the time the two of you returned to find Jonas's dead body."

"That sounds right to me," Alberta concurred.

"Which means that whoever was in the tree house with Jonas probably saw the two of you run by . . ."

Books by J.D. Griffo

MURDER ON MEMORY LAKE

MURDER IN TRANQUILITY PARK

Published by Kensington Publishing Corporation

MURDER in TRANQUILITY PARK

J.D. Griffo

KENSINGTON PUBLISHING CORP.
www.kensingtonbooks.com

To Jean Dolores—the original J.D. Griffo.
Otherwise known as Mom.

ACKNOWLEDGMENTS

Special thanks to the Cozy Mystery writing community for embracing me with open arms. I also want to thank my agent, Evan Marshall, and the entire team at Kensington Books—the artists, proofreaders, social media experts, and my editor John Scognamiglio—for guiding me through this latest adventure.

CHAPTER 1

Dove c'è la vita, c'è la morte.

There's no place like home.

Alberta repeated those words to herself several times, and while she knew they were true she couldn't believe all of this was hers and that this was her home. How could it be possible? The Cape Cod cottage was traditional, ordinary even with its gray shiplap walls, faded black shutters, and the front door painted a cheerful yellow. But it was the view from her kitchen window that never failed to take her breath away. And it should because it was magnificent.

Parting the yellow and white gingham curtains to get an unrestricted look at the immense body of water that was essentially her backyard, Alberta marveled at the crystal blue water of Memory Lake just as she did most mornings. Undisturbed, the lake looked like a sheet of ice, strong and solemn, its liquidity only apparent when a stray bird flew by and dipped its beak into the water in search of food or when ripples gurgled on the surface, the result of some unknown activity underneath.

The lake was almost entirely surrounded by an array

of trees and bushes in various sizes and multiple shades of green although a few houses, almost identical to Alberta's, popped up here and there along the circumference. None were close enough to disrupt Alberta's solitude, and the houses on the opposite side of the lake were hardly visible due to the distance that separated them and the lush foliage that kept them tucked away from easy sight.

Alberta watched as the morning sun crept up slowly from the horizon to introduce bright yellows and oranges to the cloudless dark blue sky. The view was majestic and it was hers, and yet she still couldn't believe her good fortune. *None of this makes any sense*, she thought, *this has got to be some crazy mistake.*

"Alberta Marie Teresa Ferrara Scaglione," she muttered out loud. "What in the world are you doing here?"

It had been almost six months since she moved into the house on Memory Lake, and Alberta still felt like an intruder. It was as if she was living inside a dream, but not one of her own making, someone else's. Alberta was not someone prone to indulge in fanciful possibilities, of what could happen if all her fantasies came true or if she hit the lottery, so she never imagined she would own a quaint little cottage in a quaint little town overlooking a quaint, but not-so-little, lake. She had assumed she'd be spending her golden years living by herself in a modest-sized condo or among a bunch of other old ladies in a senior citizens building, and she had been fine with those scenarios. Life, however, had other plans for Alberta's future.

Thanks to the very generous inheritance she received from her late Aunt Carmela, instead of looking forward to Bingo games on Tuesday nights, Alberta looked forward to the view from her kitchen window every morning. A part of her kept thinking that she didn't belong here, and the other part kept reminding her that this was exactly where she was supposed to be.

Alberta bent down to scoop up her cat, Lola, whose black fur was the same color as her own hair, although the cat's fur was natural and the shade of Alberta's hair was the product of chemistry, and held her close to her chest so they could both enjoy the scenery.

"My life was supposed to be coming to an end," she whispered into Lola's ear. "It wasn't supposed to be starting over."

But that's exactly what had happened. At the ripe old age of sixty-four, Alberta was surprised to learn that her favorite aunt was a secret multimillionaire and Alberta, for some still unknown reason, her only heir. Just when she thought she was going to have to start watching her pennies and invent new ways to stretch her late husband Sammy's social security and pension checks, she was given a new lease on life thanks to the millions she received from Carmela, not to mention the keys to the cottage at 22 Memory Lake Road in the lakeside enclave of Tranquility, New Jersey.

Alberta had spent joyful summer vacations here with her family as a child, but she never thought she'd return as a homeowner to embark on a whole new chapter of her life. As a widow, she also assumed that she'd have to learn to live life by herself, but ever since she moved to Tranquility the reverse was true. She seemed to be surrounded by more family and friends than ever before.

Her sister, Helen, who recently left the convent where she had been a nun for forty-one years, was now living as a civilian nearby; her sister-in-law, Joyce, who retired from years of working on Wall Street, lived on the other side of the lake; her childhood friend, Vinny D'Angelo, was the chief of police; Lola, who liked to appear aloof and disinterested, was never far from her side; and then there was the *mela dell'occhio,* the apple of Alberta's eye, her granddaughter, Jinx.

After years of being separated, Alberta and Jinx—whose real name was Gina, but thanks to the comical and complicated circumstances surrounding her birth in an Atlantic City casino on Friday the 13th would forever be known by her nickname—had been reunited and their relationship was growing stronger every day. Even when there were a thousand miles between them while Jinx was growing up in Eufala, Florida, of all places, their love for each other never faded, but now that they lived a few minutes from each other, it was in full bloom like the fragrant hydrangeas and honeysuckle flowers that dotted Alberta's property. What was better, and perhaps even more unexpected, was that their respect and curiosity for each other had also blossomed.

At twenty-five, Jinx was at an age when most women wouldn't want to spend the time and energy to get to know an estranged grandparent. Maybe an occasional Sunday afternoon dinner or a mandatory holiday visit to alleviate feelings of guilt and to convince herself that she was being a dutiful granddaughter, but Jinx was different. She, like Alberta, understood the importance of family. The wonderful revelation, however, was that they were both finding out that family members could be linked together not only by blood, but by friendship, too.

Alberta and Jinx liked each other. Alberta admired Jinx's determination to have a career and her willingness to work hard to become the best journalist she could be. She marveled at her fearlessness and the fact that she faced the unknown armed with courage instead of walking down a safer, more familiar path.

Jinx was impressed with Alberta's emotional strength and her devotion to her family and those she loved. She respected the fact that her grandmother embraced the curves life had thrown her and hadn't allowed the past to defeat her, but only became more capable to overcome the next hurdle. And they both adored each other's spunk and senses of humor.

Despite the forty-year age gap and the countless differences in their upbringings, they had so many common interests and beliefs it was as if they had filled out personality questionnaires and a computer chose them to be best friends. On those certain occasions when they didn't see eye-to-eye on a particular topic, they almost always considered it an opportunity to learn something new. Except, of course, when it came to cooking. No matter how many times Jinx had tried to get Alberta to substitute tofu for sausage or incorporate vegan ingredients into her traditional Italian recipes, she'd failed. As Alberta once told her, "Jinx, I love you, but don't make me choose between you and lasagna."

Despite many obvious obstacles, Alberta and Jinx became friends, confidants, and recently with Helen and Joyce as willing sidekicks, partners in solving crime. Much to their joy and surprise as well as the slight embarrassment of Vinny and his police force, Alberta and Jinx, as the leaders and cofounders of the unofficial Ferrara Family Detective Agency, discovered who killed Lucy Agostino, Alberta's childhood nemesis. With that mystery resolved and peace restored to

Tranquility, the women had found yet another unlikely, but equally dangerous way to bond—as jogging partners.

With her sixty-fifth birthday looming only a few weeks away, Alberta realized if time wasn't going to stand still she probably shouldn't either. But when Jinx suggested Alberta join her for her morning runs to lose some weight and adopt a healthier lifestyle, Alberta initially balked.

"There is no way that my fat ass is going to keep up with your skinny legs," Alberta claimed.

"And just how do you think I prevent my skinny legs from being attached to a fat ass?" Jinx replied.

"*O dio mio!* Because you're *bellissima* and young and you can eat whatever you want and not gain a pound," Alberta groused. "I'm an old lady who looks at a bowl of pasta and breaks the scale!"

"If you would eat my no-carb, gluten-free pasta, instead of the unhealthy stuff you insist on making . . ." Jinx began.

"I'd rather run ten miles every day!" Alberta shouted without thinking.

"It's a deal!" Jinx shouted triumphantly.

After some tense negotiations, Alberta agreed to accompany Jinx three mornings a week and jog—not run—a mile and a half from her house, through Tranquility Park and back, as a way to reclaim her health and get back in shape. As an added incentive she had bought herself a new dress in a size smaller than she usually wore, hoping to squeeze into it in time to wear it for the holidays. Even though she now had enough money to waste on buying clothes she would never wear, her frugal nature refused to allow her to buy a dress she would never be able to fit into. Some habits would never change. Old ladies, however, could still learn new tricks.

Alberta noticed the white hairs above Lola's left eye wiggle, a sure sign Jinx was about to arrive. "My coach is right on time per usual," she announced.

Lola squirmed in Alberta's arms when she saw Jinx pass by the kitchen window at precisely six a.m. Punctuality was definitely a trait Jinx inherited from her grandmother.

"Morning, Gram," Jinx announced, entering the kitchen. "Ready to start the week off right?"

Her cheerful nature, however, was not something that had been passed on from grandmother to granddaughter. Alberta's personality fell somewhere in between pessimistic and cautiously optimistic. She wasn't dour or cranky, like her sister, Helen, could be, but she wasn't the cockeyed optimist Jinx was either. She was a realist and this led her to have a more grounded view of the world around her. Being around Jinx meant that her guarded skepticism was starting to soften, but a sense of world-weariness still clung to her, which prohibited her from enjoying events to the fullest. Still, she never failed to smile when Jinx burst into the room. And Lola never failed to leap from Alberta's arms to greet Jinx with a deep purr.

"You want to come running with us, Lola?" Jinx asked, while sitting on the kitchen floor and rubbing the cat's belly.

"Are you *pazzo*?" Alberta asked. "That one's lazier than me."

"You're far from lazy, Gram," Jinx protested. "In no time at all you'll be outpacing me and I'll be struggling to keep up with you."

"*Mamma mia!* You are *pazzo* if you believe that," Alberta said.

While Jinx continued to rub Lola's stomach and under her neck causing the cat to lie flat on her back and purr in sheer ecstasy, she spread her legs into an almost full-on Russian split position and with her free hand grabbed the tip of her left sneaker. Alberta rolled her eyes at her granddaughter's easy display of flexibility and began her own series of pre-jogging stretches.

Raising her arms over her head, Alberta twisted to the right a few times and then to the left, and felt the muscles in her sides and her shoulders reluctantly start to come alive. Clasping her hands in front of her chest, she continued to twist vigorously from side to side and was astonished, yet again, by the miracle that was the sports bra. It really did what the salesgirl had promised it would, her boobs didn't jiggle or bounce despite the quick movements, but stayed firmly in place. She was so glad she let Jinx talk her into buying it, and after a lifetime of wearing bras with painful underwire and straps that cut into her flesh, she couldn't believe how comfortable the thing was either. This new exercise regimen was worth it if only to introduce her to a whole new world of undergarments.

But Alberta forgot how impressed she was with herself when she saw Jinx bend her head forward to rub noses with Lola so her torso lay flat against the floor. It was an ungodly position that Alberta didn't think she was ever able to get into even when she was Jinx's age. She thought about it and couldn't recall anyone trying to contort their bodies into such a position when she was young. Alberta shook her head, a lot had changed since she was Jinx's age, from appropriate physical fitness to appropriate subject matter between a grandmother and granddaughter.

"So how was your date with Mr. McLelland last night?" Jinx asked. "Have you two made out yet?"

"Jinx!" Alberta gasped. "What kind of a question is that?"

"The kind I want an answer to."

"Fuhgettabout it!" Alberta replied, sounding like a New York cab driver. "I am not comfortable talking about such things with you."

Alberta wasn't entirely sure she was comfortable in her relationship with Sloan McLelland, a librarian at the Tranquility Public Library and the unofficial town historian, who had taken her to dinner several times. He was a true gentleman and she enjoyed his company, but it was odd dating a man after forty years of marriage. Even if those forty years of marriage weren't always blissful and idyllic. Alberta felt even less comfortable when she bent over and attempted to touch her toes, but enduring physical pain was better than enduring the conversation Jinx was trying to have. She let her head hang upside down and desperately tried to elongate her fingers so they could reach the edges of her sneakers, but only succeeded in grabbing hold of her shins. Meanwhile, Jinx continued her questioning in an even more inappropriate manner.

"Does that mean that the two of you have done it already?!"

In response to Jinx's question, Alberta raised her head so quickly she got dizzy and had to hold onto the kitchen counter to steady herself. Only when the room stopped spinning was she able to reply.

"That, Signorina Maldonado, is none of your business," Alberta said. "But, of course, the answer is absolutely not. What kind of woman do you take me for?"

"The normal kind."

Standing up, Jinx bent her leg at the knee and grabbed her ankle with her hand, pressing the heel of her foot into her buttock. Alberta tried to mimic the position, but could only manage to bend her leg until it was half a foot away from her own bum. Normally, Jinx would get behind Alberta and coax her into a full stretch, but this morning she was more interested in coaxing her grandmother into spilling the salacious details of her sex life.

Waving her finger at Jinx, Alberta declared, "A normal girl doesn't talk about such personal things, you remember that."

"I don't want all the details," Jinx started, then corrected herself. "That's a lie, actually I do, but I'll take what I can get. I've been patient long enough, Gram, I want to know all about your boyfriend."

"Sloan McLelland isn't my boyfriend!"

"He is, too!"

"He's taken me out to a few dinners, that's all."

"That is so not all!" Jinx contradicted, "He was also your date for the Tranquility Waterfest Aqua Ball. How can you forget such a special event like that? Which, by the way, was your first date."

"So we've gone out to a few dinners . . . *and* the Aqua Ball."

"Which was back in August and it's now October, which means Sloan McLelland is officially your boyfriend."

Alberta had been around Jinx's company long enough now to know that she wasn't going to win the conversation so while she didn't necessarily agree with her granddaughter that she had a boyfriend, she knew that it was futile to convince her otherwise.

"Fine, you win!" Alberta exclaimed. "Your grandmother's got a boyfriend."

"I knew it!"

Jinx squealed so loudly it made Lola run out of the kitchen. Alberta shook her head, but couldn't suppress a smile as she watched Jinx do a happy dance in the middle of her kitchen. Her display of unbridled joy was almost infectious, and if Alberta didn't need to conserve all her energy to run for over a mile, she might have joined in. But she knew that within a few minutes she was going to be huffing and puffing and silently cursing herself for ever agreeing to such a cockamamie scheme, and that if she didn't take control of the situation and get them both out of the house immediately, she was going to flop on the couch next to Lola and watch the morning news shows. Grabbing the bottle of water she wouldn't dare leave behind, Alberta knew it was time to start their workout.

"C'mon, let's defy every law of nature and trick this body of mine into thinking it can do something more stressful than walk," Alberta announced, leading them both out of the house.

"Try to keep up, Alberta," Jinx said as she began to jog in place. "Or should I say the future Mrs. McLelland."

"You listen to me, Jinx!"

But Jinx was already several feet ahead so if Alberta wanted her granddaughter to hear what she had to say she was going to have to pick up the pace. Grumbling, she moved her legs as fast as possible and pumped her arms at her sides, but was still jogging several strides behind Jinx. Alberta sighed heavily and muttered, "I guess it's going to be one of those mornings."

Fifteen minutes later the women trotted through the ornate archway that signified the entrance to Tranquility Park. Over twelve feet high, the black metal structure was a recent addition to the park and designed and built by a local artist. The sides depicted branches that twisted and intertwined with one another and were embellished with leaves, birds, and even a few squirrels. On the top, Tranquility Park was written in script and directly underneath the lettering, at the arch's midpoint, hung a fixture that Jinx had told Alberta was the Chinese symbol for tranquility. It was comprised of a period on top of a horizontal line that had vertical etchings on either ends, and below the line was what looked like a *J*. The individual components of the design were welded together with thin pieces of metal and since it dangled several feet above even the tallest person's head, each element appeared to be floating in space. It was meant to offer tranquility and peace to all who entered the park, which Alberta thought was a lovely sentiment, but the main reason she liked it was because the *J* made her think of Jinx. It also served as a reminder that whenever they jogged underneath it they had hit the halfway mark of their run.

"You should drink some water, Gram."

Jinx made the same comment every time they entered the park, and it always made Alberta smile because it reminded her of the old Italian women from her childhood, who could be counted on to utter the same remark over and over again. In a flash, Alberta was whisked back to Hoboken, New Jersey, and could clearly see Mrs. Esposito, a widow of thirty-some-odd years, leaning out of her second story window, elbows resting on a folded dish towel, yelling, "Careful crossing that street, Berta, the traffic lights are no good over there, no good at all." She said the same thing every single time she saw Alberta headed toward Washington Street, which was at least twice a week, and the words always sounded as if they were being spoken for the first time. Some things really never did change.

Surprisingly Alberta didn't feel the need to hydrate even though it had become habit to take a swig of water when she entered the park. She figured she might as well continue the status quo and take a drink so she wouldn't disappoint her granddaughter. During the pause in their run, she thought it would be a good time to remind Jinx that she also hadn't forgotten their earlier conversation and that Alberta could be just as meddlesome.

"So how's *your* boyfriend, lovey?" Alberta asked.

Unlike Alberta, however, Jinx was delighted to talk about her boyfriend.

"Freddy's wonderful," Jinx shared. "He's smart, sweet, funny, and not preoccupied with sex like most guys his age."

That was a tad more information than Alberta had hoped Jinx would share about Freddy Frangelico, nonetheless, she was relieved to hear that Freddy was respectful. The disclosure, however, made Alberta realize she felt even more uncomfortable talking about her granddaughter's sex life than she was talking about her own, so she deliberately turned away from Jinx to avoid eye contact and took in the scenery.

The park grounds were vibrant, fertile, and not overly manicured so it possessed a hint of an uncivilized landscape. Small enclaves looked like they had been left untouched from before the time the park was built so as to become a window into the town's past; this is what it had looked like before structure and order took over. Alberta didn't remember coming here as a young girl when her family visited the lake area, but she had an idea that it had been more forest than park. It would've been fun to explore the area with her siblings and cousins playing adventurers on the hunt for some hidden treasure. Just as Alberta was about to turn back to Jinx, she discovered that some treasures were lying right out in the open.

About five hundred yards away was something Alberta had never seen before, a tree house tucked into the branches of a very large and presumably very old oak tree.

"Jinx, do you see that over there?"

Looking in Alberta's direction, it took Jinx a few seconds and a few squints to see what her grandmother was referring to. "Looks like a tree house."

"I've never noticed that before, have you?"

"No," Jinx admitted. "Guess I'm too busy listening to music or talking to you to notice my surroundings when I jog through here."

The tree house wasn't large, less than fifty square feet and made out of plywood that was weather-beaten but still in decent condition. There were a few patches of the slanted roof that were threadbare, but otherwise it looked like whoever built the structure used quality materials and knew what he was doing. There was a window next to the front door that Alberta imagined was once adorned with curtains that would blow in the breeze. Now, the window was just an opening that offered a view right into the interior of the tree house.

"Did you see that?!"

"What now?" Jinx asked as she started to jog in place.

"I saw a shadow or something inside the tree house," Alberta said. "Through the window."

"I can't see anything."

"I could've sworn I saw something," Alberta insisted, jogging in place alongside Jinx.

"Probably just a bird living the high life," Jinx surmised. "Can you imagine how roomy that thing must be to some bird family after having to live cramped together in a little bird's nest?"

"Maybe," Alberta said, though she was unconvinced of Jinx's theory.

Alberta felt a tingle in her chest and although it could have been a muscle spasm, her intuition told her Jinx was off the mark.

"Alberta and Sloan sittin' in a tree," Jinx sang.

She was also off-key.

"Ah *cavolo*! You sing worse than you cook."

Laughing, Jinx replied, "That may be true, but I still sing the truth!"

Once again Jinx sprinted ahead and Alberta had to increase her speed if she wanted to keep up with her granddaughter. After about thirty seconds of a fast-paced run, Jinx slowed down her pace dramatically allowing Alberta to pass her by.

"Hurry up, lovey!" Alberta cried. "You don't want to get beat by an old lady."

But Jinx didn't care. She held back knowing, instinctively, that sometimes the old lady was the best person to lead the way.

The women continued to jog around the circumference of the park, and on their way back, Alberta steered them on a slightly different route than the one they usually took so they could wind up directly underneath the tree house. Alberta wasn't sure why, but she wanted to take a closer look. Maybe she found it odd that she had never noticed the tree house before, or maybe it was intriguing to her because she had never seen any kind of tree house up close. There was also a third option: that her earlier intuition was right and she subconsciously knew the house snuggled into the body of the tree was soon to become a crime scene.

Alberta and Jinx stopped in their tracks at the same time when they saw the body lying in the grass just underneath the tree house. There was no reason to search for a pulse because they could tell from the unnatural position the man's body was in that he was dead.

"*Dove c'è la vita, c'è la morte,*" Alberta gasped.

Jinx's Italian was getting better since she had been spending time around her older relatives, who spoke the language fluently, but she was too preoccupied staring at the dead body to translate. "What did you say, Gram?"

"Where there's life, there's death."

Alberta's tingle in her chest hadn't been a muscle spasm. It had been her instinct telling her that death, once again, had disturbed the peaceful town of Tranquility.

CHAPTER 2

Guarda prima di saltare.

"Here we go again!"

Jinx didn't have to say another word for Alberta to understand exactly what she was talking about. They had been in this position before, remarkably just a few months ago, and as unbelievable as it was, history was already repeating itself.

"Another dead body showing up right at your feet, Gram. And I mean *literally* right at your feet."

What were the odds, Alberta thought, that something like this could happen again? And so soon? Weren't there rules according to the laws of the universe that prevented such things from happening? Wasn't stumbling on a dead body once in a person's lifetime enough to fill a quota? Regardless of how much of a long shot it was, there was no denying that Alberta was again the witness to death.

"Please do not tell me that you know this one, too," Jinx said. "That would be way too much of an eerie co-incidence."

Ignoring Jinx, Alberta touched the gold crucifix she always wore around her neck and silently recited the

Hail Mary, her go-to prayer. This time she didn't know the lifeless body lying on the grass in front of her and she had no obvious history with the man, but she still felt a connection. She didn't know who the man was or if he had been Catholic, Jewish, or religious at all, but she knew that every recently departed soul deserved some kind of acknowledgment.

Following Alberta's lead, Jinx bowed her head to add her own silent prayer to the unspoken ceremony. After Alberta kissed her crucifix, Jinx joined her in making the sign of the cross, though she was a few beats behind her grandmother. Still, she had participated and hoped God would understand that she was a bit rusty when executing spiritual formalities. When it came to more material matters, Jinx was much more focused. And yet she still wasn't as quick as her grandmother.

Alberta knelt down to take a closer look at the man's body, and like an obedient student Jinx took the same position on the other side of the corpse. From a distance they resembled experienced professionals objectively conducting a forensic examination instead of the amateur sleuths that they were. But even though they had no formal training, they had plenty of street smarts.

The man looked to be in his sixties, but Alberta sensed that he was younger and only appeared older because he had led a hardscrabble life. She recognized the craggy lines on the sides of the man's face, the splotchy skin, the receding hairline, and especially the thick, red veins decorating his nose. It was all physical evidence that, for whatever reason, the man had not had an easy life.

He reminded Alberta of her Uncle Paolo, her father's older brother. Paolo had the same upbringing as Frank, Alberta's father, the same advantages and disadvantages, and yet the two men couldn't have turned out any different. They both married and had three children, but the comparison stopped there. While Frank was the strong and silent, family-oriented man, Paolo was loud, obnoxious and got even louder and more obnoxious when he drank, which was almost daily. Where Alberta's father died at eighty-two, surrounded by his family, Uncle Paolo died from a stroke a few days after his sixty-first birthday, alone in a neighborhood bar. Alberta would never forget how ancient he looked lying in his casket because no amount of mortician's magic had been able to wipe away the years of self-induced physical trauma.

Looking at this unknown man, Alberta didn't know if his countenance was the result of his own reckless choices or if life simply had been unkind to him. Either way, she could feel the tears well up in her eyes because she understood what it was like to buckle under pressure. She didn't approve of her Uncle Paolo's lifestyle, but she understood what could drive a person to act so irresponsibly.

Alberta shook her head roughly and wiped away a few defiant tears. It wasn't time to contemplate this man's past, whatever that might be, it was time to try and figure out how he had come to his present state. And what a state he was in.

His eyes were closed and his head was twisted to the right so if you looked no further, he appeared to be asleep. From the neck down, unfortunately, he didn't look as restful. His left arm was bent at the elbow with his hand reaching overhead, while his right arm lay limp against his side. His left leg looked normal, but his right must have taken the brunt of the fall as it appeared to be pulled from its socket and was lying almost horizontal from his hip. Improperly, it reminded

Alberta of Jinx stretching on the floor of her kitchen, but she knew that there was no way this man would have been able to achieve that position while he was alive. His flexibility was a result of his death.

But how did he die? Alberta bent closer to the man's face searching for a clue and once again she was overcome by an unwelcome feeling of déjà vu. She couldn't believe that for the second time in only a few months she was face-to-face with a deceased body. And not the preserved, embalmed body on display at a wake, but the raw, untouched body with the kiss of death still fresh on its lips. Leaning back, Alberta examined the face in its entirety and not each individual feature, and she concluded that something was off.

Just as she leaned in closer to get a better look there was a banging so loud that it startled her and Jinx, causing them to gasp at the same time.

"What was that?" they screamed in unison.

Looking around to see who or what was nearby and making such a ruckus, it wasn't until they heard the noise again that they realized it was coming from above. The door to the tree house swung outward and banged a third time against the front wall as it revealed itself to be the culprit. Somehow the door had been opened but never locked. Perhaps that was because the person who unlocked the door was now lying at their feet.

"He must've accidentally fallen out of the tree house?" Jinx surmised.

Alberta looked at the dead body and then up at the door that was still moving to and fro languidly in the now stagnant air and judged Jinx to be right.

"*Guarda prima di saltare.*"

Again, Jinx was confused by the foreign phrase.

This time, however, she didn't have to ask for it to be translated as Alberta could tell by her expression that she was still far from mastering their family's native tongue so she interpreted the phrase into English. "Look before you leap."

Nodding her head, Jinx replied, "That would've been some good advice, *before* he took his final step."

The scenario made sense to Alberta, that the man could've taken a step without looking first and wound up falling to his death. But while it was logical, it didn't feel like the truth, and for some reason, she wasn't fully convinced. She had no reason to suspect there was more to the story, and she wondered if she was allowing her imagination to overpower the facts.

She needed to clear her mind so she tilted her head back and inhaled deeply through her nose. Just when she opened her mouth to release her breath, a black crow flew overhead and screeched loudly, its hard caw echoing through the air.

"Then why didn't we hear him scream?"

"What do you mean?" Jinx asked.

"We weren't that far away so if he screamed, we should've heard him," Alberta explained. "If you were to fall from such a height, wouldn't your natural reaction be to scream?"

"Mine would, at least I think it would," Jinx agreed. "But that doesn't mean everyone would have the same response. I hate to pull the gender card, but a guy might also be less likely to scream than a woman."

For the second time, Alberta had to admit that what Jinx said made sense, but just like before she wasn't buying it. This time when an unexpected wind swept by them she wasn't startled by the sound of the door slamming against the side of the tree house, she was drawn to the potent smell that accompanied the strong breeze. She didn't get a whiff of grass or dirt or even the fragrance of the nearby rose garden, she was overwhelmed by the distinct smell of alcohol.

Making sure not to come into contact with the corpse, Alberta leaned in even closer than before, until she was about an inch from the dead man's face, and looked like she was going to perform mouth-to-mouth resuscitation.

"Gram, that's so gross!" Jinx cried. "What are you doing?"

"Confirming my suspicion."

"That he's really dead?"

"No," Alberta replied. "That he's dead drunk."

Shocked by her grandmother's announcement, Jinx fell back on her haunches. "How in the world did you guess that?"

Shrugging her shoulders, Alberta said, "Some things come with age."

She didn't want to tell Jinx the truth because that would tarnish the image she had of her grandfather, but the fact of the matter was that Sammy Scaglione had liked to drink almost as much as Uncle Paolo. The main difference between the two men was that while Paolo was an indiscriminate alcoholic and would drink whatever was cheap or handy, Sammy's drink of choice was bourbon. Most often he preferred to drink it on the rocks after he got home from work or with his lunch, but he was also known to use it in his morning coffee in lieu of milk. After such a long marriage, Alberta had become familiar with the strong scent, and she could smell it on the dead man's breath. It wasn't pure bourbon though, there was another, sweeter smell mixed in so it was clear to Alberta that the man was more like her uncle than her husband and had been mixing his alcohol.

"So he was probably too drunk to scream when he fell out of the tree house," Jinx concluded.

Probably, Alberta thought, unless the alcohol had some help.

"Where's the ladder?" Alberta asked.

Looking up, Jinx realized her grandmother was right and there was no ladder attached to the tree house where it should have been, either leaning up against the side of the house or hanging from the bottom of the doorframe. It might be easy to fall out of a tree house that doesn't have a ladder, but it would prove incredibly difficult to climb into a tree house without one.

"Oh my God, Gram! It's like you notice everything."

They quickly surveyed the area, but didn't find a ladder or anything that could have been used as one. They also agreed that when they saw the tree house for the first time on their run, they hadn't noticed a ladder so it wasn't as if it was there at one point and then some thief or vandal took it away.

"That's really weird," Jinx said. "I mean there has to be one, otherwise, how else are you going to get inside. Jump?"

Taking a few steps back, Alberta tried to look through the open window, but from the steep angle, she couldn't see anything. "Maybe he pulled the ladder up after him."

"Why would he do that?"

"So nobody else could climb up?"

"He might've wanted to drink alone," Jinx concurred. "But then he got so drunk that when he went to leave he forgot that he had brought up the ladder, took a step, and fell to his death."

Grimacing at the thought, Alberta nodded her head, "That's very possible."

"I think it's more than possible," Jinx stated. "I think that's exactly what happened."

Smiling at her granddaughter, Alberta couldn't help but feel a twinge of disappointment. "Oh, lovey, haven't you learned that things aren't always what they seem at first glance?"

"Seriously, Gram? You think this is more than just an unfortunate accident?"

Staring at the oddly contorted body of the dead man lying on the grass, Alberta didn't have proof, but she knew that this man, whoever he was, had not come to his current situation by accident.

"What I think," Alberta said. "Is that the Ferrara Family Detective Agency has found its next case."

A smile formed on Jinx's face and her eyes grew wide. She knew that her reaction was not appropriate given the circumstances, but she was thrilled to get another chance to flex her investigative journalism muscles.

Seeing the excitement race through her granddaughter's body, Alberta knew that if she didn't intervene immediately Jinx's enthusiasm might get out of control. She needed to prevent her granddaughter from doing another happy dance next to a dead man, getting videotaped by some stranger's cell phone, and then going viral on the Internet, thus, ruining her career before it even got started.

"Before we get ahead of ourselves," Alberta said. "Let's call for backup."

Simultaneously, they each whipped out their cell phones, Jinx's from her arm band and Alberta's from her fanny pack, and called the other members of their team.

"Aunt Joyce!" Jinx shouted, her voice brimming with exhilaration. "We have another case."

"A what?" Joyce asked.

"A case! Another dead body."

"Are you serious?" Joyce replied, her voice filled with shock as well as a tiny bit of excitement.

"Meet me and Gram at the tree house in Tranquility Park and see for yourself," Jinx instructed.

"I'll be right there," Joyce said.

"Wait a second, you know where the tree house is?"

"Of course, I do," Joyce affirmed. "Doesn't everyone?"

"Are *you* serious?" Jinx asked. "I didn't even know the thing existed, and I'm a reporter."

"Don't be too hard on yourself, honey, you haven't lived in the area that long," Joyce said. "Also too, you're young and young people don't spend as much time looking at the sights as you do when you're older."

"If I want to make it as a reporter, I'm going to have to start paying more attention to the world around me," Jinx admitted.

"Until then you have us old ladies to help," Joyce said. "I'm on my way."

At least one Ferrara family member was being cooperative.

"What do you mean you can't leave now?"

Alberta was not having as easy a time convincing her sister to join them at the park as Jinx had with Joyce. True to form, Helen was not being cooperative.

"I'm having breakfast," Helen replied, munching loudly.

"You sound like a cow chomping on a bale of hay!" Alberta yelled. "What the hell are you eating?"

"Eggs Benedict."

"You don't like eggs Benedict."

"I do, too."

"No you don't," Alberta insisted. "I made them last week and you had a bowl of Cheerios instead."

"I don't like *your* eggs Benedict."

Alberta's face looked like someone had just shoved a knife in her back and twisted it several times. Figuratively, her sister did just that.

"Gram . . . are you alright?"

One of the main things Alberta took pride in was her cooking. She freely admitted that she couldn't bake a proper cake if her life depended on it, but when it came to cooking she had a gift. The fact that her sister would deliberately state the opposite was close to blasphemy as far as Alberta was concerned. Thankfully, she understood that Helen was crotchety and often didn't censor her thoughts before speaking so Alberta expected her to say outlandish things. Still, Alberta thought her sister was very close to crossing a line.

"So whose eggs Benedict are you eating?" Alberta asked, as if she was asking her husband who he just spent the night with.

"I'm at Veronica's," Helen replied, still chewing with gusto.

"And who, pray tell, is this Veronica?"

"Veronica's *Diner*," Helen clarified. "Right near St. Winifred's. Which you would know if you went to church more than once a month."

"Don't start that again," Alberta said, clearly not up to having an ecclesiastical debate while standing over a dead body. "Just hurry up and get over here, there's been another . . . death."

"It isn't someone else we know, is it?" Helen asked warily as she put down her fork and clutched the rosary beads that she always kept in the pocket of her skirt.

Looking at the man, Alberta replied, "No, neither of us recognize him. But will you get over here now? The park is going to start to get crowded soon and I want to make sure we have enough time to gather clues before the police get here."

"You're becoming a regular Agatha Christie, aren't you?" Helen quipped.

Alberta knew her sister was ribbing her, but she couldn't help feeling proud. She had spent decades not trusting her instinct or acting on her intuition and instead lived the life that her husband and so many others around her wanted her to live that it felt good to be doing something that she wanted to do on her own terms. Even if that something involved the more gruesome aspects of life.

"I just have to pay and then I'm leaving," Helen advised, nodding at her waitress and moving her fingers across the air in the universal sign that meant, I'm ready for my check.

"Good," Alberta said. "Because we're needed."

After Alberta hung up, her words pounded in her ear. She hadn't thought about them before she spoke, they just tumbled out of her mouth, but they hit her as forcefully as the poor man's body must have hit the ground. The reason she felt drawn to solving murders wasn't only because it was something that brought her closer to Jinx and something that bizarrely brought her family together, it was something that brought closure to those who died. She solved the mystery of who killed Lucy, and she knew that she and her family would find out who killed Tranquility's latest victim.

Because the more she thought about it, the more she was convinced that this was not an accident.

Fueled with confidence, Alberta dialed another number on her cell phone.

"Who are you calling now Gram?"

The person on the other line picked up before Alberta could answer Jinx's question. But when she spoke it was obvious who she was talking to.

"Hello Vinny, it's me."

"Alfie?" Vinny asked, using the nickname he coined for Alberta when they were teenagers by utilizing the first two letters of Alberta's first and last names, *A, l, f,* and *e.* Pronounced as one word, it became Alfie. "You realize it's barely after seven o'clock, right?"

"Sorry about that, but you need to get to Tranquility Park immediately."

"Why? What's going on?"

Alberta glanced at the unmoving body on the ground and replied, "There's been another murder."

CHAPTER 3

Albero della morte.

Alberta had never heard Vinny scream so loudly. She put the phone on speaker so both she and Jinx could hear every angry and off-color word Vinny shouted. Despite the fact that they were being yelled at by the chief of police and there was a dead body less than a foot from their feet, Alberta and Jinx both had to put their hands over their mouths to prevent themselves from laughing out loud. Even the most serious situations could take a ridiculous turn.

"What do you mean there's been another murder?" Vinny's voice shrieked into the otherwise calm early morning atmosphere of Tranquility Park. "Did you see something? Did you see someone get murdered? There hasn't been a murder here in decades and you show up and poof! There's not one murder, but now there's two! What is going on? I mean seriously, what's this all about, Alfie?"

Hearing Vinny reference, albeit unknowingly, the phrase from the famous movie starring Michael Caine as a randy Brit searching for love in all the wrong places was too much for the women and even with their hands over their mouths, their laughter rang through their fingers to conjoin with Vinny's screaming voice and further disturb the peaceful surroundings. The sound didn't bring Vinny any peace either.

"Are you laughing at me, Alfie?"

Forcing herself to turn her laughter into a coughing fit, Alberta replied, "Never! This is serious police business."

Unfortunately, her attempt at a cover-up failed. Although Vinny and Alberta saw very little of each other after graduating from high school, each going their separate ways to pursue their adulthood only to reunite months ago when she moved back to Tranquility, their bond, like so many made during childhood, was strong and everlasting. They knew each other very well and Vinny knew that Alberta was lying.

"First of all, I'll be the judge if this is serious police business because I am still the chief of police!" Vinny bellowed. "And second of all, don't tell me you're not laughing when I can hear you and Jinx yucking it up."

"You got me, Vinny," Alberta replied, her laughter ending for good. "This really is very serious, but I'm sorry . . . your shouting is comical. I think you made some birds fly south for the winter prematurely."

Once again Alberta was impressed with herself. After years of marriage to a man who could fly off the handle at the slightest provocation, whether tipsy or sober, Alberta had developed the skill of saying whatever she thought would appease Sammy, and more often than not what she knew her husband wanted to hear wasn't the truth. Now that Vinny had called her out and her back was against a proverbial wall, she was happy that she hadn't reverted back to her usual practice of saying whatever she thought would make someone happy, but instead told the truth. It was a small victory, but another sign that even at the age of sixty-four she was able to change.

"We're at the tree house in Tranquility Park," Alberta said.

"Right next to the dead body," Jinx added.

Ignoring Jinx's more descriptive remark, Vinny focused on Alberta's comment.

"What are you doing there at this time of the morning?"

"We were jogging through the park and on our way back we saw—"

Before Alberta could finish her sentence, Vinny interrupted. "You were jogging?! What are you trying to do, Alfie? Become Tranquility's next statistic?"

In her mind, Alberta knew that somewhere deep within Vinny's questioning there was concern. But in her heart, Vinny's words resonated differently. She heard what she had heard so many times before, ever since she was a little girl, that someone—and that someone was usually a man—thought she was too fat or too female or too fragile to attempt something new, let alone accomplish a new feat. So when she responded to Vinny's comment, she screamed even louder than Vinny had and did, in fact, disturb some birds in a nearby tree, causing them to fly from their resting place to search for a quieter location.

"I'll have you know that I am in perfect physical condition! Go ask Dr. Del Baglivio!" she yelled. "He told me there's no reason why I can't jog a few mornings every week, and that's just what I'm doing. And what's more, *Vincenzo*, this morning I didn't even get that stitch in my side that I usually get so yes, you *can* teach an old dog a new trick every now and again!"

It was Vinny's turn to laugh. "Alright, alright, Alfie! Don't get your knickers in a twist, I was only concerned that you were pushing yourself too hard."

"Pushing yourself is the only way you can move forward," she replied.

"Just be careful," he warned, then asked, "By the way, are you wearing knickers?"

"No, but I have a bright red sports bra on!" Alberta yelled.

"Size thirty-six C," Jinx shouted.

Shocked that Jinx would offer such personal information, Alberta slapped her on the shoulder and pointed a finger at her. She didn't have to speak a word for Jinx to know that she wasn't happy with her disclosure. But Jinx, as a member of a less-conservative generation unbothered by old-fashioned rules of propriety, didn't think she said anything wrong.

"You should be proud of your bust size, Gram," Jinx said. "Just like you should be proud that you instinctively know this poor guy was murdered and didn't die from an accident."

Jinx's compliment reminded Alberta of why she called Vinny in the first place.

"If you really want to be helpful, you'll get yourself to the tree house in Tranquility Park," Alberta advised. "Because we have another murder to investigate."

And Alberta's comment initiated another round of screaming from her old friend.

"You mean the police department has another murder to investigate!"

"Well, sure, Mr. D'Angelo," Jinx interrupted. "With our help."

"Hey Jinx, if you're trying to sound like you respect me, you should call me chief and not mister!" Vinny yelled. "I know you're just like your grandmother and you think that you can get away with murder because we know each other."

Before either woman could point out Vinny's poor choice of words, he did it himself.

"And yes I know that was a poor choice of words, but I'm short staffed here today and I'm cranky."

"Then stop acting like my sister and get over here before the park gets too crowded," Alberta commanded. "In fact, Helen and Joyce are on their way over so we might have some answers for you by the time you show up."

Alberta disconnected the call but wasn't quick enough, and they heard Vinny shout something about them meddling in official police business. It was probably because Alberta had grown up surrounded by a large, and very loud, extended Italian family, but the shouting didn't bother her. Other than when she felt Vinny was attacking her personally for not being physically fit to jog a mile or so every other day, of course. Otherwise she was used to the loud volume. It's how Italians have communicated for centuries, whether they were angry, happy, or feeling some emotion in between. Even now in her seventh decade she could still hear the cacophony of sounds that accompanied almost every dinner while growing up and the endless high-decibel chatter that lasted throughout every family holiday. She was grateful for the peace and quiet she now had, but there were times when she found herself feeling sentimental for the raucous Sunday dinners of her past.

Jinx, on the other hand, had only experienced a small sampling of the loud Italian family lifestyle before her parents moved her to a very unItalian part of Florida to live, so she was a bit more unnerved by Vinny's reaction.

"I don't think Mr. D'Angelo, I mean Chief D'Angelo, likes us very much," she conceded.

"Oh lovey, don't let the sound of a man's voice fool you, especially an Italian man," Alberta replied. "They yell, that's what they do. Instead, listen to his words."

Jinx was more confused than ever. "I did listen to his words, and it's his words that make me think he doesn't like us very much."

Shaking her head and smiling, Alberta was amazed that as mature as Jinx could be, she was still a baby in so many ways. "That's because you're just listening to the words themselves and not the feeling that lies underneath them," Alberta explained. "Your generation likes to say everything that they feel and think, and they have this crazy need to share every single thing that they do and every thought they have with the entire world because they *think* that what they have to say is so incredibly important. But older people, we sometimes don't always say what we mean, but if you listen hard enough you'll hear what we're trying to say."

Jinx felt as if Alberta had just recited a very moving piece of poetry . . . in Greek. She didn't follow a word of Alberta's insight. "So what exactly was Vinny trying to say?"

"*O dio mio!* That he cares about us and doesn't want anything bad to happen to us so we should stop this crazy detective work before one of us gets hurt."

Amazed, Jinx replied, "You got all of that from his ranting and raving?"

"Sometimes it really does pay to be an old lady," Alberta gathered. "And speaking of one, here comes Joyce."

From a distance, Joyce looked nothing like an old lady and exactly like a runway model. It was only 7:30, but Joyce was perfectly dressed and accessorized, and looked like she was going to attend an early morning business meeting. Having spent so many years working in the male-dominated financial industry, Joyce had learned two things: the importance of always being well dressed and the importance of always appearing feminine. When she was part of the workforce, some women felt the need to confirm and adhere to a no-frills, almost masculine, dress code, but Joyce recognized early on that as a woman, and an African American woman at that, she was going to stand out and be marginalized by her white male colleagues regardless of how conservatively she dressed. And for the first two decades Joyce worked on Wall Street, all of her colleagues were white men so there was very little chance that she was going to blend in.

She hadn't tried to be defiant, only honest to her own fashion sense, so she wore tailored business suits in a bevy of bright colors and always adorned them with jewelry, scarves, and whatever other accessory was trendy at the time. In her retirement she didn't attend many occasions that required her to don a business suit, but whatever she wore she continued to maintain her fashion philosophy.

Walking toward Alberta and Jinx, Joyce was an explosion of color. She wore pink cropped pants and matching pink pumps, a plaid pink and black cape made out of angora wool, and pink leather gloves. Hanging from her ears were her trademark gold hoop earrings.

"Don't you look beautiful, Joyce," Alberta enthused. "I always loved that cape."

"No matter what time of day, Aunt Joyce, you always look like you walked out of a magazine."

"Hopefully *Vogue* and not *AARP!*" Joyce replied. "But look at the two of you! You're the ones who look beautiful."

Surveying their outfits, Alberta commented, "Hon, we're wearing jogging clothes."

"There is nothing more beautiful than a healthy woman!" she cried. "And Berta, I am so proud of you for starting to jog. When you get to our age you cannot take your health for granted."

Alberta nodded in agreement. "You can't take your health for granted at any age. Right there is a perfect example."

Joyce turned to where Alberta was pointing and for the first time noticed the dead man lying on the grass. With just one look she proved that she knew more about him than either Alberta or Jinx who had been in his company far longer.

"Oh, poor Jonas!"

"You know him, Aunt Joyce?"

"Everybody does," she answered. "That's Jonas Harper, he's lived in Tranquility his entire life."

Now that the man had a name, his death took on an even deeper meaning. He was no longer an unknown corpse lying on the ground, he was a man with an identity and, therefore, a history. Sadly, he might have a past, but his future was over. Alberta didn't really know anything more about this man than she had a few moments ago, but somehow hearing his name spoken out loud made the sorrow she felt for him deepen.

"I don't remember ever hearing his name before," Jinx remarked. "Did he do anything important in town?"

"He lived in this town," Joyce chided. "I think that's important enough."

Humbled by Joyce's tone, Jinx attempted to explain her comment. "I didn't mean that he, you know, himself wasn't important, I just meant did he do something that with me being a reporter I should've known about, like was he a councilman or a store owner?"

Alberta grabbed Jinx's hand to calm her. She loved her granddaughter and as independent and adventurous and confident as she was, she was still an inexperienced young girl who had a lot to learn about life. "We know, honey," Alberta said. "But just because you don't know someone's name, doesn't mean they're unimportant."

Before Joyce could explain who Jonas Harper was, Vinny arrived, marching toward the women like he was about to enter the battlefield. Which, in a way, he was.

"Get away from the dead body, ladies," Vinny barked. "I don't want you messing up my crime scene."

"Technically it's our crime scene, Vinny," Alberta affirmed. "We got here first."

Stopping a foot from the women, Vinny raised a finger in the air and was about to unleash another scolding before Alberta defused the situation. "I'm joking. And don't worry, we little ladies haven't touched a thing. Jonas is just the way we found him."

Turning around to face the corpse, Vinny's entire demeanor changed when he saw who was lying on the grass. His shoulders dropped and he let out an audible sigh. Clearly, he also knew who Jonas was and he was greatly affected by seeing his body unmoving on the ground.

For a moment no one spoke a word and allowed Vinny some time to catch his breath and regain his composure. With his hands on his hips and his head bowed, he didn't make the sign of the cross or kiss a crucifix, but Alberta could tell by the way his lips were moving, almost imperceptibly, that he was offering his own prayer for Jonas's soul. More proof that people might be different, but in many ways they're all the same.

"Why didn't you tell me it was Jonas Harper?" Vinny asked, his voice much quieter than it had been earlier.

"We didn't know who it was until Joyce showed up and identified him," Alberta explained.

A strong wind blew by lifting up and ruffling Jonas's untucked shirt. It looked odd to all of them to see activity on a dead man. A dead man, who while living, had his share of demons.

"Jonas worked for the Department of Public Works," Vinny informed. "And among his many duties was taking care of the park."

"Which could easily explain why he's here," Alberta commented. But then she noticed Joyce and Vinny share a quick conspiratorial look and realized that she had been too quick to form an opinion. "Unless there's another reason why he liked to be in the park early in the morning."

"It's hardly a secret," Joyce began. "But Jonas liked to drink a little . . . every now and again."

Smirking at Joyce's attempt to romanticize the recent past, Vinny contradicted her, "Jonas liked to drink period. No way to sugarcoat it, he was a drunk. And a tree house is no place for a drunk."

"*Albero della morte,*" Alberta muttered.

Before Jinx could translate the phrase in her head, Joyce beat her to it. "True, but it's the most beautiful tree of death I've ever seen."

And Joyce was right, the tree *was* beautiful. Its thick trunk measured about eight feet around and at its full height it reached almost twenty feet. Its branches extended from its center like powerful arms greeting the world ready to offer it comfort and protection, and the tree's crown was a robust cluster of leaves, a few still green, but most had already turned a deep orange and yellow. No one knew how old the tree was, but it could definitely be considered mature as some of its roots were exposed above the ground to create a carved, dynamic landscape at its base.

While the women discussed the juxtaposition between something so pretty being the cause of something so ugly, Vinny's tone was getting uglier by the second as he tried to get in touch with his deputy.

"Kichiro! Where the hell are you?" Vinny yelled into his phone.

When he continued to scream and not wait for an answer, it was obvious that he was leaving a voice message and wasn't having a heated conversation. "I need you at the tree house in Tranquility Park, and I need you here now!"

Now this kind of yelling was a reason for concern, Alberta thought. Squabbling among family members even in public was normal Italian fare, but public-display squabbling with coworkers was different. Then again, Alberta reminded herself, cops were a close-knit group of people, the nature of their profession and the need to trust each other implicitly with their lives leads them to create their own family so maybe there wasn't anything peculiar about Vinny's bellowing. Something, however, didn't sound right to Alberta, and once again it wasn't the words Vinny spoke, but how he spoke them.

"Trouble with the underlings, Vin?" she whispered.

"No," Vinny answered immediately. He didn't look at Alberta but was still engrossed in trying to communicate with Kichiro and was texting him, presumably to repeat the message he just left for him on his voice mail. When Vinny was finished, he turned to face the women, and Alberta thought he looked a bit more tired than usual.

"No," he said again, a bit softer this time. "Everything's fine with Kichiro, he's a good man, but lately . . . I don't know, he just hasn't been himself."

A stronger wind blew past them and some of the leaves that had fallen onto the ground became airborne. A few landed on top of Jonas's body, and when Vinny squatted, Alberta thought he was going to remove them, but he only wanted to get a closer look at his friend. "Maybe if Jonas had been a bit more like Kichiro, he wouldn't have gotten himself killed."

"What do you mean?" Jinx asked.

"It doesn't take fancy detective work or a bunch of amateur lady sleuths to see what happened here," Vinny replied. "Jonas was up in the tree house, got drunk, and accidentally fell out. Case closed."

Rolling her eyes and shaking her head, Alberta couldn't believe what she was hearing. "You, Vinny D'Angelo, should know better. Jonas Harper was murdered and we can prove it."

CHAPTER 4

Ciò che sale deve scendere.

Looking at Vinny, Alberta was transported to the past once more and marveled, yet again, how some things never changed.

Almost half a century ago, Alberta had been Vinny's babysitter. Even as a boy, Vinny was respectful, introspective, and quiet, but he was also a man-in-training, which meant from time to time he would rebel and try to undermine Alberta's authority. She would sometimes let him feel as if he won a battle by letting him stay up past his bedtime or have a few more ricotta-cheese cookies, which were his favorite, but most often she reminded him that she was in charge. Good-natured and nonaggressive at heart, Vinny would usually retreat to acting like the quiet, obedient boy he was. But that was then. Now as the chief of police Vinny was used to being the head honcho, and as even-keeled as he could be, he didn't like anyone questioning his rank.

"Let's not get carried away, Alfie," Vinny snapped. "We need to take this one step at a time."

"*Di preciso!*" Alberta exclaimed. "Where are the steps?"

"What?" Vinny asked.

"Ah *madon*! There's no ladder!" Alberta pointed out. "By the way the poor man's body is twisted, he obviously didn't fall from running through the park so he must've fallen out of the tree house."

"We've already established that, Alfie," Vinny stated, his patience growing thin.

"But if there's no ladder," Alberta remarked. "How in the world did he get up into the tree house in order to fall out of it?"

Jinx and Joyce, flanking Alberta on either side, beamed with pride. "Gram's right about that."

The group looked at Jonas's dead body and then up to the door of the tree house in search of an alternative route that could get a man from the ground to about ten feet in the air without the use of a ladder. Unless the person had stilts, was freakishly tall, or had a pet giraffe, the only real possibility would be to climb the tree itself. But that would be a difficult feat for any person and almost impossible if that person were drunk.

"It might be an impossible task for you, Alfie," Vinny claimed. "But not for a guy."

Shocked to hear Vinny utter such a misogynistic statement as fact, Alberta felt a chunk of anger rise up to her throat. Sure, Vinny was a man of a certain age and had spent his career in law enforcement, a male-dominated profession despite the attempts to diversify, but still it was a surprising proclamation. One she was going to enjoy watching her old friend prove.

"Oh really, hot stuff?" Alberta asked. "Why don't you show us how easy it is?"

And just like that, Alberta and Vinny were no longer senior citizens having a conversation but were teenagers having a confrontation. Like most teenagers, Vinny knew that the smart choice would be to apologize and confirm that Alberta was right, but like most teenagers the smartest choices were often the most elusive so instead Vinny succumbed to the peer pressure and accepted the challenge.

"Stand back," he declared, waving his arms so the women would back away from the tree.

"This should be good," Alberta mumbled.

"Even though I was born in a casino, I'm not a betting woman," Jinx announced. "But if I were, I'd put down a C-note on the tree."

"I happen to have one in my purse in case anyone would like to place a bet," Joyce shared.

Vinny shot Jinx and Joyce a glance that spoke volumes about how men feel when being teased by women. It was such a deadly glare it was enough to make Jinx feel bad for making her comment, but not enough to keep Joyce silent.

"Are you wearing your medic alert bracelet, Vinny?"

"Will you all stop jabbering?!" Vinny shouted. "And watch how it's done."

Angry, Vinny slammed his foot onto the trunk of the tree and reached up to grab hold of a bulbous, knotty growth. He took a few seconds to maintain his footing, but when he tried to lift himself up, the growth turned out to be loose bark and he tore it off with his hand. Caught off guard by this unexpected glitch, his body swung to the right, causing him to wobble. He reached out to try and grab the side of the tree, but the trunk was so big that he couldn't make any kind of secure connection and only succeeded in slamming the palm of his hand into the tree. At the same time his foot slipped down the side of the trunk and landed with a thud on the ground.

"Careful," Alberta advised.

Vinny muttered something under his breath that Alberta couldn't understand, but she understood by the look on Vinny's face that he hadn't said, "Thank you."

For his second attempt he took a different approach. Vinny placed his foot onto the tree trunk like he did before, but this time he jumped up to grab hold of a low hanging branch. Less confident after his first failure, Vinny tugged on the branch a few times with his left hand to make sure that it wouldn't break and would hold his weight. When convinced that he wouldn't fall once again, he lifted himself up and started to climb the tree with his feet gripping the sides of the trunk until he was high enough for his right hand to reach another, sturdier-looking branch. So far, so good. Unfortunately, when Vinny lifted his left hand to reach up and grab another branch, his fingers were at least a foot away.

He tried again, this time shifting his weight as far to the left as possible, and while his fingers got a little closer to the branch, he was still unable to grab it. Ignoring the chattering from the women below him, both nervous and nurturing, Vinny swung himself to the left and became airborne, which reminded Alberta of her favorite childhood comic strip—*Tarzan*. Unlike Tarzan, however, Vinny lacked the jungle man's agility and grace, and never made his destination. Unless that destination was to be lying flat on his back on the ground.

"*Ciò che sale deve scendere*," Alberta said.

"Shut up, Alfie," he groaned.

"I have no idea what my grandmother said, but I'm pretty sure it proves our point," Jinx declared. "If you couldn't climb up the tree stone-cold sober, how could Jonas ever have done it drunk?"

"He did prove our point, lovey," Alberta confirmed. "*Ciò che sale deve scendere.* What goes up, must come down."

"Also too, come down hard," Joyce added. "Are you okay, Vinny? Should we call someone?"

"I'm fine," he groaned again, still not moving.

"No you're not, you're just being a *stunod*," Alberta corrected. "You're lucky you didn't get yourself killed like poor Jonas."

Wincing, Vinny rolled onto his side, maneuvered himself onto his knees, and then hoisted himself up into a standing position before replying. "He probably pulled the ladder up after him, but forgot to put it back out when he left."

"I guess that's possible," Alberta acquiesced. "But the only way to know for sure is to get inside the tree house and inspect it ourselves."

Whatever Vinny was going to say in response was interrupted by his ringing cell phone. He looked at his phone and was visibly relieved when he saw the caller's identity. "Kichiro! Where in heaven's name have you been? Wait, I don't have the time, just get yourself to the tree house in Tranquility Park." Vinny was about to end the call, but then shouted one final command, "And bring a ladder!"

Fifteen minutes later, Kichiro entered the park carrying a large, metal ladder under his arm. Behind him holding her pocketbook in the crook of her arm was Helen.

"What do we have here, Vinny?" Helen queried. "Another murder?"

"No," Vinny replied.

"We think so," Joyce said.

"Yes," Alberta and Jinx declared.

"I'm glad to hear we're all in agreement," Helen quipped.

Nodding to the women, Kichiro stopped in his tracks when he saw Jonas's unmoving body. "Oh my God! No!" He was so shaken by the sight that he dropped the back of the ladder and Vinny had to grab the front of it to prevent it from falling to the ground and possibly disrupting the potential crime scene or landing on one of the women's feet.

"I'm sorry, Kich," Vinny apologized. "I should've warned you."

"I . . . I can't believe this," Kichiro stuttered.

"Neither can I," Vinny said, his voice adopting a fatherly tone. "But we have a job to do."

Kichiro only hesitated a moment, but in that moment it was clear that Jonas may have had a rough life, but he had friends. Despite the circumstances, however, Kichiro still had a boss.

"Why didn't you answer your phone when I called?" Vinny whispered.

"Sorry, I-I . . . overslept," Kichiro replied, almost bashful.

"That's a first," Vinny said, sounding as if he didn't entirely believe Kichiro's excuse.

"Yeah, well, it was a rough night," Kichiro confessed.

"It looks it," Jinx interrupted, her voice much louder than the two men. "What happened to your finger?"

Startled, Kichiro didn't immediately know what Jinx was referring to until he lifted up his right arm, the one holding the ladder, and noticed the Band-Aid wrapped around his finger. "Oh this . . . It's nothing," Kichiro answered dismissively. "Just cut myself."

"In that case it must've been a *really* rough night," Jinx said.

As Kichiro followed Vinny's instructions and placed the ladder underneath the tree house door, unfolding it, and locking it in place, Jinx couldn't take her eyes off him. The last time they were standing near a dead body he was animated, even belligerent, and now he was quiet and sullen. Kichiro wasn't acting anything like the pompous, hotheaded cop Jinx, from previous experience, knew him to be. It could be that her journalistic instincts were being honed or that her own inquisitive nature was working overtime, but she believed there was more to Kichiro's story and that he had deliberately left out important facts. She would dwell on that later. Right now Vinny was commanding everyone's attention.

After snapping on a pair of protective gloves, Vinny climbed the ladder with much more speed and dexterity than he had exhibited trying to climb the tree. At the same time a few more policemen arrived, who immediately blocked off the area with yellow police tape to prevent a crowd from interfering with their work. Already, some onlookers walking their dogs in the park and other early-morning joggers had gathered around hoping to get a closer look at the action. Alberta and Jinx looked around and couldn't help feeling a teensy bit superior to the rest of the people since they had VIP access to the event. An event that was about to take an interesting turn.

With Kichiro still at the base of the ladder holding it firmly into position, Vinny positioned himself near the top with each foot one rung above the other. After a pause to make sure that he could maintain his balance without holding onto the ladder with his hands and that the ladder itself wasn't going to shift from not standing on level ground, he leaned his left hand against the tree house wall and with his right turned the door knob to pull the door open. He was momentarily in a precarious position because he had to lean backward in order to open the door fully, and the women let out a collective gasp thinking that history was going to repeat itself and Vinny was going to fall once more onto the ground, knowing that from this higher height he would bruise more than his ego.

When the door was fully open and he could see inside, Vinny shouted, *"Mucca sacra!"* one of his favorite Italianisms since childhood that roughly translated to "Holy cow!"

"What is it, Vinny?" Alberta asked.

"This tree house is more like a love nest," he announced.

Now that he saw the tree house was very likely a hotbed of clues, Vinny remained on the ladder and didn't enter the interior so he wouldn't contaminate it. He offered a commentary of the tree house's contents while taking pictures with his cell phone and described it as containing pillows, a few quilts, an empty Tupperware container, a bottle of wine that looked like pinot grigio, and two glasses.

"I knew I saw someone else in there!" Alberta shouted proudly.

Vinny twisted around so abruptly to face Alberta that Kichiro had to add more pressure to the side rails of the ladder to steady it so his boss wouldn't fall off.

"You saw someone else! Why didn't you say something?"

"It was when we first entered the park, near the archway, so we were a little distance away," Alberta clarified. "I thought it was just a bird."

"You saw two people?" Vinny asked.

Alberta saw that not only were Jinx, Helen, Joyce, and Kichiro staring at her waiting for her to respond, but so too were the other policemen and onlookers. She felt like she was on trial, and while she hadn't placed her hand on a bible and sworn to tell the truth, the whole truth, and nothing but the truth, she knew it wasn't the right time to embroider the facts with possibilities.

"Not exactly," Alberta confessed. "I only saw one shadow and I'm not sure if it was a bird's or a person's . . ."

"Or maybe even a squirrel's," Helen added, not altogether helpfully.

"I would've been able to tell if it was a squirrel, Helen," Alberta scoffed.

"You aren't sure if you saw a man or a blue jay," Helen corrected. "For all we know you saw a squirrel playing house. Rumor has it they love climbing all over trees."

Stepping down from the ladder onto the grass, Vinny shook his head. "You're not helping, ladies."

"No you aren't, Helen," Alberta said, disregarding the fact that Vinny spoke in the plural. "I'm not exactly sure what I saw, but with two glasses and a bottle of wine, Jonas must have had a guest."

"You don't know that, Alfie, and you gotta stop guessing. Sure, we have to follow a hunch every now and again, but police work is mainly following the facts."

"Then can you explain how Jonas climbed up the tree if there wasn't a ladder?" she asked.

"No I can't, not just yet," he admitted. "But Jonas did live in Tranquility his entire life and he worked in the park so he knew the area better than anyone. If there was a way to get up there, he'd know it."

"If I may speak as a woman who dedicated her entire adult life to an organization that deals almost exclusively in hunches and faith," Helen said, referring to the Catholic Church. "Facts aren't always as factual as they may seem, and they often need to be taken with a grain of salt. Or some sacrificial wine."

Wiping a few beads of sweat from his brow, Vinny sighed. "I have no idea what you're saying, Helen."

"Two glasses and a bottle of wine sound more like a romantic getaway than a drunkard's hideaway," she asserted. "So Berta's right and you know it. If Jonas was up there, chances are very good that he wasn't up there alone."

"There's only one problem though," Joyce interjected.

"What would that be?" Helen asked, not thrilled to hear that there was a flaw in her theory.

"Jonas's drink of choice was vodka."

All heads turned to Joyce following her pronouncement. After years of having to prove herself in the corporate world and always having her business judgment questioned because of her gender and the color of her skin and not the validity of her rationale, Joyce was used to being put in the position of having to offer a further explanation to support a claim. This situation was no different.

"Jonas saw me buying a few bottles of flavored vodka once at Luigi's Liquor over in Sparta," Joyce started.

"They have very good prices over there," Helen said.

"How do you know that, Aunt Helen?"

"Father Sal swears by it," she answered. "And if you can't trust a priest about wine, who can you trust?"

Vinny took a deep breath and looked over at Kichiro presumably in search of professional camaraderie, but Kichiro was staring at Jonas's body and lost in thought. Knowing he wasn't going to get the support he needed from his deputy, he turned his sights on trying to corral the chorus of amateur detectives.

"Can you all please shut up so Joyce can continue?" Vinny asked wearily.

"Thank you, Vincent," Joyce said demurely. "Jonas told me that he was something of a vodka connoisseur and that his favorite was butterscotch."

"He had good taste," Helen added. "For a drunk, that is."

Just as one of the medical technicians was about to pull the sheet up to cover Jonas's face, Alberta stopped her. "Hold on a second, please. What's wrong with Jonas's face?"

"Other than the fact that he's dead?" Helen asked.

"Helen!" Alberta chastised. "I'm talking about his nose and his lips. I noticed it before, but it seems to be getting worse."

They all peered closer at Jonas's face and noticed that Alberta was right; there were some physical traits that could simply be the man's ordinary features, postmortem abnormalities, or they could be clues. His nose seemed redder than before and his lips were severely chapped. They all knew that a red, veiny nose was a symptom of alcoholism and not an uncommon physical trait, but the chapped lips were a bit of an anomaly.

"If he was drinking only alcohol and not enough water, he could've gotten dehydrated," Kichiro offered.

It was a simple comment, but again Jinx noticed something strange in the detective's voice. The timber was lower than his usual high-pitched tone, and there was a sadness to it. She quickly corrected herself when she realized that just because she didn't particularly like Kichiro, he did have feelings and his relationship with Jonas might have been more than just professional. The two men could've been friends.

Despite the evident despondency of Vinny and Kichiro because of the death of their friend and Jinx's own sorrow knowing that a human being had lost his life, what she mainly felt was excited at the possibility of solving another murder.

"I think we really might've found our next case, Gram."

"I think so too, lovey," Alberta whispered in Jinx's ear. "But let's not count our chickens before they're hatched."

"You think there's a chance Vinny could be right?"

"A very small chance," Alberta admitted. "But nobody likes a sore winner so let's not say, 'I told you so,' until, of course, we have proof."

As they rolled the stretcher away, Alberta silently added, "Don't worry Jonas, you may not know us, but we'll get to the bottom of how you died. You can count on that."

CHAPTER 5

I morti non rimangono in silenzio.

"To Jonas!"

After Alberta's salute, all four women raised a jelly glass full of butterscotch vodka in the air to celebrate the life of Tranquility's latest fallen resident. They were sitting around Alberta's kitchen table, the canasta cards spread out on the harvest-themed tablecloth, but no one was in the mood to play, not even Helen, who almost always wound up winning each hand. They were more interested in discussing and speculating what the results would be of the preliminary investigation into Jonas's death.

"I agree with Gram, this was no accident."

Joyce wasn't so sure. "I know it's unusual that there wasn't a ladder around, but that in itself doesn't mean there was foul play. I hate to speak ill of the dead, but Jonas could be his own worst enemy."

"Like cousin Patty?" Alberta questioned.

"Exactly," Joyce confirmed.

Since it had been over a decade since Jinx had lived close to the bulk of her relatives, her knowledge of family details and closet-dwelling skeletons was limited, and even the facts that she did remember had become cloudy with age. As the de facto matriarch of the Ferrara clan, Alberta was always looked upon to fill in any gaps in order to educate the younger generation and even to repair the memories of the older, more forgetful, relatives. As much as Alberta wanted to keep moving forward toward the next chapter of her life, she understood the importance of knowing what had come before and was always happy to share her wisdom.

"Food was to cousin Patty, what alcohol was to Jonas," Alberta explained. "It was a crutch, maybe an addiction, though I'm no psychiatrist so what do I know about that?"

"It doesn't take a shrink to know that Patty was obsessed with food, still is," Helen said. "At one time or another we all tried to get her to go on a diet or at least eat healthier, though nothing as insane as the way you eat, Jinx."

"I take that as a compliment, Aunt Helen."

"That's because you've destroyed your taste buds with all that vegan, gluten-free nonsense you insist on eating," Helen remarked. "I even got Patty an appointment with one of those gastric bypass doctors."

Joyce was so surprised to hear this revelation that she almost spit out a mouthful of butterscotch vodka. "You did that?"

"Of course I did that!" Helen snapped. "I don't know why you all think that I'm heartless."

Suppressing a smile, Alberta couldn't help herself from stating the obvious. "Maybe because all you do is yell and criticize."

"It's called 'tough love,' Berta!" Helen yelled as she leaned forward to gather all the stray cards. "If Jesus could bear it from his father, you people can handle it from me."

Although it was apparent that no one was in the mood to play a game of canasta, out of habit Helen started shuffling and then dealing the cards around the table. Absentmindedly, Jinx stroked Lola's fur while the cat napped contentedly in her lap. Until Jinx spoke, the only sounds in the kitchen were Lola's purring, the snapping of the cards, and the water from the faucet as Alberta washed a few dishes that had been left in the sink. "How well did you know Jonas, Aunt Joyce? Other than the flavor of his favorite vodka."

"Not very well, honey," she replied. "Jonas was a loner and kept to himself, but he could address every resident by their first name."

"So he was kind of on the outside looking in," Jinx observed. "Even though he had a front row seat to the show."

"That about sums him up," Joyce confirmed. "He was born and raised in this town, and like I said, I didn't know him very well, but I don't think he traveled farther than New York his entire life."

"That doesn't sound possible," Jinx remarked.

"The most important thing I learned in the convent, Jinxie, is not to judge other people by your own experiences or desires," Helen advised. "What's good for the goose isn't necessarily good for the gander."

"Or the neighbor's dog."

No one responded to Alberta's comment because no one understood it. But in the silence that followed her remark they were able to at least figure out where her non sequitur came from. In the distance they could hear a dog barking. The sound wasn't the gruff, commanding bark of a guard dog or the excited, almost breathy, cry of a dog roughhousing with its owner, it was the annoying yelp of a dog that wanted nothing more than to be noticed. It was also a sound from Alberta's childhood.

"Oh my God, Helen, that sounds just like Bocce."

While arranging the cards she held in her hand in numerical order, Helen tilted her head toward the kitchen window so she could hear the sound better. After a few more yips from the clearly agitated dog filtered into the kitchen, the sound also transported Helen to the past.

"It's not only the same pitch, it's the same rhythm," Helen confirmed. "One bark, then a pause, then two more barks. Always the same, like he was trying to tell us something that we would never understand."

"*Caro signore,* I haven't thought about that dog in years," Alberta reflected.

"Maybe he's come back from the dead to haunt us."

Although they should have been used to it, Helen's blunt comment caught the ladies by surprise. Even Lola propped up in Jinx's lap, raised an eyebrow, and gave Helen a questioning look.

"Um, Aunt Helen, why do you think your childhood pet would return from the grave to haunt you?" Jinx asked.

"Because we were never able to prosecute his murderer and sufficiently avenge his death," Helen replied oh-so-nonchalantly. "That's why."

"Helen, I mean no disrespect when I ask this question, and not to use Lola's namesake in vain," Joyce started. "But Holy Gina Lollobrigida! What are you talking about?"

Both Alberta and Helen were so wrapped up in the emotions of long-ago events that they responded simultaneously, each offering individual snippets of information that when strung together told the story of how their beloved childhood spaniel, Bocce, died.

"Bocce was an angel," Alberta said. "Most beautiful chestnut brown hair."

"Best dog ever," Helen concurred. "But when he got excited, he yelped."

"I loved the sound of his voice."

"Everyone did."

"Except old lady Sanducci."

"'Cause she was evil."

"A regular Eva Braun that one. 'Cept she was Molfetesse."

"She hated Bocce."

"For no reason."

"Said that he ate her tomato plants."

"Bocce hated tomatoes, everybody knew that!"

"We tried to tell her it was the Irish setter from down the block, but she wouldn't believe us."

"She said Irish setters were gentle."

"I said not Winky, that dog was no good."

"No good at all."

"She said she was going to make Bocce pay for ruining her garden."

"We told Daddy, but he wouldn't believe us."

"Then one day when we were at school old lady Sanducci poisoned Bocce."

"We came home and found him dead in the backyard, and I saw that evil woman looking at us through her kitchen window."

"Smiling! She was *smiling*!"

"We could never prove it, but we knew she had murdered Bocce."

"It was written all over his little face."

"That's it!" Alberta screamed, throwing her dishtowel down on the kitchen counter. "Jonas looked just like Bocce!"

Ignoring the requests to explain herself further, Alberta raced to the phone on the kitchen wall and pounded some numbers into the keypad while muttering *I morti non rimangono in silenzio.*

"Amen," Helen replied.

Jinx whispered to Joyce if she understood what the sisters were talking about, but she was just as much in the dark as Jinx was. Noticing their confusion, Helen translated.

"The dead don't stay silent," she translated. "Now, let's see what Bocce has to say for himself."

If they were expecting Alberta to convey a message from Bocce, they were going to have to wait, for she was on a mission and was not going to be disturbed until she could share her thoughts with whoever was on the other end of the line. When Vinny finally picked up his phone, he didn't even get a chance to say hello before Alberta started to speak.

"Vinny! I know why I was so curious about Jonas's red nose and chapped lips. He was poisoned!"

Alberta only paused because Vinny started yelling louder than she had been speaking. He screamed so loud the other women in the room could hear him clearly through the receiver.

"Are you losing your mind, Alfie? First you know Jonas didn't die from an accident, and now you know he was poisoned. How, Alfie? How on God's green earth do you know that?"

"Because he looks the same way Bocce did when he was poisoned by old lady Sanducci!"

"Who?!"

"You remember! Gloria Sanducci, the *vegliarda*, the old crone who lived next door to us in Hoboken. She poisoned Bocce and when we found him dead in the backyard, his nose and lips looked exactly the same way Jonas's did. That's why I was so bothered by it."

The silence on the other end of the line stymied the women. Was it possible Vinny believed Alberta and didn't think she was crazy? The silence continued and just when the suspense became almost too impossible for the women to bear, Alberta placed the phone back in its cradle and conveyed that Vinny was going to order a toxicology report to determine if her suspicions were correct.

Proud that Vinny had taken her seriously, Alberta sat down at the table, took a sip of butterscotch vodka, savoring the sweet taste in her mouth before swallowing, and placed her glass back down in the middle of some uneaten cookies and a pile of cards.

"Now, who wants to play canasta?"

Three days later Alberta and Jinx visited the one place at St. Clare's Hospital they thought they'd never have to step foot in again—the morgue. Since it was Thursday, Helen had her shift as a volunteer at the animal shelter and Joyce had an appointment with a former colleague who wanted to buy a few of her paintings for his daughter's new restaurant so, as a result, only half of the Ferrara Family Detective Agency was greeted by Luke, the orderly, when Vinny escorted them into the, unfortunately, familiar room.

Luke had obviously learned his lesson and looked much more professional than he did the last time he met the ladies. Gone were the earphones and the half-eaten sandwich, and in their place were a small transistor radio playing a soft rock classic from the seventies and a bowl of blueberries and granola. It was like they had entered a time warp.

"Hi, Chief," Luke said when they walked through the door.

"How's it going, Luke?" Vinny asked.

"Just fine, thanks," he replied. "And nice to see you ladies again, too." He quickly realized that the morgue might not be a place where people want to make a repeat visit and added, "Sorry, I guess you're not as happy to see me."

"Nonsense," Alberta said. "It's always nice to see you. Plus, we're only here on business this time and not to identify one of your . . . um, guests."

"That's good news," Luke said. "I know this is no one's favorite place."

Although she was eager to find out whatever she could about how Jonas died, Jinx was not thrilled to be surrounded by death and felt the need to change the subject with some small talk. "What happened to the earphones?"

"One too many people snuck up on me while I was wearing them so it was time to upgrade," he explained.

"To a transistor radio?" she asked incredulously.

"Wi-Fi stinks down here," Luke replied. "So, old school is the new upgrade."

"I think it makes you look more professional," Alberta added. "And I'm happy to see that you're eating healthier, too."

Looking around the morgue impishly, Luke said, "Thought I better improve the old diet before I took up permanent residence around here."

Even though his joke wasn't entirely appropriate, they all understood that in order to keep sane while working in such a profession, not to mention, setting, having a sense of humor was a job requirement.

"What can I do for you?" Luke asked.

"Is Lori around?"

Luke swiveled in his chair to the right and pointed to a door in the far corner of the room. The last time the women were here they didn't even notice there was another door in the room, but then again the last time they were here they also had other things on their mind. "She's right in there, go on in."

"Thanks," Vinny said.

"Keep up the good work, Luke," Alberta said, walking right behind Vinny.

"Thanks, Mrs. Scaglione," he replied, and then added with a wink, "You, too."

Vinny knocked on the door with his knuckles, but before waiting for a reply opened the door and entered a room that looked more like a large supply closet than an office. He held the door open and gestured for Alberta and Jinx to enter, and as they did they both made note of the nameplate on the door. Vinny didn't have to introduce them to the woman sitting behind the desk for them to know that they were barging into the office of Lori LaGuardia, the medical examiner. Turns out Vinny didn't have to introduce Alberta and Jinx to Lori either as she was expecting them.

"Hey Vin," Lori said, getting up from her chair and walking around her desk to greet her visitors. "And this must be Alberta and Jinx."

They all shook hands and, despite herself, Alberta was a bit surprised to see a woman in such an important and, in her opinion, difficult position. She knew that women could be as rational and scientific as men, but she didn't think that they could be as detached. Personally, she couldn't imagine having to cut up a cadaver on a daily basis or simply having to look at and touch dead bodies in order to receive a paycheck. She knew it was an arrogant thought and being a medical examiner was a vital and worthwhile position that suited some people's personalities perfectly, but she just couldn't believe that a woman would want such a job. And she couldn't believe that she could hold such a misogynistic belief after she had felt held down by men all her life. *Ah well,* she thought, *the mind is a complicated thing.*

So was Lori's professional journey.

"Lori was a doctor here at St. Clare's years ago before she was whisked away to Europe by some brilliant scientist," Vinny conveyed.

"That sounds exciting!" Jinx exclaimed.

"It was . . . for a long time," Lori confirmed. "Until my husband, the aforementioned brilliant scientist, starting cheating on me with his lab assistant. All of them actually. And there were quite a lot."

"Oh . . . well, that kind of puts a damper on things," Jinx stammered.

"It did for him," Lori started. "I divorced the slime bag, took him for every cent he was worth, which was a nice chunk of change whether you added it up in euros or American dollars, and moved back here to start my life over. Not a bad way for a fifty-seven-year-old broad to reboot her life if I do say so myself."

"And we couldn't be happier to have her," Vinny added.

"And I couldn't be happier to be here," Lori confirmed.

Despite the smiles plastered on Vinny's and Lori's faces, Alberta detected a dent in the clay, a strain underneath the cheery surface that made the smiles appear unnatural. But when Lori spoke, all of her suspicions were put at ease.

"It's also refreshing to see the chief of police take such a revolutionary approach to solving crime by bringing in some local sleuths who aren't hindered by following all of those pesky police rules and regulations to help fight the good fight," Lori enthused.

In spite of her initial concerns about her job choice, Alberta liked Lori, and it wasn't because of the compliment. She was reminded of what a noble profession Lori was in. Where else could you help right the wrongs of the world and at the same time be disassociated from it. As a medical examiner, Lori could assist in solving crimes or give a family solace as to how a loved one passed away, while never having to make an emotional connection with the prime subject. For a woman recently scorned, it seemed like she had chosen the perfect career. If not the perfect choice of words.

"Thanks a lot, Loretta," Vinny joked.

"No *problemo*, Vincenzo," she replied.

"I'd like to say I keep them on a short leash," Vinny said. "But we all know I'd be lying."

Once the laughter died down, Vinny cleared his throat and plunged into the real reason they had all gathered in Lori's office. "So you said in your text that you got the toxicology report back."

"Yes, came in this morning," Lori said as she reached over and grabbed a file from her desk.

"Did it confirm that Jonas was poisoned?" Alberta asked, unable to wait for Lori to reveal the results.

"It most certainly did," she confirmed.

"I knew it!" Alberta cried.

"That's pretty impressive that you were able to figure that out, Alberta," Lori remarked. "A red nose and chapped lips are hardly telltale signs of poisoning."

"But he was poisoned, right?" Jinx asked.

"Yes, in addition to quite a high level of alcohol poisoning, there were high traces of a pesticide in his bloodstream," Lori described. "I'm not yet sure what kind, but we're doing additional tests to find that out."

Alberta knew nothing about pesticides, but she was curious about alcohol.

"Had he been drinking bourbon?" Alberta asked.

"What are you, Tranquility's version of Shirley Mac-Laine?" Lori asked. "How'd you know that?"

"I have a bit of history with that particular type of liquor," she admitted.

Lori paused and nodded, her expression taking on a more serious demeanor as if she understood what Alberta was saying. "Well, however you figured it out, you're right," Lori confirmed. "Jonas had mainly been drinking lots of white wine, but also some bourbon."

"So what are you going to put on your report as the cause of death?" Vinny asked, even though he already knew the answer.

"The fall may have broken his back, but based on even this partial toxicology and the postmortem blood work, he was dead before he hit the ground," Lori stated. "I'm not sure how the poison got into his system or exactly what type of poison it was, but that's what killed him."

Neither Alberta nor Jinx had to say "I told you so" out loud. The words hung in the air like a blinking neon sign in the middle of a pitch-black night for all to see. Alberta was right, Jonas didn't die from some freak tree house accident. The cause of death was much simpler and far scarier: he was murdered.

CHAPTER 6

Sorpresa!

Upon Lori's announcement the temperature in the office plummeted. It was as if icicles suddenly sprouted from the ceiling to dangle inches from their heads and as if the cheap linoleum floor started to freeze over to become a skating rink. But Alberta wasn't sure if it was because Lori confirmed her suspicions that Jonas had been murdered, or if it had more to do with the icy glares Vinny and Lori were casting in each other's direction. She had been right; their relationship was not as friendly and good-natured as they tried to make it appear.

Maybe it was professional rivalry, Alberta thought. Even though they were both supposed to be fighting on the same side hoping to achieve the same outcome, it wasn't uncommon for one person in such a race to want to cross the finish line first and be the recipient of all the glory. But she had never known Vinny to be competitive or to think of himself before his position. As the chief of police he had made a pledge to achieve justice, not celebrity.

So if it wasn't Vinny initiating the stare down, per-

haps it was Lori. As a divorcée of a certain age returning to her old stomping ground after a long absence, it
was very possible that Lori was hoping to make a name
for herself, and very possible that she would try to do it
at Vinny's expense. Make him look bad in order to
make herself look good. Alberta hadn't been in town
for that long, but she had quickly learned that Vinny
was held in the highest regard by everyone—colleagues, subordinates, and residents alike—so if his
authority and role in the community were suddenly
being challenged by a newcomer, it would be an unfa-
miliar attack and would only be natural that he would
get defensive. It was human nature even for the best of
humans. But as Alberta examined the newest member
of Tranquility's extended law enforcement team closer,
she noticed a flicker in Lori's eyes that was more personal than professional. There wasn't animosity between them, but awkwardness. She couldn't believe
she hadn't noticed it earlier, but unless she was wildly
mistaken, the woman was flirting.

The look hovered in between rascally and kittenish.
It was a clumsy expression, but Alberta figured that
Lori, like herself, was out of practice when it came to
seducing a man with her eyes and trying to capture his
attention while in the presence of others. But admit-
tedly, it also looked odd because Lori, although Alberta hated to even think it, wasn't pretty. At best she
could be described as a handsome woman with deep-
set eyes, a high forehead, and an unfortunate chin. So
when she tried to be flirtatious, if that was even her
goal, she wandered closer to bawdy than sexy and
looked more like a late-in-life Mae West than a nubile
Marilyn Monroe.

Once again Alberta silently scolded herself for judging Lori, first about her chosen profession and then

about her physical appearance. It really was shameful that she would have such an immediate, harsh reaction to a woman she had just met. Wasn't there this thing called "girl power"? And shouldn't women support other women instead of falling into the age-old trap of trying to knock each other down like Krystle and Alexis having a catfight in a lily pond viciously determined for only one to emerge the victor? There should be enough room at the top where all women could stand as a united group, and if they did that, Alberta thought, instead of trying to tear each other down with insults and assumptions like she just did to Lori, maybe they'd finally be able to break through that glass ceiling.

Duly admonished, Alberta thought to herself, *I certainly learned a valuable lesson today.* Then again she may have just fallen into a trap.

"Maybe you should put Alberta on your payroll, Vin," Lori suggested. "She's more astute than most of the cops in this town."

There was that look again in her eyes, but this time Alberta recognized it for what it truly was. Lori wasn't a flirt or an unpolished vixen, she was an instigator, someone who liked to push other people's buttons, a *piantagrane*, kind of like Helen. Whereas Alberta had a lifetime to adjust to Helen's character, Vinny had yet to warm up to Lori's personality.

His forced smile was a rather good indicator that despite his earlier bulletin that Lori had been welcomed into the community with open arms, the novelty of her arrival was already beginning to wear thin. Since Alberta got the distinct impression Vinny was desperately trying to maintain decorum, she felt that it was time for her to voice her approval of Vinny and his staff.

"Thank you, but I think you're giving me too much credit, Lori," Alberta fussed. "We just put in our two cents and follow the lead of Vinny and his team."

"Then it wasn't you who deduced that there was someone else in the tree house who poisoned Jonas and more than likely pushed him out the front door to his death?" Lori inquired, her thick eyebrows arching.

Blushing slightly, Alberta was about to answer when Jinx beat her to it. "Nobody else but my Gram."

Swooshing the air with the back of her hand, Alberta dismissed the idea that she had insight others didn't. "*Sono diventato fortunate.*"

"It was more than luck. You're too modest and you know it," Lori said. "And I think the chief here knows it too, don't you, Vin?"

This time Lori flashed a huge smile and immediately all her features softened. Her appearance didn't magically transform into a Marilyn Monroe at any stage of the icon's life, but she at least got closer to an attractive mid-career Barbara Stanwyck. Alberta couldn't help but notice that Lori didn't wear a stitch of makeup so the dark circles under her eyes and the dry patches of skin on her cheeks and forehead were magnified. Or that she wasn't as obsessed with dyeing her hair like Alberta was so her mousy brown hair fell limply at the top of her broad shoulders and proudly showed off strands of gray at her temples like a man's sideburns. Flaws aside, however, when Lori smiled her homely features faded and revealed a prettier exterior.

And when she threw her head back to laugh at Vinny's apparent discomfort with her comments, she revealed two long horizontal lines on her neck and droopy skin that jiggled as she chuckled. Alberta realized this was a woman who didn't care about outward appearances. She might possess strong, borderline mas-

culine features, but she didn't feel the need to camou-
flage them with expensive products and spend time
each day transforming herself into something she wasn't
and someone the rest of the world expected her to be.
Alberta wanted to applaud her for her self-confidence
and bravery, but instead she just laughed along with
her.

"Looks like you've found yourself a worthy sparring
partner, Vinny."

"Not sure about that, Alberta," Lori said. "I think
you might've beaten me to the punch."

It was Vinny's turn to blush, and Alberta thought it
positively endearing to watch her childhood friend's
face turn a subtle shade of red. Since their relationship was purely platonic, she knew he wasn't turning
colors because of the possibility that they might embark on a romance so it had to be the idea that he and
Lori could be a couple that was making his olive skin
appear sunburnt. There was a thin line between love
and hate after all.

Alberta looked at Lori, who even in her flats was almost five feet ten inches, and then at the over-six-foot
Vinny and decided that they might make a nice pair-
ing after all. She didn't get a chance to do any match-
making because Lori was otherwise engaged. But
luckily with a man who had no pulse.

Lori opened up the toxicology report and flipped
through to the last page. She grabbed a pen from the
pocket of her white lab coat and signed her name to
the report. Alberta noticed her signature also had a
unique style—both *L*'s were large and written in cursive, while the rest of the letters in both her names
were printed.

"Here's the report, Vin," she said, handing over the
file. "Once I get the results from the follow-up tests, I'll

write up an addendum. Now I hafta run. I'm due in Morristown. Their examiner is away at a conference, and they've got a thirty-nine-year-old male on a slab waiting for my gentle touch."

She took off her lab coat and tossed it on top of a filing cabinet in the corner of the room. She then leaned over her desk and grabbed her jacket that was draped over her chair. But when she turned around, her hip accidentally brushed against the blue and white porcelain vase on her desk that contained a small bouquet of white roses—the only personal touch in the otherwise antiseptic room—causing it to slide to the edge of the desk, totter back and forth, and slowly tip over the side. Jinx leaped forward, bent down on one knee, and grabbed the vase just before it was about to crash on the floor.

Lori whipped around to see Jinx holding up the vase almost like an offering to her, and a few tears sprang up to the corners of her eyes.

"Oh my God," Lori gasped. "Thank you so much."

Turning her back to the others, Lori placed the vase back on her desk and fiddled with the flowers for a moment. With her back to her visitors, she said, "Guess I'm not so gentle after all." When she turned back around she was dry eyed and smiling. "Sorry, I've had that vase for years and I'd hate for it to break."

"You don't have to tell me about sentimental value," Alberta said. "I still have the pantyhose I wore on my wedding day tucked away in a box."

"I hope they didn't stay on too long," Lori teased.

The women laughed uproariously, their voices echoing throughout the small room, while Vinny and Jinx merely smiled. Vinny, because he just didn't think the comment was funny and Jinx because she knew Lori made the comment to hide her true feelings.

* * *

Later that afternoon it was Jinx who was trying, unsuccessfully, to hide her true feelings.

"Get ready to wear your big girl pants, Jinx, 'cause you're officially on the varsity squad."

"Could you maybe speak in English and not sports metaphors?" Jinx asked. "You know I don't know my football from my hockey puck."

Wyck Wycknowski, the editor-in-chief of *The Upper Sussex Herald*, and Jinx's boss, frowned. Wyck, whose real name was Troy, but had been known by the shortened version of his last name since the day he was born, brushed some stray strands of his flaming red hair back over his ears and sighed, "That's one of your few faults, Jinx, but I'm willing to overlook it because you have the makings of a fine reporter."

"Thank you, sir," she replied, thrilled by the acknowledgment, but still a bit confused as to why she had been summoned into the boss's office. "Going back to my original question, could you please de-sportify that comment and explain why I need to amend my wardrobe?"

"What? Oh right, of course," he stammered. "Jonas Harper's been murdered."

News really did travel fast in a small town. Good news traveled even faster.

"And I want you to investigate this one."

Jinx couldn't believe her ears. She was actually being handed a murder investigation without having to beg for it. She had planned to tell Wyck about the murder, but she couldn't figure out how to massage the message to include her desire to report on it without appearing mercenary. She also felt it would be a waste of her time since most often the more senior editors like Sylvester Calhoun, her biggest competitor, got to work on the juiciest stories. As the newbie, it was a constant struggle for Jinx to get the chance to write about anything more exciting than shouting matches at the local PTA meetings. She did get to share the byline with Calhoun on some articles about the last murder that took place in Tranquility a few months ago, but since then, she had gone back to her unenviable position as Queen of the Soft News. Wyck was about to change all of that. Unfortunately, with change came some strings.

"Before you start jumping up and down and doing that happy dance thing that you do, I have to warn you," Wyck cautioned. "Calhoun is going to be working the case as well."

"Why?" Jinx protested. "I can do this on my own, you know I can."

Wyck's faced formed into a doubtful half smile. "You're good, Jinx, but you're inexperienced, and the fact of the matter is if you'd look at Calhoun like a mentor instead of your competition you could learn a lot from him."

It was Jinx's turn to smile doubtfully.

"And anyway, Calhoun came to me with the story first so there's no way I can't let him run with it," Wyck disclosed. "His buddy, Luke, at the morgue filled him in on the medical examiner's findings."

"He must've bribed Luke to give him that information," Jinx whined.

"Of course he did!" Wyck confirmed. "You think you can get info like that just by tossing your hair back and smiling?"

"Um, well, yeah," Jinx confessed sheepishly involuntarily tossing her long black wavy hair from side to side.

For the second time in one day Jinx was in a room rippling with laughter while she remained silent. "You got so much to learn, Jinxie, I love it! Trust me, in no time at all, you'll be the one scooping Calhoun."

Deflated, but not entirely depressed, Jinx realized that sharing top billing with Calhoun once again was hardly the worst thing for her career. She had only been a reporter for less than a year, after all, and she reminded herself that sometimes it was important to look at the whole picture and not dwell on the smallest detail. In other words, it was time to party, not sulk.

"Nola!" she screamed into her cell phone. "Tell me you're free tonight, we need to celebrate."

On the other end of the line, Jinx's roommate, Nola Kirkpatrick, was sitting behind her desk at St. Winifred's Academy, marking up a student's essay with her favorite fine-tipped red marker.

"I'm free," Nola said, grabbing a hold of her long blonde hair and twirling it with her fingers. "But what do you want to celebrate?"

"Wyck's letting me be the lead on an investigative story!" Jinx gushed. "Co-lead with Calhoun to be exact, but I'll take it."

"That's wonderful, Jinx, you're really moving up in the world," Nola replied. "What's the story about?"

"That's the sad part . . . there's been another murder."

"Another one!" Nola shouted. "Maybe we should rename this town Cabot Cove."

Jinx rolled her eyes at the reference to the setting of the old TV series *Murder, She Wrote*. Nola also taught theater at St. Winifred's and sometimes she forgot to leave the drama in the classroom. "It isn't that bad and you know it," Jinx said. "Murder is a fact of life."

"Wow! Listen to you. You're already sounding like a hard-boiled reporter," Nola joked. "Lucky for you I can offset your grisly news with some news of my own."

"Really? What's going on with you?!" Jinx yelled. "Tell me! Tell me now!"

Jinx was practically hyperventilating, completely unaware that she sounded even more melodramatic than Nola.

"I've been waiting for the right time to tell you, but I have my own reason to celebrate," Nola confessed. "I have a new boyfriend."

The two girls squealed for about a minute over the news, and Jinx forgot all about Jonas's murder. Instead, she was more consumed with making plans for their celebration tonight, which would simply be dinner at their apartment with their boyfriends.

Later that night sitting on the couch next to her boyfriend, Freddy, Jinx couldn't believe her eyes when Nola opened the door and introduced them to her new boyfriend. If it was possible, Kichiro Miyahara looked even more uncomfortable standing in Jinx's apartment than he did next to Jonas's dead body.

"Surprise," he said impishly when he saw Jinx's jaw drop.

Channeling her grandmother, Jinx replied, "*Sorpresa* indeed!"

CHAPTER 7

In vino veritas.

Jinx was dying to talk to Alberta and her aunts about her recent discovery that Kichiro was not only Vinny's right-hand man, but Nola's new number one guy, but a funeral service wasn't the most appropriate place to gossip. Plus, her grandmother was preoccupied with her own romantic relationship, and Jinx didn't want to interrupt them.

Walking up the steps of Ippolito Stellato's funeral parlor, Jinx held onto her boyfriend Freddy's hand, but her eyes were on another fella entirely. She couldn't help but smile when she saw Sloan place his hand on Alberta's elbow to guide her inside the funeral parlor. Jinx knew her grandmother didn't need his help, but she was thrilled to see that Alberta didn't push his hand away and accepted his touch for the kind gesture that it was. She quickened her pace, dragging Freddy behind her so she could catch up to Alberta and Sloan before they got lost in the crowd. Jonas Harper's wake was jampacked and turning out to be the event of the season.

As Jinx passed her grandmother, she didn't say anything, she merely winked. Alberta knew exactly what Jinx was trying to say—that she wholeheartedly approved of Sloan. And Alberta wholeheartedly agreed.

Sloan McClelland was unlike any other man Alberta had ever known, let alone dated. Not that she had much experience dating since she married Sammy so soon after high school. Still, his intelligence, his cultured air, his physical charms, his non-Italian-ness were all very refreshing to Alberta. She also had to admit that she liked the stares that she was getting from people in the town now that the rumor was bubbling that she and Sloan were a couple. In her heart she wasn't sure how true that was. She enjoyed his company, she found him a delight to talk to, but she didn't know if she wanted another man in her life on a permanent basis. She was just getting to know herself better, and she wasn't sure if she wanted to throw another person into the mix.

If Lola had her way, however, Sloan would move in to the cottage tomorrow.

"Your pants are still covered in cat fur," Alberta noted. "It's seems like Lola's got a crush on you."

"That makes two of us," Sloan said, grinning. "And her mama's not so bad either."

Alberta feigned shock and slapped Sloan playfully on the shoulder, "Don't be such a dirty old man this close to an open casket."

"God will understand," Sloan said, then sighed heavily. "Plus, He's busy right now getting Jonas acclimated to his new home."

That was another thing Alberta liked about Sloan— he was spiritual and wasn't afraid to talk about it. In all the years of her marriage to Sammy, she could only recall a few times when he spoke of God or heaven in a way that wasn't a regurgitation of a bible lesson he remembered from Catholic school or a pithy platitude that he might have seen on a bumper sticker. Come to think of it, she didn't even know what Sammy believed. She assumed because he was Italian Catholic that he subscribed to the theories of the church, but in hindsight she wasn't certain. She had learned more about Sloan's spiritual beliefs and background in the few months she'd known him than she did of her husband after several decades of marriage.

"I hope Jonas finds more peace up there than he ever did down here on earth," Sloan remarked.

"I wonder if he was searching for peace and quiet from this world inside the tree house that night," Alberta commented.

"Possibly," Sloan said. "It was the reason his father built the thing for him in the first place."

"What?" Alberta exclaimed.

She shouted just loud enough so her voice echoed throughout the viewing room and caused most of the people in the nearby vicinity to look around to see who was making such a disrespectful commotion. Not wanting to be pointed out as the culprit, Alberta joined them in looking around and even shook her head and tsk-tsked under her breath as if to chide the guilty party. When the interest from the attendees in finding the loudmouth subsided, she refocused her attention on getting Sloan to elaborate. But this time in a whisper.

"Jonas's father did what?"

"After Jonas's mother died, which happened when Jonas was very young, his father built him the tree house when the park was nothing more than an open plot of land as a sort of refuge because Jonas took his mother's death very hard," Sloan explained. "She died from cancer and it was a long illness."

"Losing your mother so young and having to watch her pass, that's a tragedy," Alberta said, shaking her head in sympathy. "But what a wonderful father."

"Yes, Aaron Harper was a good man," Sloan reminisced. "But Jonas could never get over his mother's death. His father tried, but he could never reach his son."

Before Sloan could elaborate any further, Alberta saw Helen and Joyce sitting on the other side of the room, and Helen was waving them over. Even though they weren't in a church it was always difficult for Alberta to see Helen at a religious ceremony without her being dressed as a nun. It had been almost a year since Helen left the convent, and while Helen seemed to be adapting to a secular life very nicely, Alberta often found herself having a problem accepting her sister's metamorphosis because she didn't know why Helen left the convent in the first place. The only explanation Helen had given was that it was time for a change. Alberta knew there was more to it than that, and it was a mystery she was determined to solve, one that she might focus on once they found Jonas's killer.

The prayers were led by Father Sal, Helen's former colleague and would-be professional nemesis. She didn't hold him in the highest regard, but he did quite a wonderful job and managed to highlight all the positive points of Jonas's life, while circumventing the negatives. He impressed those in attendance, however, by not ignoring the fact that Jonas battled alcoholism for a large portion of his life, but defied every person in the church to think lesser of him. He preached that every person has their demons and, in the end, the only one able to pass judgment of any kind was God.

Alberta looked around and saw many people, including Vinny and Lori, though they were sitting nowhere near each other, nodding or bowing their heads in either prayer for Jonas or as part of their own self-reflection. For all of his flaws, Father Sal was touching the hearts of the community.

"He might turn out to be a decent priest after all," Helen whispered sarcastically to Joyce.

Father Sal was about to gain even more of Helen's praise.

"Thank you all for coming today to celebrate the life of one of our own, Jonas Harper," Sal said. "Due to the police investigation, the church mass and the funeral itself will take place at a later date and will be private, but for now we would like to continue the celebration so please join us at Veronica's Diner where we'll raise a glass of wine in Jonas's honor."

"Well, isn't that a nice surprise," Helen cooed.

Alberta, however, thought that Sal had made a huge faux pas by suggesting that the entire town should raise a glass of wine to celebrate the life of a man who spent so much of his life abusing alcohol, but then she saw by the sea of excited faces that everyone fully condoned the idea. Especially Helen.

"Isn't that thoughtful of Sal," Helen said.

"Also too, it's Saturday."

"What so special about that?" Alberta asked.

"Saturday's dessert is fresh blueberry pie and Helen can't resist."

Arching her eyebrows, Alberta scoffed, "At least it isn't eggs Benedict."

An hour later nestled into a periwinkle blue vinyl

booth at the diner, Helen, Alberta, and Joyce ate their slices of blueberry pie in virtual silence pausing only to sigh contentedly or smack their lips in delight.

"From the sounds you're making, Berta, I can tell you agree," Helen said. "This is one of the best pies you've ever tasted, right?"

"If I could bake a pie half as good as this, I would give that Martha Stewart a run for her money," Alberta said pushing her empty plate into the center of the table to join the others.

"It almost makes me want to give up Entenmann's," Joyce added. "But I think we can agree that Veronica's pies are for special occasions only. Too much of a good thing is no good."

Something on the other side of the diner caught Helen's attention and she didn't respond to Joyce's comment immediately. When she did, all thoughts of pie were gone. In their place were thoughts that weren't as sweet.

"I see something else that's no good," Helen said. "Follow me, ladies."

Confused, but obedient, Alberta and Joyce grabbed their pocketbooks and followed Helen through the crowd until the reason for Helen's sudden departure became apparent. In a corner of the diner Nola was surrounded by a group of teenage girls who mistook the unorthodox funeral service as a field trip. Yes it had been made known that this was to be a celebration and not a dour event, but their loud voices and raucous laughter were definitely out of place.

As the women got closer, the girls' conversation became clearer, and they could hear what the girls said instead of just nondescript, high-volume cackling.

"I'm sorry he's dead and all, but he was such a weirdo," said one girl with thick black eyeliner.

"Right? The way he used to stare was creepy," her friend replied. "Especially at Miss Kirkpatrick, gave me eye cooties."

"I told him once that he should take a picture and that it would last longer," the first girl added. "But I told him that he probably couldn't afford a smart-phone on his salary."

"You didn't!"

"Of course I did! The freak should've known better."

Alberta grabbed Helen's arm because she was certain she was going to slap the girl with the heavy-duty eyeliner in the head with her purse. There was no need for violence, however, as Nola intervened and proved why she was a three-peat for the Teacher of the Year award.

"Kylie, you need to apologize," Nola demanded.

"For what? Telling the truth?" Kylie snapped back.

"For being nasty," Nola said. "Mr. Harper had to work hard for his money because he wasn't lucky enough to be born into a family like yours that owns several international companies and a few hotels. I'm sure your *joke* made him feel like nothing more than a piece of garbage."

Alberta, Helen, and Joyce looked at each other and were impressed by Nola's direct approach and no-nonsense attitude in handling her student. It reminded them of the teachers from their youth, who were much sterner than the ones today. Kylie seemed to appreciate being called out for her mistake as well.

"You're right, Miss Kirkpatrick," she said, her voice no longer haughty, but humble. "I never thought about how it made him feel."

"Now you know," Nola replied.

"I'm sorry, really, I am," Kylie said. "And Jonas wherever you are, I hope you accept my apology."

"That's more like it."

"I do have to say one thing, Miss Kirkpatrick," Jinx said, coming up behind Nola.

"What's that?"

"You really know how to ruin a party."

Laughing, Nola said, "That's what teachers do best."

When the two girls walked away to join their other friends at the ice cream sundae station, Alberta noticed two things about Nola: she deliberately stood with her back to Jinx and her expression changed. Her face dropped, her smile faded, and she took on a much more serious countenance. Could Kylie have spoken the truth about Jonas and was Nola's reprimand merely an act? When Nola saw Alberta her face automatically lit up and Alberta had all the proof she needed that her suspicion was true.

"Mrs. Scaglione," Nola beamed. "So nice to see you . . . even at a time like this."

"I know, honey," Alberta replied, giving Nola a hug. "You remember my sister, Helen, and my sister-in-law, Joyce, don't you?"

"Of course I do," she said, exchanging more hugs. "Jinx here never shuts up about the three of you."

"Because these three fabulous, *stupefacente* women are my idols," Jinx beamed.

Before Alberta could morph from doting grandmother into private detective, Helen interrupted her. "I couldn't help overhear your conversation with those girls," she said. "You handled them like a pro."

"That's sweet of you to say. Jinx told me you spent some time in the trenches teaching as well."

"Feels like a lifetime ago," Helen confirmed. "But I see kids haven't changed. They can still be cruel, but honest. Is what they said about Jonas true? Did he ever cross a line?"

Before Nola spoke a word, her slightly outraged expression told them all they needed to know about Jonas's behavior. Her emphatic and heartfelt veneration told them the rest. "Absolutely not. Jonas was harmless, sure he was a bit off, but who isn't? The kids were doing what kids do, exaggerating and like you said being cruel."

"That answers that question then," Jinx stated. "So the only question remaining is, Why is your boyfriend huddled so close to that woman over there?"

"Boyfriend?" Helen asked.

"Who's got a boyfriend?" Alberta added.

"Also too, *that's* your boyfriend?" Joyce gasped.

All heads snapped to see Kichiro hunched over whispering into the ear of a blonde-haired woman.

"Kichiro Miyahara, Vinny's Kichiro, is your boyfriend?" Alberta questioned. "And you knew about this, Jinx?"

"I just found out," Jinx replied apologetically. "Like almost literally."

Alberta eyed Jinx suspiciously, surprised that her granddaughter would keep such an interesting kernel of juicy gossip a secret. But then, she thought, they were at a memorial service where gossip, juicy or otherwise, wasn't appropriate conversation so she understood Jinx's silence. She didn't understand what she was witnessing, however, and the scene was unusual at best.

Even with her back to them, the woman appeared to be several years older than Kichiro, which only made their intimacy, not to mention the short length of her skirt, look odder. When Nola identified the woman it made things even worse.

"That's my boss," she explained. "Principal Basco."

"*Sharon* Basco?" Joyce asked.

At the mention of her name, the principal spun around. "Joyce Ferrara? Is that really you?"

"In the flesh!"

Joyce and Sharon hugged each other warmly, and Joyce introduced the woman as the principal of St. Winifred's Academy and, therefore, Nola's boss. Joyce continued to explain how Sharon bought some of Joyce's paintings years ago to hang in the school's hallways, which is how they got to know one another.

"Those paintings are yours?" Nola squealed. "They're beautiful."

"They most certainly are," Sharon interjected.

"I always thought they were done by a real artist."

"Nola!" Sharon chided.

"Oh I'm so sorry," Nola said. "I didn't mean to insult you, not at all. I meant, you know, somebody famous and not—"

"Some old lady from town," Joyce finished with a laugh so Nola would know that she didn't inadvertently hurt her feelings.

"Look at me, I'm telling the kids not to be rude and I go ahead and do the exact same thing," Nola confessed. "I feel awful."

"Nonsense," Helen said. "Joyce knows she's old. The only surprise is that people keep buying those things that she paints. I'll never understand it as long as I live."

"What I don't understand is why you and Kichiro were huddled in the corner whispering to each other."

Alberta's comment brought the non-party party to a standstill. Everyone was silent and shocked until Sharon started to crack up laughing. Alberta ignored the sound and focused on Sharon's appearance, which she found to be unnaturally youthful. Curly blonde hair, round face, button nose, shimmering green eyes. The only sign that she was probably in her late forties or maybe even her early fifties was the crepey skin around her neck that wiggled when she laughed. Which she was still doing.

When Sharon finally stopped she explained her conversation with Kichiro was completely innocent and about the only thing they had in common: Nola.

"We overheard Nola reprimanding Kylie and we were both saying how well she defused the situation," Sharon said.

"She sure did," Kichiro added, pushing himself in between Nola and Sharon and putting his arm around Nola's shoulder. "My girl is an incredible teacher in and out of the classroom."

"Unfortunately some of our students are quite immature even though they think they're adults," Sharon conveyed.

When Alberta saw that Helen's brow was wrinkled and her lips pursed, she knew exactly what her sister was thinking because she was thinking the same thing: Sharon was a phony. It wasn't only her appearance that was fake, but also her pronunciation. She pronounced the word "immature" with a soft *t* like imma*tour* and adult with the accent on the first syllable and an *a* like in Alice. Alberta knew her sister as well as Helen knew the bible so she knew that if she didn't put an end to this gathering pronto Helen would make a rude comment they would all regret. Sharon, however, did it for her.

"Joyce is there any chance that you have more paintings I could look at?" Sharon asked. "The school could use some sprucing up, and I think it's time we did some redecorating."

"I have tons of canvases you could choose from,"

Joyce confirmed. "Why don't you pick a day and come over, and I'll give you a private viewing of my collection?"

"That sounds perfect," Sharon cried.

She turned her left hand over to read the watch face on the inside of her wrist and remarked that she had another appointment. She then whipped out her cell phone from her purse and said, "Let's make a date right now." When Sharon huddled next to Joyce as close as she had been to Kichiro, Alberta took it as an opportunity to escape.

"C'mon, sis," Alberta said, locking arms with Helen. "I need a drink."

"After listening to Miss Fancypants talk and fawn all over Joyce like she was Picasso's lovechild, I need a double."

"Lovey," Alberta whispered.

"Yes, Gram?"

"We'll catch up with you later."

"Okay," Jinx said, waving Freddy to join her, Nola, and Kichiro.

Alberta and Helen pushed through the crowd until they joined Sloan and Father Sal at the counter. "Barkeep," Helen barked at Sal. "We need some adult beverages."

They all laughed at Helen's request, but only Alberta laughed at how Helen pronounced the word "adult" as an homage to Sharon's attempt at sounding erudite.

Dutifully, Father Sal walked around the counter and placed four plastic cups onto the surface and proceeded to fill them with red wine.

"Wait a second," Alberta interrupted. "We have to drink white wine because that was Jonas's favorite."

"It most certainly was not," Sal corrected.

"No, I'm sure it was white," Alberta said. "They found a bottle of pinot grigio in the tree house and Lori, she's the new medical examiner, said they found large quantities of alcohol in his system."

"Alberta, I hate to contradict you in front of your new beau, but you're wrong," Sal said. "Jonas Harper was allergic to white wine."

"What?"

"Whenever he would come over to seek my counsel, I had to switch to red," Sal explained. "Now don't get me wrong, I'll drink red wine if that's all the somme-lier has on his menu, as Helen knows I'm much more of a Chardonnay connoisseur. However, red wine is the only kind of wine Jonas would drink because that's the only kind of wine Jonas *could* drink. He was allergic to white wine and if he drank it he got a terrible reac-tion and his face would get all puffy and his lips would get all dry and chapped."

"*In vino veritas,*" Alberta gasped.

"There's more than truth in that wine," Helen added. "There are also allergens."

"You know what else that means?" Sloan asked the group.

"What?" Alberta replied.

"Aaron Harper may have built the tree house for his son, but Aaron Harper's son wasn't the only one using it."

CHAPTER 8

Persone invisibile.

"**M**iss Gina Lollobrigida, get off my table," Alberta commanded. "We're having company."

As expected, Lola completely ignored the directive and remained sprawled out on top of the kitchen table surrounded by canasta cards, jelly glasses, a bottle of fluffy marshmallow vodka, and one of Entenmann's specialty creations, a s'mores coffee cake. She then purred loudly, rolled over onto her back with her front paws overhead looking both comical and obscene.

"Nice way to raise your cat, Berta," Helen said gathering the cards so she could shuffle. "I wonder where she learned that pose."

"Maybe we should call up Mr. McLelland and ask if he finds it familiar?" Jinx joked.

"Ooh, is Sloan tonight's very special guest star?" Joyce asked.

Rolling her eyes at the barbs from her family, Alberta scooped up Lola in her arms and explained, "Sorry to disappoint you all, but I invited Lori over so she could fill us in on the details from the additional toxicology report in person."

"Is she allowed to share that information, Gram, you know, outside of police headquarters or her office?"

"Of course she is," Alberta confirmed. "We are unofficial members of the police force."

"We are?" Helen and Joyce asked at the same time.

"Yes," Alberta replied, her tone adamant. She then added just as adamantly, "But don't tell Vinny."

"Don't you think Lori is going to tell Vinny you invited her over to pump her for classified information?" Helen asked.

"Let's just say I think Lori wants to see the best *woman* solve this crime and stick it to the good old boys' club."

"Reminds me of how I felt in the convent," Helen mused. "I think I like this Lori already."

Just then there was a knock at the kitchen door.

"We're about to find out how much she likes us," Alberta whispered.

Still holding Lola in her arms, Alberta swept from one end of the kitchen to the other like Loretta Young in search of a stairway and opened the door. "Lori! I'm so glad you could make it. Come on in."

Wearing three-inch heels, Lori had to duck before entering the kitchen to make sure she didn't bang her head into the doorjamb. The first thing Alberta noticed, which she regretted immediately, is that Lori didn't look much more attractive in heels, a little makeup, and wearing a tailored black business suit with a cream blouse instead of a white lab coat. But then she flashed that smile of hers and it was like a glaring light went off from somewhere inside of her that showed her real character and distracted from her physical imperfections.

"Thank you so much for inviting me," Lori said standing in the middle of the kitchen and literally towering over Alberta and the rest of the ladies. "After the day I've had this is a real treat."

"Then come inside and make yourself at home," Alberta instructed. "Are you hungry? I can heat up some lasagna. Or we have cake."

"How about both?" Lori suggested. "The only thing I've eaten today were greasy hors d'oeuvres, and I think both lasagna and cake would go with this."

Lori handled Alberta a bottle of vodka that Lola immediately started to scratch. "You don't like root beer, Lola, so hands off," Alberta said.

"Root beer vodka!" Joyce exclaimed. "I don't think we ever tried that flavor."

"I picked it up in Philly today," Lori explained. "I was there as part of a panel discussing proper medical examination procedures when dealing with deadly and contagious pathogens in less than ideal situations."

"That sounds like a fun field trip," Helen joked.

Lori laughed good-naturedly as she kicked off her heels and placed them underneath the bench of the hutch that stood next to the front door. "Actually it was! It makes you appreciate the relative calm and normalcy of real life. Plus, I never met a deadly pathogen I didn't like."

Laughing even louder, Lori sat down between Helen and Joyce as Jinx brought in a chair from the dining room to accommodate the extra seat around the table. Alberta handed off Lola to Jinx and went about preparing a plate of lasagna for Lori. It seemed like it took Alberta longer to microwave the meal than it did for Lori to devour it.

"Ah *cavolo!* That has got to be the best lasagna I've ever tasted in my entire life," Lori proclaimed.

Blushing, Alberta replied, "I'm sure your mother's was just as good."

"My mother was not what you'd call a domestic," Lori shared. "I did a lot of the cooking for us and nothing ever tasted like that."

"Jinx, maybe you should cook for Lori sometime," Helen hinted. "She won't notice there's any difference.

Alberta cleared Lori's empty plate and put it in the sink. She was going to let it sit until later, but out of habit she turned on the faucet and started cleaning.

"So Lori, do you come from a large family?" Alberta asked.

"No," Lori replied. "It's just me and—"

Before she could finish, Joyce interrupted. "Did you grow up in Tranquility?"

Before she could respond, Jinx answered for her. "You did, right? Isn't that what Vinny said?"

Talking loudly to be heard over the running water, Alberta confirmed, "Yes, grew up here, but moved away to Europe when you got married, right?"

Once again Lori was interrupted before she could confirm or deny.

"Ladies! It's like I've time traveled back to the Inquisition," Helen chastised. "Give the woman a chance to breathe and answer the really important question."

"Which is?" Alberta asked washing her hands with a dishtowel.

"What kind of pesticide was Jonas's pinot laced with?"

Alberta laughed and threw the towel down on the kitchen counter. "Holy Anna Maria Alberghetti! I am *pazzo!* With all our kibitzin' I almost forgot."

When Lori spoke again it was like she was a different person. She was precise, articulate, and spoke so quickly that no one could interrupt her even if they wanted to.

"The second toxicology report, unfortunately, came

back inconclusive and we're unable to pinpoint the type of pesticide that was found in Jonas's system," Lori conveyed, "but the results did help us narrow it down to a member of the organophosphate family, which is a common, but deadly, toxin found in readily available pesticides and insecticides. However, even with the final results, we still have to speculate as to how Jonas was poisoned."

Lori stared off into space and took a deep breath before continuing.

"It's hard to tell definitively," Lori cautioned. "But it's very likely that the white wine and the pesticide, whichever one it was, combined together to cause an allergic reaction that resulted in respiratory failure."

"Probably the same way Bocce died," Alberta said as she made the sign of the cross.

"So Father Sal was right," Helen added. "Jonas was allergic to white wine."

"Yes," Lori confirmed. "The report supports that, but Alberta knew it before we did. Impressive work, Mrs. Scaglione."

"Thank you," Alberta said, curtseying slightly. "I understand what killed Jonas, but I don't understand *how* it killed him. Why would he drink wine he knew he was allergic to?"

"Drunks have been known to drink the most outrageous substances when they're desperate," Lori explained. "Rubbing alcohol, cough syrup, hand sanitizer, lemon extract."

"Lemon extract?" Alberta exclaimed. "Grandma used that in her cookies."

Raising her eyebrows, Lori said, "It contains eighty-three percent alcohol."

"No wonder she loved baking so much," Helen remarked.

Ignoring her sister, Alberta continued with her line of questioning. "So, Jonas could have mistakenly drank the pesticide. I mean not for nothing, but as a park custodian he must have had access to products that contained the substance."

"Of course he did, Gram, maybe he mistook some weed killer for his wine."

"That's a bit of a stretch," Joyce said. "It's hard to mistake a bottle of pesticide for a bottle of pinot grigio, don't you think Lori?"

Lori scrunched up her face and shook her head while sipping a glass of fluffy marshmallow vodka. "First of all, it's a tie between root beer and fluffy marshmallow, I'm not sure which one is more delicious. Second of all, you're right, but I've seen it happen before. Alcoholics like all addicts come in many shapes and sizes so not everyone acts the same. Jonas could have been in a blind rage or was so drunk he was hallucinating and downed the first thing he reached for, but not knowing the man I can't rely on his personal habits, I can only focus on the facts."

"And the facts tell you he didn't make a lethal mistake?" Helen asked.

"Correct," Lori replied. "And I come to that conclusion not because I think Jonas was a discerning alcoholic who wouldn't stoop to drinking pesticide if he was desperate for a high, but because of the lack of evidence. There were no traces of the pesticide found in the tree house."

"Not even inside the wine bottle?" Alberta asked.

"None," Lori confirmed.

"What about the glasses?" Jinx asked, holding up her own jelly glass.

"Both glasses were wiped pretty thoroughly so it doesn't take a brain surgeon, or a medical examiner for that matter, to conclude that someone was trying to get rid of any trace of the poison," Lori stated. "But if I had to hazard a guess it would be that before that wipe down only Jonas's glass contained both the wine and the pesticide."

"Which means someone played the role of deadly bartender," Jinx surmised. "Spiked Jonas's wine before he showed up or when he wasn't looking and then left with the pesticide when he fled the scene."

Sighing expressively, Lori agreed, "That's how I see it, too."

"So this is premeditated murder," Alberta said, almost to herself.

The statement and all the ugliness it brought with it lingered in the room for a while. It was as if each woman was trying to figure out a way that it couldn't be true, but failed. If there was pesticide in Jonas's system, but no traces of it in the tree house, he either drank it before he entered the house, or whoever gave him the tainted liquid took the evidence when they left.

"Who could've wanted that poor man dead that badly?" Alberta asked.

"I haven't been back in Tranquility for very long and most of the people I grew up with have moved away," Lori advised. "But did Jonas have any enemies?"

"None as far as I can tell from my investigation."

All heads turned to look at Joyce, who was too busy munching on a piece of s'mores cake to notice how much attention her comment had garnered.

"What do you mean *your* investigation?" Alberta asked.

"I made a few phone calls to some friends," Joyce started.

"You have friends?" Helen asked sarcastically.

"Would you shush?" Alberta scolded. "Joyce, what did you learn?"

"Nothing, that's the problem," she replied. "Jonas wasn't in debt, his credit score was decent, he didn't have a criminal record, and he was never married. At first glance there aren't any red flags in his past or his present to indicate he'd have an enemy."

"He must have done something that ticked someone off," Jinx said.

"Those girls at the diner did say he was creepy," Alberta added. "Though Nola denied it."

Refilling her jelly glass with a combination of both root beer and fluffy marshmallow vodka, Lori suggested, "Maybe you amateur detectives need to investigate the Academy."

"I think you mean *ama-tour*," Alberta corrected.

"What?" Lori asked.

She would have to wait for a reply because the four women laughed hysterically at Alberta's imitation of Sharon. Joyce couldn't resist joining in even though Sharon was a patron of hers.

"Sorry, that woman is going to ruin all her students with her phony airs," Helen remarked.

"Sharon?" Lori said. "The principal?"

"I don't know her very well and I don't like to make fun," Alberta claimed. "But I have to agree with Helen, Sharon acts like her you know what doesn't stink."

"She might also want to dress a bit more age appropriate," Jinx commented. "Did you check out the hemline on the skirt she wore at Jonas's service? A bit high for such an event *and* definitely too high for a woman her age."

"It was more like a handkerchief," Alberta said.

"C'mon," Joyce interjected, "I thought she looked terrific."

A thick silence greeted Joyce's comment, broken only by Helen's shriek.

"For a fifteen-year-old hussy!"

Once again the women erupted into laughter that only ended when Lori accidentally knocked over her jelly glass and spilled vodka all over the table.

"Oh dammit!" Lori shouted, mopping up the spill with some napkins. "Sorry, I'm starting to crash, I must confess it's been a very long day."

"Confess! That's it!" Alberta squealed, uncharacteristically ignoring the mess.

"What do you mean?" Lori asked.

"Jonas might not have done something to get himself killed," Alberta said. "But maybe he knew something that he felt compelled to confess."

"Confess to what?" Joyce asked. "I told you he didn't have a criminal record."

"Maybe not to a serious crime or one that went reported or was uncovered," Alberta explained. "But why else would you have to meet with a priest if not to confess something. And Father Sal said that they met regularly."

No one had to say a word for Helen to know what three out of the four women were thinking. Smirking, she replied, "Don't say it, I need to have a clandestine rendezvous with Father Sal."

"It doesn't have to be secret," Alberta said. "You can do it in broad daylight."

"Well, gee, thanks, sis."

"Don't mention it."

"Jinxie," Helen said. "You know I don't really like Sal so will you come with me?"

"Sure thing, I'll pick you up first thing in the morning," she replied.

"And don't be like Miss Sharon, remember to, you know, dress *appropriately*," Helen said cryptically.

"What? Oh, yeah, right," Jinx said, then two seconds later shouted, "Oh my God!"

"What's wrong?" Alberta asked.

"I just realized that the person Jonas knew, trusted, and murdered him, could very well have been at the service."

The cool evening breeze suddenly turned into a strong wind, and the gingham curtain on the window over the kitchen sink rose and fell against the window screen. Most disturbingly, the small statue of the Blessed Mother that Alberta kept on the window sill next to the photos of her parents and children, and the porcelain Bambi that she had since she was a child, toppled over and fell into the sink. Alberta raced over to the kitchen counter to lower the window and breathed a sigh of relief when she saw that the statue wasn't broken. It was hardly expensive, but symbolic.

Lori joined Alberta and helped her put back the fallen photos and tchotchkes. "It's nice to be able to see loved ones," Lori remarked. "Otherwise we're *persone invisibili*."

"The invisible man?" Jinx questioned, not sure if her translation was accurate.

She was close.

"Invisible people," Alberta said. "What do you mean by that, Lori?"

"For all the people at Jonas's service, did anyone really know him?" she asked rhetorically. "He was on this earth, like the rest of us, but he was hardly noticed until he was killed."

Lori looked out the window and watched the moon reflected on Memory Lake. Alberta thought Lori looked like she was lost in memories of her very own, but like the song said, memories that might be too painful to remember.

"I think it's time for me to go before I have us all crying in our vodka," Lori announced.

"Me too," Jinx said. "Gram could you drive me? Freddy dropped me off here so I don't have my car."

"Nonsense, I'll take you home," Lori said. "Although my Prius isn't as fancy as your grandmother's Mercedes."

"The Mercedes is mine," Joyce corrected. "Berta drives the new baby blue BMW."

"Same color as my eyeglasses," Helen remarked.

"First new car I've had in years," Alberta said. "I thought I might as well live a little."

"Might as well live while you can," Lori said. "Because like Jinx said, somewhere close by, there's a killer among us."

CHAPTER 9

Correre dietro alle farfalle.

Father Sal's office looked the same as the last time Helen and Jinx visited, except this time scattered among the brown leather chesterfield sofa, plush burnt orange rug, and antique mahogany desk were boxes both empty and overflowing. Since Sal was months away from retirement, the mementos and gifts he had accumulated over a lifetime in the priesthood were now encased in bubble wrap and securely resting in boxes anxiously awaiting their new home. Almost as anxiously as Father Sal himself. He loved being a priest, but he loved the prospect of being a retired priest even more. Until then, Helen and Jinx were going to make sure he continued playing the role of informant.

"More wine, Father?" Jinx asked, pouring more Chardonnay into his glass before he even responded.

"Thank you, Sister Maria," Sal said.

Jinx smiled and bowed her head. She felt blasphemous dressing up as a novitiate yet again in Sal's presence, but since she had impersonated one the last

time she and Helen met Sal they both decided they
should err on the side of consistency and continue the
charade so Jinx donned the habit once more. She figured if Helen could ignore her true feelings about Father Sal to pump him for information, the least Jinx
could do was play her part. In costume.

Seeing Father Sal lounging back in his Italian leather
desk chair, Jinx thought he too was wearing a costume
and had decided to show up today as a priest who once
appeared on *The Sopranos*. His jet black hair was con-
spicuously absent of any strands of gray that should
have appeared on the man's head and perfectly
matched the thick frames of his vintage eyeglasses. His
left hand was adorned with two gold rings, one high-
lighting a ruby, the other a sparkling diamond, which
Jinx could tell weren't fakes. And his skin, smooth and
unlined, was either covered in theatrical makeup or
was the result of a few trips to the Botox clinic. Even
though she knew Sal had spent even more years in the
employ of the Catholic Church than Helen had, Jinx
couldn't shake the feeling that he was playacting the
role. As a result she felt a little less guilty that she was
impersonating a woman of the cloth. It was all about a
means to an end anyway, and the quicker she got
there, the quicker she could end the charade.

"Such an excellent vintage, isn't it?" Jinx remarked.

"Yes, quite a good one," Sal answered. "One of my
favorites."

"Speaking of favorites," Helen interrupted. "You
were quite fond of Jonas, weren't you?"

A shadow brushed past Sal's face. "Very much so,"
he said. "I knew him his whole life."

"How long did you know him professionally?" Jinx
asked.

"Oh my, well . . . quite a long time," was all Sal would

say. He took a long drink of wine and finally clarified his vagueness, "Over thirty years at least."

"Such dedication," Helen remarked. "You and he must have had a strong bond."

"We did, unbreakable."

Jinx realized it was time for something to shatter.

"Why did Jonas come to you, Father? Was it for the wine? Or the absolution?"

Sal looked at Jinx as if he knew she was a fraud, but if he did he gave no indication when he spoke. "Some souls are lost and simply ache to be heard. Jonas wanted someone to hear what was in his heart."

"And what was that, Sal?" Helen demanded. "Tell us."

Sal paused for a moment, but it was clear that he, like Jonas, felt the need to be heard. "The age-old illness from time immemorial that poets, scholars, and philosophers have spent untold hours pondering and never really getting close to the miracle. He was in love."

Helen and Jinx exchanged confused glances. There had to be more to it. Jonas wouldn't maintain a thirty-year relationship with a priest just to talk about his love life. Unless there was something corrupt about that love.

"In love with who?" Jinx asked.

"His high school sweetheart."

"Did she love him back?"

"Unfortunately, it was an unrequited affection."

"Does this sweetheart have a name?"

"I'm sure she does, but he never mentioned it to me."

"And you never asked?"

"No, Sister Maria, I never did," Sal replied, appearing to be offended by the very question. "You see when a parishioner needs counseling, it's best to allow the parishioner to lead the conversation. Let them feel that they are in control even when, by their mere presence in a pastor's office, they feel completely out of control."

"Is that how Jonas felt?" Helen inquired. "Out of control?"

The grandfather clock in the corner of the office chimed ten times, and the trio collectively chose silence during the musical pronouncement.

"The heart wants what the heart wants and when the heart is told it can't have what it wants the result can be painful," Sal mused. "It can make you do things you normally wouldn't do."

"What kind of things did Jonas do?" Jinx questioned.

"Don't let your imagination get the best of you, Sister," Sal cautioned. "It isn't like he stalked her or did anything requiring police intervention, he merely sent her flowers."

"A very romantic gesture," Helen remarked.

"The roses were sweet," Sal continued. "It was something he started while he was in high school and he kept it up long after they graduated and long after they were a couple."

"Which now sounds a little less romantic," Jinx added.

"Jonas was trapped in the past," Sal explained. "He would speak of this girl, this woman actually, as if he had just met her or as if they had only returned from their first date, instead of as a woman he'd known for over twenty-five years. I guess it's because they were almost engaged."

"Engaged?" Jinx cried. "Don't you think that's an important piece of the puzzle?"

"It was an engagement in Jonas's mind only," Sal clarified, waving his left hand in the air dismissively, which reminded Jinx of one of Helen's more notorious gestures, except when Helen did it her hand wasn't dripping in jewels. "He never asked the girl for her hand in marriage, he never bought a ring, he only thought that when she returned to town about twenty years ago that this time he would win her hand and they'd be wed. When things didn't work out as he planned . . . well, that's, unfortunately, when things got worse for him and he began to drink even more heavily."

"And never stopped," Jinx added. "Until the day he died."

"Correre dietro alle farfalle," Helen said.

"I have no idea what you just said, Sister . . . I mean *former* Sister Helen, but it sounded beautiful," Jinx remarked.

"To run after butterflies," Helen translated.

"It even sounds beautiful in English," Jinx said.

Smiling, Helen looked at Jinx like she was a little girl taking her first steps into the real world, and in some instances she was just that. She was intelligent and at times could be street smart, but she was, at her core, innocent. She was also wrong.

"The phrase is far from beautiful, but rather tragic," Sal explained. "It means to chase an unrealistic dream. Jonas wasted his entire life chasing after a woman who didn't return his love. So instead of moving forward to find a love he could call his own, he retreated into the past and found solace in the bottle." Sal paused a moment and looked as if his own words had caught him off guard and were more personal than he had intended. "A very common human tragedy that no amount of prayer could rectify."

Prayer might not help, but some good old-fashioned reporting might.

* * *

An hour later Jinx was back in her street clothes at her desk at work rifling through the back issues of *The Herald* searching for any clue she could find about Jonas and his mystery girlfriend. She didn't find his high school sweetheart, but the woman she discovered he was linked to stunned her. The article frightened her so much, she printed it out, and only read it in its entirety when she was safely ensconced in her car.

Jinx couldn't believe that she was reading about a connection she never imagined existed. Several years ago a school teacher took out a restraining order against Jonas because he was harassing her at school.

"Nola?"

Jinx read the article again and unless there was another Nola Kirkpatrick who taught English and drama at St. Winifred's Academy, the article was about her. Which meant that the gossipy goth girls at Jonas's service weren't being gossipy at all, but were telling the truth. And Nola and even Sharon covered up the facts about Jonas's past behavior. But why would they do such a thing?

And why would Freddy be sending me a one-word text, Jinx thought. Since the one word was "urgent," she thought she should reply immediately.

Fifteen minutes later just as Jinx was about to put the key into her front door, it opened. Standing in front of her wasn't her boyfriend, but Nola's. They both appeared disappointed.

"Kichiro, what's wrong?"

Motionless, the detective stood in the doorway with his hands balled into fists. His left one was at his side, but his right was pressed against his lips as if he were contemplating punching himself in the face.

"Nothing, I'm just leaving."

"No, I mean with your finger."

The last time Jinx saw Kichiro at the impromptu celebration dinner for Jinx's new assignment he was still sporting a Band-Aid around his finger from the cut that he endured the night before Jonas was killed. But now the Band-Aid had been replaced with a larger white bandage that covered his entire index finger.

"Oh this," he said.

When it was obvious that he wasn't going to elaborate, Jinx continued her questioning. "Yes that, are you alright?"

"Oh yeah, it's . . . that, that splinter I got, you know it became infected so I had to get some antibiotic cream and need to keep it bandaged."

Jinx was speechless. Not because she was grossed out or felt bad for Kichiro, but because the cop was lying to her.

"You said you cut yourself, now it's a splinter?"

Kichiro didn't say a word, he merely glared at Jinx. Finally when the façade thawed, he looked like his old self, like he did when they first met. It was a relief to see his dismissive glare that said he felt Jinx was a complete moron, at least that was familiar. The quiet, introspective Kichiro she witnessed when they found Jonas's body and the cheerful, upbeat Kichiro, who she had dinner with recently, were alien to her. So while she wasn't thrilled that his eyes were drilling imaginary daggers into her forehead, she was happy to be reunited with the Kichiro she loved to hate.

"Would you knock it off with your fact-checking?" he finally spat. "It's really annoying."

"I can't help it, I'm a reporter, fact-checking's in my blood."

"You're a real reporter, like I'm gonna be chief of police someday," Kichiro said. "It's never gonna happen."

"Do not compare your lack of ambition to my aspirations," she scoffed. "If you want something in this life, Kichiro, you have to go for it."

Kichiro shook his head and his eyes lost all their fire. He seemed to age right in front of Jinx's eyes. "If you believe you can really have something just because you want it, you're stupider than I thought."

Jinx wasn't hurt or upset by Kichiro's comment because it wasn't said in anger, but rather pity. And not for Jinx, but for Kichiro himself. She watched the cop slowly descend the stairs and couldn't help feeling sorry for him. Like Jonas, Kichiro clearly had his own personal demons to contend with; what they were she had no idea, but they were causing him to lie, act differently, and be very un-coplike. Luckily, one man in Jinx's life was behaving consistently and exactly the way she wanted him to.

Just as she stepped into her apartment and closed the front door, Freddy had his arms around Jinx's waist and was nuzzling his mouth against her neck.

"It's about time you got home," he said gruffly.

Jinx turned around and let her keys and bag fall to the floor so she could return the favor. She wrapped her arms around Freddy and allowed his lips to move north from her neck to her mouth. She loved the way he tasted, fresh like the morning rain even in the early evening. She also loved the way he felt, soft lips, smooth skin, strong shoulders, and most of all how his floppy ears felt in between her fingers when she pulled on them.

"Stop it," Freddy giggled. "You're gonna make me look like Dumbo."

"Dumbo was cute," Jinx teased. "Plus, he *was* an elephant."

Pleasantly surprised by Jinx's innuendo, Freddy took her comment to mean that he was going to get an invitation to spend the night. And he probably would have if Nola's crying in the other room didn't spoil their romantic mood.

"What's that?" Jinx asked.

"What else?" Freddy said, rolling his eyes. "She's been crying non-stop."

"Seriously? But Kichiro just left."

"I don't know what's going on between them, but when I came over he was already here and she didn't look happy," Freddy explained. "Then they went in her room and must have had a fight. I had to keep turning up the volume on the TV to shut them out."

"They were fighting?"

"Dude! That's why I texted you," he said. "I couldn't hear exactly what they were saying, but they were loud."

"What do you mean you couldn't hear what they were saying? They were right in the other room."

"I'm only the reporter's boyfriend," he declared. "If you want me to eavesdrop, you have to give me some lessons first."

From the way Jinx looked over at Nola's bedroom door, Freddy knew that he wasn't going to get anything from Jinx tonight other than a raincheck.

"I'm sorry," Jinx said. "I have to get up early anyway. Why don't you plan to come over tomorrow night and we can spend it doing . . . whatever."

Exhaling deeply, Freddy kissed Jinx long and passionately before speaking. "And I'm going to hold you to that offer to do . . . whatever."

"I hope you do," Jinx replied unable to hide a mischievous smile.

After Freddy left, Jinx took several cleansing breaths to expel sultry thoughts of her boyfriend from her mind, picked up her things from the floor, and turned her attention to lifting up her roommate's spirits.

"Hey Nola, it's me, open up," she shouted, knocking on Nola's bedroom door.

It took her roommate almost a minute to obey and when she did it was evident that she had taken the time to wipe her eyes.

"What did Kichiro do?"

Confused, Nola shook her head and said, "He didn't do anything."

"Then why have you been crying?"

Nola's eyes grew wide. Jinx thought for sure that words were going to tumble out of her mouth like they had so many times before and Nola was going to explain exactly what was going on in her life in excruciating detail. But she was wrong and instead Nola swallowed hard and looked away.

"You wouldn't understand."

"Try me," Jinx said. "When have I ever not understood something that's bothering you?"

"This is different."

When Nola tried to shut her bedroom door in her face, Jinx put her arm up and placed her hand on the door pushing it wide open. "Don't lie to me Nola. What did Kichiro do?"

"This has nothing do to with him," Nola stated. "Well, not entirely."

"What's that supposed to mean?"

Stuttering, Nola started to say something, then stopped, then started to cry, and then she started to talk again. Jinx found it frustrating to watch her and even more frustrating to hear her rationale for keeping quiet. "I know you don't like him so just leave it alone."

"This has nothing to do with whether or not I like him, Nola, this has everything to do with the fact that he's made you cry."

"I'm not crying over him!"

"Then why are you crying?"

"Because I'm an idiot! I've been an idiot my entire life and nothing is ever going to change!"

Luckily, the venom associated with Nola's words made Jinx take a step back so when Nola slammed her bedroom door closed, Jinx was a little more than an inch away from getting hit in the face. The last thing she needed was a broken nose considering that her roommate already had a broken heart.

Jinx knew that she wasn't going to be able to make Nola feel better at that moment or divulge any more information as to why she was in such a frantic state. But she would. She also knew that despite what her roommate claimed, Kichiro was very much the reason why she was crying her eyes out. First, Nola defended Jonas for stalking her and now she defended her boyfriend for breaking her heart. An icy shiver ran down Jinx's spine as she asked herself a frightening question: What other secret is my roommate keeping from me?

CHAPTER 10

L'erba è sempre più verde.

Two women, two destinations, one goal: find out why Jonas's secret past as a stalker has been kept hidden.

When Alberta entered the police station, she was alarmed that Vinny was not trying to keep his own feelings secret or hidden.

In the middle of the station, in front of the main desk, Vinny was standing next to Kichiro, and Alberta didn't need to hear a word of what he was saying to his deputy to know the two men were arguing. Vinny was about a half foot taller than Kichiro under normal circumstances, but with Kichiro's head bowed staring down at the black-and-white linoleum tiles and Vinny standing with his chest puffed and arms waving, the difference in their height was exaggerated. Not only that, but once again Kichiro's defiant attitude was subdued, and Vinny, who despite his role as chief of police was not known to capitalize on his position of authority and throw his power around, looked furious. The anger in Vinny's voice matched his posturing.

"What is wrong with you lately?" Vinny shouted.

"I'm sorry, Chief," Kichiro mumbled.

"I'm tired of hearing you say, 'I'm sorry.' I want an explanation! What is going on? And don't tell me you didn't get enough sleep again and you're tired because I don't buy it!"

Aware that he was being stared at not only by Alberta but the rest of his colleagues on the police force, Kichiro's cheeks turned red, and he gazed with even deeper intensity at the floor. He was staring so intently, Alberta expected lasers to fly out of his eyes and dig a tunnel in the floor, creating an escape route. The lasers didn't come, but the tears did. And no one expected them, least of all Kichiro.

The young detective wiped his eyes so furiously it was as if he was smacking his tears like a desperate father might smack an unruly child on his backside to get him to be quiet. Something was definitely going on with Kichiro, and it had nothing to do with a few sleepless nights. Vinny didn't notice or, more likely, comprehend, what was going on until midway through his next tirade.

"You've been late, unresponsive, unfocused!" Vinny yelled. "It's like you've forgotten how to do your job. And I just can't. . . What the . . . ?"

Seeing Kichiro cry made matters worse. Vinny was stunned to watch Kichiro hold his hands against his face for a few moments and breathe deeply. The rest of the police officers in the room tried to act as if they didn't notice the scene unfolding a few feet in front of them, but it was impossible. They saw it, but like Vinny, they didn't understand it. Alberta felt that Kichiro didn't understand it either. Finally, Kichiro dropped his hands to his side and raised his gaze higher than the floor. He couldn't meet Vinny's eyes, but at least he was now focusing on his shoulder.

"I-I'm just going through some personal stuff," Kichiro said with quiet honesty.

Thankfully, Vinny had not changed much from the person Alberta remembered him to be and was still a kind man, and not someone who kicked another when he was down.

"Why don't you take some time off?" Vinny suggested, his voice decibels lower. "To work through whatever it is you need to work through."

Perhaps it was the combination of the fatherly tone of his voice or the kindness of his words, but whatever the reason, Kichiro finally had the strength to look Vinny in the eye. What Alberta saw in Kichiro's eyes when he did broke her heart because she had seen that look in the mirror before. It was the look of someone who needed help but didn't have the courage to ask for it.

"Thank you," Kichiro said. "But I'll be fine."

Unconvinced, but unwilling to push the subject while an audience was still gathered, Vinny replied, "Good. Now get back to work."

Kichiro stared at Vinny, and Alberta thought he was about to tell the truth of what was going on inside his mind, but instead he nodded his head and started to walk into the bowels of the building. As he passed by, Vinny patted him on the shoulder, and it was more than a reflex, more than a mindless gesture, it told Kichiro that he wasn't alone and that Vinny would be around whenever he was ready to talk.

When Alberta waved at Vinny, she could tell by his expression that he didn't feel like talking to her, but despite the scene she just witnessed, she wasn't going to take no for an answer.

"I'm sorry to barge in here like this, but I need to talk to you."

"If I ask you to come back later, I assume you're going to tell me you can't wait and what you have to tell me is of the utmost importance."

"I might not have used those exact words," Alberta hedged. "But the gist of it would be the same."

Vinny frowned, let out a deep breath, and said, "Follow me."

At least he isn't afraid to show his true feelings to me, Alberta thought.

Vinny closed the door to his office behind them and put out a hand indicating that Alberta should take a seat in the one chair on the other side of his desk. It was faux leather in a sandy brown color with chrome piping that had seen a better day. He plopped into his slightly larger, but equally outdated and beaten up, chair behind his desk and reclined so the back of his chair almost rested against the wall. He folded his hands on his chest like he was prepping to take a nap, but instead told Alberta to start talking.

"Okay, what's so important?"

Since Vinny wasn't wasting any time on pleasantries, neither was she.

"Did you know that Jonas's father built the tree house just for him?" Alberta asked.

"No I did not."

"How come?"

"Because I'm the chief of police, not a mind reader."

"But that could be an important piece of information, don't you think?"

"Not really. It doesn't matter if Jonas was emotionally connected to the tree house or he had never seen it before, I just need to figure out why he died a few feet below it."

"But if it *was* someplace he was emotionally connected to, don't you think he could have visited the tree house with much more frequency than just one random morning?"

"Very possible, but again it doesn't matter. Most everyone in town knew the tree house had become a kind of landmark in the park. A few years ago I tried to get it torn down because I was afraid it was going to get destroyed by vandals or become a hideout for some kids who would use it as a place to party and get hurt, but the town fought me on it."

"So no one had ever gotten hurt or fallen out of the tree house before?"

"If anyone had, it went unreported, but I knew it was only a matter of time before something serious would happen. Now, of course, I'm the bad guy because somebody, in fact, did get killed."

Leaning forward, Vinny kept his hands clasped and placed them on the desk. "Is there anything else, *Detective?*"

Alberta was surprised to hear the agitated tone in Vinny's voice, but chalked it up to his earlier conversation with Kichiro, which she was dying to ask him about. But Alberta knew it would only serve to get Vinny madder, and she wanted him to remain cooperative and share whatever information he had with her.

"That's *Mrs.* Detective to you," Alberta said trying to defuse what was starting to become a heated discussion.

Smiling, Vinny relaxed in his chair. "Duly noted." Alberta's tactic worked. Briefly.

"Why didn't you reveal that Jonas had a restraining order against him?"

Vinny tried to conceal his surprise, but was unsuccessful. He also was unsuccessful in concealing his anger. "What idiot told you that?!"

Before Alberta knew what she was saying, she gave away her source. "My granddaughter is hardly an idiot."

"She has no right spreading that information around."

"Why not? It's public record isn't it?"

"It happened a long time ago and that girl recanted her story."

"Nola?"

Vinny tilted his head to the side and smirked, "You know exactly who I'm talking about."

"Why would she recant her story after asking the court to issue a restraining order?" Alberta questioned. "Getting one of those things isn't automatic. You have to prove that there's a reason, no?"

Vinny sighed heavily and Alberta noticed that his hands were no longer clasped in front of him but opening and closing as if he couldn't decide if he wanted to strangle Alberta or clock her in the nose. "Because Nola was and still is a very dramatic young woman, and she jumped to a very wrong conclusion. Once she realized her mistake she did the right thing, which was to clear a good man's name."

Alberta noticed the same tone in Vinny's voice as when he was talking to Kichiro. He was trying to protect Jonas for some reason. Maybe he couldn't bring him back to life, but at least he could protect his character.

"So Jonas hadn't been stalking Nola?"

"No, Alberta, he hadn't!"

"Then what exactly had he been doing?"

"Why don't you and your granddaughter stick your noses further where they don't belong and find out?"

They were both startled by Vinny's words and their intensity. Although she knew she was pushing the limits of their friendship and delving into police matters that really didn't concern her, and Vinny's outburst was the result of his frustration about the case as well as his genuine concern for her and Jinx, all she could hear was that another man was trying to control her life.

"Thanks for the suggestion, Vinny," Alberta said tersely. "Jinx and I will do just that."

Swiveling in his chair to face his computer, Vinny added, "I didn't expect anything less."

While Alberta gathered her thoughts to think of something witty or civil to say in order to end her visit on friendlier or at least less ambiguous terms, Vinny beat her to it by being blunt.

"And shut the door behind you on your way out."

Before Jinx opened the door to St. Winifred's Academy, she heard the screaming. She had no way of knowing that Sharon was yelling at Nola in an even louder voice than Vinny had been shouting at Kichiro, she only knew that she was walking in on a volatile conversation. She also had no way of knowing that Sharon was using almost the same words that Vinny had.

"What is wrong with you lately?" Sharon screamed. "And don't give me that 'I'm sorry' crap because I don't want to hear it."

"Sharon, you of all people, should know that I'm dealing with a lot of personal stuff right now," Nola replied.

"You think you're the only one?!"

Jinx didn't know if Nola agreed or challenged Sharon's question because whatever Nola said in reply, she said it quietly. Jinx had followed the voices down the hallway right up to the door of Nola's classroom,

but by the time she arrived could only hear the muffled sounds of a normal conversation. The argument
had been intense, but short, and was now over. When
Sharon flung the door open, however, it was obvious
that the tension remained.

"Mrs. Basco," Jinx blurted out. "Hi."

Flustered, it took Sharon a moment to focus her attention on Jinx and reply. "Hello . . . oh . . . Jinx . . .
well . . . yes . . . hi."

Looking like a woman out of one of those old Dou-
glas Sirk melodramas of the 1950s, Sharon smoothed
out her tight, houndstooth skirt and then put a wayward strand of hair back into place by brushing her
palm across the side of her face. It was a theatrical gesture, unnecessary, but effective in allowing Sharon to
appear as if she was adjusting her physical appearance
when what she was doing was modifying her mood for
her audience. Finished, Sharon flashed Jinx a smile
that positively beamed. *Wow,* Jinx thought, *Sharon's a
darn good actress.* Had Jinx not heard the arguing that
directly preceded her performance, she would have
considered Sharon's expression genuine.

"What brings you to our neck of the woods?"
Sharon asked. "And might I add that you look amazing
in red. It should be your signature color."

Jinx became flustered, not because of the compliment—she knew the red leather jacket was the perfect
accent to her long black hair and olive complexion—
but because the ease in which Sharon switched gears
from hostile to hostess was frightening.

"Really? You think so? Okay . . . thank you," Jinx
stammered, sounding like Sharon did a few moments
earlier. "The jacket is my Aunt Joyce's, she's not only a
great painter, a former financial bigwig, but a fashion
maven, too."

At the mention of Joyce's name, Sharon's demeanor relapsed a bit, but the retreat into calmer territory was short-lived. "She does have a wonderfully creative flair about her," Sharon gushed. "Especially for a former Wall Street wizard . . . or wizardess . . . number crunchers are usually so boringly unartistic."

"Like most women she has multiple sides to her personality," Jinx praised.

"That is true, most of us do," Sharon agreed, then quickly apologized and shifted the conversation once again. "I wish I could stay longer and chat, but I have so much work to catch up on, and if I don't get home at a reasonable hour tonight to start dinner, I think my husband will finally make good on his threat to file for divorce."

"Don't let me stop you," Jinx replied. "I would never come between a man and his wife."

Sharon started walking down the hallway and then turned around to address Nola, but never stopped moving so she was walking backward. "And remember, Nola, I need those assessments on my desk by nine a.m. tomorrow morning." When she was finished she turned around to continue walking without missing a beat. Sharon Basco was not someone who wasted time.

Closing the classroom door behind her, Jinx pulled one of the student chairs closer to Nola's and sat down. "What was that all about?"

Shrugging her shoulders, Nola smiled, "Just a regular day here at St. Winnie's."

"You get screamed at like that every day?"

"Not me personally," Nola said, "But . . . each day someone gets yelled at. It's nothing, just the way Sharon lets off steam."

"Doesn't seem right to me," Jinx stated. "I mean Wyck will throw a tantrum every once in a while, but he rarely screams at someone unless they really screwed up. And since this is a Catholic school shouldn't people be nicer to each other?"

In response, Nola laughed so hard that she almost fell out of her chair. She slammed her hand down on her desk to stop herself from falling over and hit a small porcelain bowl filled with paper clips. Jinx lunged forward and grabbed the bowl before it crashed to the ground but couldn't stop the paper clips from scattering all over the floor.

The incident reminded her of when she caught Lori's vase, stopping it from smashing on the floor. So did the bowl. The pattern was the same, a very common blue and white Chinese porcelain.

"Thank you!" Nola squealed. "This . . . this was a gift."

"From Kichiro?" Jinx teased, scooping up the paper clips from the floor.

Nola paused and looked at Jinx as if trying to determine if she was joking in a friendly manner or being bitchy. "Maybe," she replied inconclusively. "So what brings you by? Are you here as a roomie or reporter?"

Jinx's instinct was to lie and say the former, but Nola knew her quite well and would see through her ruse only to get annoyed at the deception. Better to be honest.

"I found out something about Jonas that I'm hoping you can clarify," she said.

"Sure," Nola replied, dragging out the word to sound much longer than its one syllable. "What did you find out?"

Nola began to fumble through papers on her desk. She didn't look at them, only shuffled them from side to side. Jinx knew this was a tactic Nola employed whenever she wanted to avoid a subject so in order to put her friend at ease, Jinx thought it best to act as nonchalant as possible and not make Nola feel as if she was being interrogated. To create some distance between them, Jinx walked to the window and gazed out at the school grounds.

"Did you file a restraining order against Jonas a few years ago?" Jinx asked.

Jinx immediately cursed her positioning because instead of looking at Nola's face to see how she responded to her questioning, she was staring outside. She fought the impulse to turn around abruptly because that felt like a maneuver from an old crime show—ask a volatile question and then turn violently on your heel. Not the kind of action that inspires unguarded dialogue. Maintaining her stance proved to be the right choice.

"You know something, yes, yes I did do that," Nola finally replied. "It was such a long time ago I forgot about it."

Jinx sat on the windowsill and turned to face Nola, but continued to steal glances out the window to keep up her air of indifference. "Really? I mean it isn't every day that you take legal action against someone, especially someone who was creepy like your students said."

"Creepy? Jonas? Not at all."

"But Nola, you don't take out a restraining order on someone who isn't creepy. You only call in the police to protect you when someone scares you and makes you feel unsafe," Jinx asserted. "Why were you scared of Jonas?"

"Scared of Jonas?" Nola cried. "Don't be silly. He was a gentle soul. A bit kooky, but gentle."

"So you weren't frightened of him, but you still wanted him to keep his distance from you?"

"I overreacted," Nola admitted. "I think you should know me well enough to know that I have a teeny tiny tendency to do that."

Jinx didn't have to think that one over for a second. She agreed completely with Nola's self-description. But her silence did the trick and it compelled Nola to explain herself in further detail.

"He had been staring at me in a way that I thought was maybe a bit too much," Nola explained. "I wasn't going to say anything, but some of the students picked up on it and I got nervous and a bit overprotective as their teacher so I filed the restraining order. Almost immediately I realized such a drastic action was unnecessary. I spoke with Jonas, which I should've done in the first place, asked him to please stop, and he did."

"Just like that?" Jinx asked.

"Yup, just like that."

Nola started rambling on about something that Jinx thought included Kichiro and Freddy, but she wasn't listening fully, she was digesting the information Nola had shared and she was even more interested in what she noticed on the lawn. Outside almost every window were clusters of flowers. She saw daisies, some white roses, hydrangeas like the ones that decorated Alberta's cottage, even a colorful array of wildflowers. Flowers, flowers everywhere except outside of Nola's classroom window where there was only grass. And brown grass at that.

"*L'erba è sempre più verde,*" Jinx muttered to herself.

"What did you say?" Nola asked.

"Just something I read in my Italian phrase book," Jinx replied. "The grass is always greener. The, um, flowers on the school's property are beautiful."

"And ironic."

"What do you mean?"

"It's all thanks to Jonas."

"Jonas?"

"He was our groundskeeper," Nola said.

"Really?"

"That's why he was around a lot," Nola explained.

"I thought he worked for the town."

"That was his main job, but he did some work for us too, and a few other places I think. He really had a green thumb. Unfortunately, I'm just the opposite."

Nola stood next to Jinx at the window and looked at the brown patch of dead earth right underneath her window. "Jonas would say it's like I poured some kind of lethal pesticide all over the dirt to kill any life that was trying to grow."

It was as if a voice from beyond the grave had offered Jinx another clue.

CHAPTER 11

Dente avvelenato.

When Jinx heard the knock at the front door the next evening she had no idea that the voice from beyond the grave had followed her home.

She left Freddy, Nola, and Kichiro sitting in the living room to open the door and froze when she was greeted by Vinny and a young female detective, whom she recognized, but whose name she didn't remember. None of that mattered. All that was important was that the police were at her apartment and it was all her fault.

"Hi Jinx," Vinny said. His voice was that awkward mix of apologetic, professional, and forced cheerful. He didn't want to be standing at her front door, Jinx didn't want him to be standing at her front door, but both knew that Vinny and his underling were only standing at her front door because they were there on police business.

For a split second Jinx thought if she closed the door and sat back on the couch next to Freddy, they would disappear. Before she could test out her theory, Kichiro ruined everything by calling out to his boss.

"Chief, what are you doing here? Is there an emergency?"

"No," Vinny replied.

"An emergency? Here?" Nola asked.

Either Vinny forgot why he had come or he was too embarrassed to admit it, but he remained silent. Leaning back on the couch, his stocking clad feet still propped up on the coffee table, Freddy raised a hand and said, "Hey Tambra, what's going on?"

Now that the female cop had a first name it was almost as if they were just another couple who came over to hang out. Jinx and Freddy, Nola and Kichiro, Vinny and Tambra. They sounded like a real couple, so why weren't they acting like one? Why were they acting like cops?

"Tambra, seriously, what's going on?" Freddy asked.

Obviously well-trained in protocol, Tambra allowed her boss to answer Freddy's question. "We have a search warrant," he announced. "To search the, um, premises."

"*These* premises?" Nola repeated, her quizzical expression indicating that she considered it a very real possibility that the police had knocked on the wrong apartment door.

Nola looked over at Kichiro and her confusion quickly turned to amusement. She smiled and shook her head, her eyes raised like a mother bewildered, but accepting, of her naughty child. "Of course!" she squealed. "The Tranquility Police Department has nothing better to do on a Thursday night than play a practical joke on one of their own."

Nola got up and picked up the half-empty bottle of merlot from the coffee table and asked, "Are you officially on duty or can I pour two more glasses?"

Had Nola been drunk, Vinny's reply would have been enough to sober her right up.

"Please put the wine down, Nola," he ordered, quietly, but firmly. "This isn't a joke."

Slowly, Nola placed the wine bottle back onto the table without taking her eyes off of Vinny, perhaps hoping that he would flash a huge grin to let her know that he was, in fact, kidding, and his presence was, indeed, part of some police hijinks. But his dour expression didn't change, and it was clear to everyone that this was no joking matter.

"Dude, are you serious?" Freddy asked.

Jinx placed a hand on her boyfriend's shoulder and answered for Vinny. "I think it's very serious, Freddy, isn't that right, Vinny?"

"I wouldn't have a search warrant in my hand if it weren't."

"Okay, playtime is over," Nola said, unconsciously slipping into her teacher voice. "What's this all about? Why do you have a warrant to search our apartment? If you left something here, all you had to do was ask and we'd look for it."

Jinx wasn't sure if her roommate was naïve or desperate, but clearly she didn't understand the seriousness of the situation. Vinny and Tambra were standing in their living room holding a legal document that gave them the right to search every nook and cranny of the two-bedroom, two-bathroom apartment that they shared, not to search for something they had lost but to uncover evidence that they felt was integral to a current police investigation. Nola either didn't comprehend this or was acting disingenuous, and, sadly, Jinx wasn't sure which one it was. She did know, however, that no amount of stalling was going to prevent the police from doing their job.

"Nola, I don't think Vinny's here to look for something he left behind," Jinx cautioned. "He's searching for something he hasn't found yet."

"Then tell us what it is, Vinny, and we'll help you look," Nola declared. "I mean we have a cop right here who's trained to do exactly this kind of thing."

Kichiro seemed to be startled at the acknowledgment of his presence. Prior to that he had been lost in thought, far removed from the proceedings, but when Nola offered up his services he was yanked back to reality.

"Uh, yeah, su-su-sure," Kichiro stammered. "How c-can I help?"

As an afterthought, Kichiro stood up and although he didn't move forward to cross the room and join his colleagues, his body was restless. He shifted his weight from one leg to the other, he flicked the tip of his nose with his finger, he clasped his hands briefly in front of him before placing his right arm on his hip, only to change position again to wind up with his left arm crossed in front of his chest holding onto his right elbow. Even then in his chosen final position he couldn't remain still and his index finger rubbed the skin just above his elbow back and forth looking like a caterpillar stuck in one position unable to move.

"All of you can help by staying exactly where you are and letting us do our job," Vinny declared.

As a police officer Kichiro was used to accepting orders, especially from a superior, and merely nodded his head in response. Nola, as a teacher, was more familiar with being the person giving the orders so she was less cooperative. "This has gone far enough," she said. "Why in the world do you want to search our apartment?"

Vinny exhaled a long breath through his nose and then said the words he clearly dreaded speaking out loud, but knew he was legally bound to convey. "We have reason to believe that there is evidence in this apartment in connection with the murder of Jonas Harper."

"What?"

Jinx prayed no one noticed she had remained silent and wasn't part of Freddy, Nola, and Kichiro's simultaneous outburst. Ignoring the question, Vinny gave the search warrant to Jinx and then indicated to Tambra that it was time to get to work.

The female detective pulled out a Ziploc bag from her back pocket and took out plastic gloves. She passed the bag to Vinny who did the same. He put the end of the bag in his mouth as both he and Tambra put on their gloves, and when he was finished he shoved the bag into his own back pocket. Whatever it was that they were looking for, they were now ready to begin their search.

"Jinx, babe, what's going on?" Freddy whispered. "What could they possibly be looking for?"

Shrugging her shoulders, Jinx said, "I have no idea."

Looking at Jinx with eyes that were both amused and frightened, Freddy replied in a soft whisper, "Girlfriend, you are so lying to me."

On the one hand Jinx was delighted that her boyfriend knew her well enough to know that she was lying, but on the other hand she was disappointed because she knew she'd have to work on her cover-up skills. For the moment, however, she needed to focus on some other people in the room.

Jinx wasn't sure how many times Tambra and Vinny

had done this kind of thing before as a team, but they worked together in silence and with precision as if they were the only ones in the apartment.

Tambra disappeared into Nola's bedroom and Vinny lingered briefly in the living room before entering the kitchen. The moment both police officers exited the living room the mood between Nola and Kichiro changed, and Jinx noticed that they began acting as if they were as skilled and familiar a team as Vinny and Tambra.

"What are they doing here?" Nola asked.

"I have no idea," Kichiro replied.

Just as Freddy knew that Jinx was lying when she spoke the same words less than a minute before, Nola eyed her boyfriend suspiciously, and it was clear that mistrust was all that linked them. The fact that two police officers were in earshot was what kept Nola's reply to a seething whisper. "You better not."

"Chief!"

Vinny didn't verbally reply to Tambra's cry and instead rushed out of the kitchen into Nola's bedroom. In reaction to the sudden activity, Nola became frightened, but Jinx couldn't tell if it was because she knew what was going to happen next or if she was terrified of the unknown. Regardless, Kichiro did nothing to alleviate his girlfriend's concerns even though Freddy had stood up and placed his arm around Jinx's waist as both a thoughtful gesture and a lame attempt to protect her from whatever was about to come.

Jinx, however, wasn't the one who needed protection.

Vinny came out of the bedroom followed by Tambra who was holding something in another clear Ziploc bag. Their expressions were textbook, unemotional, and professional. And despite the gravity of the words Vinny spoke, his tone of voice was the same.

"Nola Kirkpatrick," he said. "You're under arrest for the murder of Jonas Harper."

Less than an hour later, Alberta, Helen, and Joyce had joined Jinx and Freddy and were all crammed into a corner of the police station while Nola was somewhere behind closed doors being fingerprinted, photographed, and told that the police believed that she was a murderess. And as Jinx explained, it was all her fault.

"Lovey, how is any of this your fault?" Alberta asked.

"Because I couldn't keep my mouth shut."

"You're going to have to elaborate a little bit," Helen said.

"Because I'm the one who shared the evidence with Lori," she replied.

"What evidence?" Joyce asked.

"The evidence they found in our apartment."

"I know you're upset," Alberta said. "But you need to be more specific?"

Jinx closed her eyes, took a deep breath, and finally found the strength to speak.

"I visited Nola at her school and I noticed something peculiar. On a hunch I went to see Lori to ask her to, you know, do her thing with it, and the next thing I know Vinny is carting off Nola in handcuffs."

"Jinxie, do I need to slap you to make you stop rambling?" Helen asked, completely serious. "Because I have no problem doing that if it'll make you talk in complete sentences."

"I'm sorry," Jinx said, tears forming in her eyes. "I'm just so upset that my friend is in there because of me."

Freddy put his arms around Jinx before Alberta had the chance, a loving gesture that almost made Alberta cry. "Hey, Jinx, unless you planted something in Nola's bedroom that the police found," Freddy said. "You're not the reason she's currently behind bars."

"You didn't plant anything in her bedroom, did you?" Helen asked.

"Helen Rose Ferrara!" Alberta gasped. "What kind of question is that?"

"Berta, if you only knew the things I've heard people say they've done," she replied. "I find it best to get the obvious questions out in the open in order to focus on the important things, like what in the name of Marcello Mastroianni is Jinx talking about."

"Honey, it would help if you could break it down from the beginning," Joyce added. "Also too, I have a flask in my purse filled with lemon-flavored vodka if that'll help calm your nerves."

"I'll have some," Helen said.

"I wasn't offering it to you," Joyce replied.

"You were always very selfish."

"Ladies can we please concentrate on why we're here," Alberta interrupted. "Jinx, sit down and tell us how this all started."

As a group, the four women and Freddy moved over to some empty chairs in the corner of the waiting room. They all turned to face Jinx, who wiped away her tears, took an even longer breath, and then began to explain.

"When I was at St. Winifred's I noticed that there were flowers all over the grounds except right underneath the window of Nola's classroom," Jinx started. "I thought that was odd and I remembered what you said about the pesticide that killed Bocce and then, of course, a huge light bulb went off in my head because Jonas was poisoned by pesticide. I realized that the soil must've been doused with a pesticide too, which prevented any flowers from growing, I mean why else would only one spot on the grounds not be filled with flowers."

"Wow! My girlfriend's a brainiac," Freddy boasted.

Once again, Freddy made Alberta smile. She was thrilled that her granddaughter had found such a worthy young man. Jinx, however, didn't feel she was worthy of anything except a dunce cap.

"Your girlfriend's also an idiot," Jinx replied. "After I left, I snuck back and took a sample of the soil underneath the window sill and brought it to Lori. I asked her to test it against the type of pesticide that was found in Jonas's system and, of course, she asked me a ton of questions about where I found it and why I suspected this sample contained the same chemical substance, and I knew whatever I said would implicate Nola."

"So what did you do, lovey?" Alberta asked.

"I told Lori that I couldn't remember where I found it and ran out," Jinx replied. "Some investigative reporter I am."

"Sometimes it's more important to be a friend first," Alberta said.

"Some friend!" Jinx shouted. "Because of me, the police got a search warrant and rummaged through our apartment thinking I was the culprit until they found the pesticide that was used to kill Jonas in a water-tight bag floating in the toilet tank in Nola's bathroom."

The three older women gasped so loudly that the rest of the people in the waiting room turned around to face them, curious as to what was so shocking. Helen turned around to face the inquisitive faces and said, "Keep walking, nothing interesting over here."

"You know what they say, honey," Joyce said. "You can't blame the messenger."

"No, I can only blame myself!" Jinx cried. "Why didn't I talk to Nola first before handing over such incriminating evidence to the medical examiner? Am I that hungry to get some inside information for an article?"

"No, you're that hungry to find out who killed an innocent man," Alberta assured.

"But Nola couldn't have possibly killed Jonas," Jinx said. "She isn't violent. She got mad at me once when I killed a bee that flew into our apartment."

"She might not be violent, but she does have a motive," Freddy suggested.

"You're talking about the restraining order?" Alberta asked.

"I know that she later changed her mind and got it rescinded," Freddy explained, "but the fact remains that Jonas did something that made Nola scared enough to go to the police to stop him from stalking her. Maybe the dude started acting weird again and Nola decided to take matters into her own hands."

"That's ridiculous!" Jinx exclaimed. "I don't care what the police found."

"The police found evidence hidden in the toilet tank in Nola's bathroom where presumably no one would ever find it," Alberta said softly. "Why would she do something like that if she had nothing to hide?"

"None of this makes sense, Gram. I know it looks bad, but Nola isn't the murdering type. I'm her roommate, her best friend, I should know."

"Maybe she's as bad a criminal as she is a drama teacher," Helen remarked.

"Aunt Helen, please don't joke about it."

"Who's joking?" Helen asked. "I told you her production of *The Sound of Music* was terrible. If she's as bad at trying to hide evidence as she was trying to hide the fact that she doesn't know how to direct, then it's no surprise that the police found her stash."

"I mean for heaven's sake she was voted Teacher of the Year three years in a row," Jinx shouted.

"Then it's another example of *dalle stelle alle stalle*," Helen added.

"What?" Freddy asked.

"A fall from grace," Alberta answered for her sister who was too busy rummaging through her pocketbook.

"Like a modern day Mrs. Roberto Rossellini," Helen said, still digging through the contents of the oversized black pocketbook she always carried with her.

"Who?" Freddy asked again.

"Ingrid Bergman, scandalized actress. Google her name," Joyce said helpfully.

"I can't believe I put Nola right in the middle of a scandal!" Jinx said.

"Stop your bellyaching, Jinx," Helen scolded. "If Nola's anything like Ingrid, she'll rebound and be back on top in no time at all."

"It's true," Joyce added. "After years of living in European exile, she came back, starred as the orphaned Russian princess in *Anastasia*, and won her second Academy Award."

"Not that Nola's ever going to win an award that has anything to do with the entertainment industry," Helen said. "But innocent or guilty she will get through this." Finally, Helen found what she was looking for and handed it to Jinx. "Here, it's about time you learned how to use these."

The tears streaming out of her eyes made it difficult for her to see what Helen had placed in her hand. "What are they?"

"My back-up rosary beads," Helen stated. "It's never too late to learn how to pray."

Distracted by the loud voices behind them, Alberta turned to witness Vinny and Kichiro in the middle of yet another argument. "Sounds like someone else might need to start praying if he wants to keep his job."

"Desk duty? You can't do this to me!"

"I just did," Vinny said. His voice was half the volume of Kichiro's, but its deep resonance carried twice the command. There was no stopping Kichiro from protesting, but anyone who heard Vinny knew he wasn't going to reverse his decision.

"You're dating the suspect, which makes you incapable of being objective, which makes you incapable of doing your job," Vinny described. "Which, not for nothing, you haven't been doing very well for the past few weeks anyway so it isn't going to be a great loss to the department to have you sitting behind a desk stamping files and putting them in alphabetical order."

Kichiro looked around the room and once again saw his colleagues and fellow citizens staring at him. He did his best to contain his fury, but Alberta noticed his fists were clenched and he was having a difficult time keeping them at his side. She knew that Kichiro could get hotheaded, but she hoped he wasn't stupid enough to punch his boss with an audience while in police headquarters.

Desperately trying to control his voice, Kichiro seethed, "I told you I've been going through some personal stuff, but . . . that's . . . all over with now."

"Why? Because your girlfriend finally got caught?" Vinny asked. "Is that what you've been struggling with lately? The fact that your girlfriend's a murderer."

"Trust me, Chief, Nola didn't do this!"

"Then tell me who did."

Silence descended on the room like a crash of thunder. The simple and soft-spoken command jolted everyone in the room including Kichiro to attention. He looked up at Vinny like a young boy peering up at his father, his face consumed with a swirl of emotions ranging from shock to fear to hurt.

Alberta recognized the look on his face as she had seen it many times on her own daughter. That look of puzzlement—how could someone I love ask me such a question? Alberta always knew how Lisa Marie would answer, and no matter what the stakes her daughter would always protect herself. Only once following their last explosive argument that ignited their decades-long silence did Lisa Marie ever speak the truth. Alberta was curious to find out if Kichiro would follow suit or act differently and tell the truth when confronted with a question that had the potential to alter the course of his life.

"I have absolutely no idea, Chief," Kichiro replied. "I swear to God."

It didn't matter if Kichiro believed in God or if Vinny believed Kichiro was telling the truth, the only thing that mattered was that Alberta knew for certain that Kichiro was lying.

CHAPTER 12

Parlare fuori dai denti.

When Alberta entered the Sussex County Prison, she was overcome with a sense of déjà vu. She felt exactly the same way she did when she walked down the aisle at St. Ann's Church on her wedding day.

The same feeling of dread clung to her throat, its clutch as powerful and unrelenting as a bear's claw, causing her to feel as if she was floating out of her body watching the experience, helpless to prevent it from happening. On her wedding day she squeezed her father's hand tightly as the organist performed an uninspired, though deafeningly loud, version of the wedding march, wishing she knew Morse code so she could use it to let him know that she wanted him to help her escape. Walking down the prison hallway, she squeezed Jinx's hand just as hard and was grateful that this time the other person on the other end of the grip squeezed back. After so many years Alberta was no longer alone. And when they reached Nola's prison cell, they realized neither was she.

"Father Sal? What are you doing here?" Alberta asked.

Both of his hands were clasped around Nola's and their foreheads had been bent so they were almost touching. It was an intimate moment that, upon reflection, Alberta was sorry she interrupted. It was obvious why the priest was in Nola's prison cell—she was frightened. But if Nola were innocent shouldn't she be angry and seeking a lawyer's help instead of a priest's?

Jinx's heart sank because this was the first time she had come face-to-face with Father Sal without wearing her Sister Maria outfit. She knew that she looked different without makeup, wearing a long black tunic, and with her hair covered in a habit, but she wasn't sure if she would be completely unrecognizable. She had fooled others before with her disguises so she hoped her current appearance would be able to fool Father Sal as well. Only one way to find out and that was to act as if she had nothing to hide.

"You still haven't answered my grandmother's question," Jinx said. "What are you doing here?"

She stared at Father Sal, searching for a shift in his expression to indicate that he recognized Jinx as Helen's sidekick, but none came. And then they were interrupted.

"I asked him to come."

The sound of Nola's voice surprised them both because up until that point they were so preoccupied with finding Sal behind bars they had almost forgotten the reason they willingly entered prison on a crisp autumn morning was to visit Nola. She also sounded more like one of the teenagers that she taught instead of the twentysomething woman she was.

Examining her face for the first time, Jinx could see the telltale dark circles underneath Nola's eyes. She looked like she sometimes did in the morning after having spent most of the night grading papers. Except now she wasn't holding a cup of her favorite hazelnut coffee hoping it would bring her back to life, she was holding the hand of a priest with the look of a desperate zealot who believes a priest's prayer will save her from spending another night in a prison cell.

"Why?" Jinx asked. "You don't need a priest, you need a lawyer."

"I needed someone to talk to," Nola replied.

"Then why didn't you call me?!" Jinx cried. "Kichiro must've told you that I tried to see you yesterday, but they wouldn't let me in because I'm not family and they said I had to wait twenty-four hours. How stupid is that? I'm your best friend, which makes me more than family!"

Nola didn't respond, bowing her head instead and gazing at the scuffed gray tiles that made up the prison cell floor. Slowly, but deliberately, she let go of Sal's hands, and Alberta thought it interesting that he didn't reach out to resume the connection, fold his hands, or do something to replace the bond Nola broke. He just let his hands dangle in front of him and kept his eyes on Nola taking his cue from her. She considered it to be a thoughtful gesture, but still got the impression that he could be doing it for his audience and not on instinct. After hearing Helen badmouth Sal for so many years, Alberta was still not certain that he was a good priest. Determined not to waste time contemplating Sal's true character, Alberta focused her attention on Nola and made a conscious effort to be sympathetic and not suspicious.

"Has anyone notified your family, honey?" Alberta asked.

Once again Nola remained silent, her body still, the only movement were the tears falling from her eyes.

Alberta recognized the despair and she didn't need Nola to answer her question—no one notified Nola's family because there was no one to notify.

"You don't have anyone?" Alberta asked quietly.

The only word Nola uttered was "No," and it was soft and filled with shame. Alberta couldn't imagine not having a family member to call during an emergency and then she was consumed with a tidal wave of guilt and depression when she wondered if her own daughter ever felt the same way as Nola did, completely alone and with no one to reach out to.

But that really wasn't true. Nola did reach out to Sal and she and Jinx had come to visit the moment they were allowed to, after Nola was booked and went through all the proper police red tape. But why a priest and not a friend? What could a priest offer that a friend couldn't?

Alberta almost gasped out loud when she realized the one thing that a priest could offer a parishioner that a friend couldn't offer another friend was the code of silence. Nola could say whatever she wanted to Sal fully confident that he would never speak another word of it, her secrets and her confessions would be hermetically sealed within Sal's memory banks and never repeated to another soul or written in a local newspaper by a young, but hungry investigative reporter. Of course Alberta knew that Sal had loose lips, but Nola wasn't aware of his less than discretionary conduct.

When Jinx spoke it was obvious that she had also realized the rationale of Nola and Sal's relationship.

"I . . . um . . . get why you'd want to talk to a priest, Nola, but like I said what you really need is a lawyer."

"I don't need a lawyer," Nola replied, her voice a bit stronger, but still shaky. "I'm innocent."

"Which is exactly why you need a lawyer," Jinx cried. "Haven't you learned that from being a cop's girl-friend?"

Jinx's head snapped in Alberta's direction, and they were both wearing the same shocked expression. When they spoke, it was in unison, "Where is Kichiro anyway?"

"How should I know?" Nola snarled.

"He's your boyfriend!"

"No he isn't!"

Silence filled the prison cell as everyone, including Nola, took in her outburst. She looked at Jinx with a combination of anger and despair, and it appeared as if she was going to continue screaming and launch into a full tirade, but Sal intervened, not with words, but by softly touching her hand with his. It was all Nola required to swallow hard and reconsider her response. When she spoke, she did her best to appear nonchalant and unflustered, but failed. Alberta could only think that Helen had been right about her, Nola really was a terrible actress.

"We're dating, that's all, we're not a couple like you and Freddy," Nola explained. "Or like you and Mr. McLelland for that matter, Mrs. Scaglione."

Alberta wanted to protest that she and Sloan were not a couple, but clarifying her relationship status wasn't really a priority and she was starting to think that it didn't matter what she said or even what she thought, the public's perception was that she was Sloan's girlfriend. Sometimes the court of public opinion was all that mattered. The thought did put a smile on her face, but smiling in a prison cell in front of a woman charged with first-degree murder somehow felt wrong so she immediately turned her smile into a scowl.

And Jinx tried to turn Nola's comment inside out.

"What are you talking about?" she asked. "You told me Kichiro was your boyfriend, that's the word you used, and then you used the b-word again when you introduced him to Fréddy."

It took Alberta a moment to figure out that the b-word meant boyfriend. She was still finding it hard to believe that Kichiro and Nola were a couple. They weren't nearly as affectionate as Freddy and Jinx. But Alberta was hardly an expert when it came to relationships so what did she know?

Nola abruptly rose from the thin, gray cot and took full advantage of the limitations of her cell by pacing from the back wall to the prison bars, all the while trying to make everyone in the room understand the truth about her relationship with Kichiro.

"Stop harping on my every word, Jinx! You know I hate that."

"No you don't," Jinx spit back. "You're an English teacher, you love words."

"Real words! Not made up words like *boyfriend*."

"Boyfriend is too a real word. So is 'lying' and so is 'I don't know what the frick you're talking about.'"

"I don't think 'frick' is technically a word, Jinx," Sal said. "More like slang."

Completely forgetting that she was trying to maintain as low a profile as possible in Father Sal's presence, she yelled, "Shut up!" She knew it was disrespectful to yell at a priest, but perhaps it would further separate her from the saintly Sister Maria and erase any thoughts in Sal's mind that the two women might be one and the same. Alberta had other concerns.

Instinctively, Alberta made the sign of the cross and

looked up to heaven to ask God to forgive her grand-daughter for yelling at a priest no matter what his reputation might be. She assumed Helen could get away with such impudent language because she had devoted herself to a life as a religious servant, but as good as Jinx was she had hardly given of herself unconditionally. Alberta wanted to make sure that neither God nor Sal would hold a grudge. Sal's smile told her that he found Jinx to be amusing and probably as endearing as he found Helen, but since Alberta was never completely sure how God reacted to the shenanigans on earth, she started to say a silent Our Father. Unfortunately, she was distracted by the yelling and stopped before she got to the Amen.

"No I won't forget it!" Jinx screamed. "This is too important. What's going on between you and the cop?"

"Will you leave me alone?!" Nola yelled.

"Tell me!"

"Kichiro isn't my real boyfriend!"

"What?" Jinx and Alberta once again asked simultaneously.

"I think you heard her," Sal replied. "Don't worry Nola. *Parlare fuori dai denti.*"

"You're correct Father," Alberta agreed. "It is good to speak openly and say what's on your mind."

"Even when what's on your mind doesn't make any sense?" Jinx questioned. "What do you mean Kichiro isn't your real boyfriend?"

"He's just . . . You know Jinx, sometimes you push too hard. He means nothing to me okay, so leave him out of this!"

Had Nola been less furious and had she been looking directly at Jinx perhaps she would've seen Jinx's eyes light up. Had she seen that she would've understood that Jinx had absolutely no intention of leaving Kichiro out of anything.

"Kichiro, I'm so glad that you could join us."

The detective squeezed into a booth next to Jinx and opposite Alberta at Veronica's Diner and looked as if he was sitting in the witness box. The periwinkle blue vinyl clashed with his greenish complexion. He looked tired, agitated, and most distressing of all, guilty.

"Do you want something to eat?" Alberta asked. "My sister tells me the eggs Benedict here are much better than mine."

"No thank you," he replied. "I really can't eat."

"Are you worried about something?" Alberta asked.

Kichiro shot her a glance as if to ask if she were an idiot. "You know why I'm worried," he said. "My girlfriend's been arrested for murder."

"But Nola's not your girlfriend."

Jinx's comment seemed to create a complicated flurry of emotions on Kichiro's face. First shock, then confusion, then relief. "Finally! I'm so glad she told you," he confessed. "I know that it's been hard on her . . . keeping our secret."

Alberta saw that Jinx's lips were forming to say, "What secret?" so she kicked her granddaughter gently, but firmly, underneath the table. She was continually astounded at how unrestrained and impatient young people could be, especially one who wanted to be an investigative journalist. Patience and strategy were required to get to the truth, not recklessness and haste.

"It's definitely taking its toll," Alberta said, opening up the small plastic container of half-and-half and pouring it into her coffee. "I'm not sure what's worse for her, being in jail or constantly lying."

Kichiro ran his fingers through his buzz cut so fiercely the women thought that his fingers were going to draw blood and stain the orange Formica table. "I know, but it's only for a bit longer, until she leaves her husband."

Alberta wasn't able to stop Jinx this time from speaking before thinking.

"Nola's got a husband?"

"No," Kichiro said, turning to face Jinx. When he saw her confused expression, he knew that she had been bluffing. "Nola didn't tell you anything, did she?"

"She told us enough, Kichiro, and you told us the rest," Alberta interrupted. "We know the two of you aren't really dating and that it's just a cover-up. What we don't know is why?"

Either because he was desperate to tell someone the truth about his relationship with Nola and the secret he'd been keeping, or, as a policeman, he was programmed to be respectful to his elders, he didn't hesitate to answer.

"Nola's pretending to be my girlfriend because I'm dating a married woman," Kichiro admitted. "And if word got out that she was having an affair, it would destroy her personally *and* professionally."

"Not to mention what it would do to her clueless husband," Alberta added.

"They haven't had a real marriage for years," Kichiro scoffed.

"How do you know that?" Jinx asked.

"Because she told me so," Kichiro replied, somewhat defiant. "I would never destroy a marriage."

"But that's exactly what you're doing," Alberta said.

Kichiro rubbed his face with his right hand and turned away from the women. His ears were turning red and since the diner was hardly overheated, Alberta knew that her words were starting a fire within the young man. Looking at him struggle to maintain his composure, Alberta was disappointed. She didn't think Kichiro was a good boyfriend, but she had thought Kichiro was one of the good guys. Sadly, she realized that Kichiro was more like her husband, Sammy, selfish and out for himself.

"So what have you been doing while your fake girlfriend has been spending a few nights behind bars?" Alberta asked. "Shacking up with your married hussy?"

"Don't you dare call her that!" Kichiro shouted, waving a finger in Alberta's face.

"And don't you dare wave your finger at me again or I'll chop it off with this knife," Alberta shouted back, waving a butter knife in the air. "Do you understand me, young man?"

Embarrassed, Kichiro put up his hands to use his palms as two symbolic white flags and whispered, "I'm sorry. I am just under a lot of stress lately."

"I guarantee you that Nola's under a lot more stress than you are right now." Alberta said, her sympathy for Kichiro waning.

"There's no way that Nola's guilty. She doesn't have a violent bone in her body," Kichiro said. "She'll be out of jail in no time and then my real girlfriend will leave her husband, and Nola and I can go our separate ways again and live our own lives."

Both Jinx and Kichiro were startled by Alberta's laughing. A few of the other patrons turned around to look at Alberta, some smiling at her, some looking at her like she had a screw loose.

"Gram, what's so funny?"

She was laughing so hard she could hardly get the word out. "Kichiro."

"Me? Why am I so funny?"

"Because you think that your girlfriend is going to leave her husband for you," she said, still cackling. "You know, sometimes I really love being old. I may not be able to do everything I used to, but at least I'm not stupid."

Trying very hard to control his anger, Kichiro looked at Alberta, his hands now folded tightly and pressing down hard on the table. "Promise me you're not going to go all amateur detective again and butt your nose in where it doesn't belong."

"Like into someone else's marriage?" Alberta asked, for some reason relishing the chance to push a man's buttons.

"I didn't barge into someone's marriage, there was no marriage to barge into, their relationship is a sham, but—"

"But what?" Jinx asked.

"But she's in the public a lot and so . . . please, I'm asking you as a friend to let this drop," Kichiro pleaded. "The truth will come out in good time. Trust me it always does."

Without saying another word, Kichiro got up and left the table. Alberta watched him leave the diner. When she turned to face Jinx, all thoughts of the wayward detective were forgotten.

"What's wrong, lovey?"

"Wyck sent me a text," Jinx said. "Calhoun is out of town on assignment and he wants me to fly solo on the Jonas Harper murder investigation."

"That's terrific."

"No it isn't. He wants me to dig up every piece of information I can find and write a tell-all article on Nola," Jinx conveyed, her face turning ashen. "Looks like the truth is going to come out sooner than anyone thought."

CHAPTER 13

Dove l'allievo è disposto, apparirà l'insegnante.

"How can I destroy Nola's life like this?" Jinx asked, slamming her laptop shut on her kitchen table.

"Because you're her friend."

"Forgive me, Aunt Helen, but that's absurd."

"No it isn't, lovey," Alberta replied. "It makes perfect sense."

"Thank you, Berta."

"You're welcome, Hel."

"Aunt Joyce, will you please talk some sense into these two. I think the vodka's gone to their heads."

"Sorry Jinx, but I agree with them," Joyce said, sipping the eggnog-flavored vodka.

"*Mamma mia!*" Jinx cried.

"Your accent is getting so much better, Jinx," Alberta remarked. "I especially like the way you held out the second to last syllable for dramatic effect."

"She's a quick learner that one," Helen added. "You, Berta, not so much."

"What are you talking about?"

"Your eggs Benedict still aren't as good as the ones I get at Veronica's."

"*Bugiardo!*" Alberta exclaimed. "You're a liar, Helen Ferrara! These are *delizioso* and you know it."

"Delicious, yes, and better than your usual attempt," Helen said swallowing a mouthful. "But the vinegar is still too overpowering. I don't know how, but the diner gets the sauce just right."

Since Jinx was on a tight deadline working on the article Wyck wanted her to write for the next edition of *The Herald,* she didn't have time to go to Alberta's for their usual Sunday dinner so Alberta, Helen, and Joyce brought dinner to Jinx. However, Alberta thought she'd mix things up and bring breakfast in the guise of dinner. She had said it reminded her of when her mother, tired of toiling in the kitchen day after day trying to come up with something new and interesting to cook for the family meal that would appeal to both her husband and her kids, would rebel and serve pancakes. Her father would always be furious, but Alberta, Helen, and their brother, Anthony, loved it because it made them feel like it was a holiday. Now, it felt like a competition.

"There is absolutely nothing wrong with my hollandaise sauce and you know it."

"Don't be upset, Berta. It's a very delicate balance mastering the culinary arts," Helen replied, finishing her plate.

Alberta threw her hands up in frustration and then grabbed Helen's plate to fill it with two more eggs. "What do you know about cooking anyway? You're used to convent food. Anything with extra salt tastes good to you."

"Could you two bicker later?" Jinx asked. "I'm in the middle of a moral dilemma."

"Morals are highly overrated, Jinx," Helen replied. "Trust the gut God gave you and you'll never go wrong."

"What's your gut say, lovey?" Alberta asked.

Jinx looked at her kitchen table strewn with papers, Post-its with handwritten notes, and files amid the dishes and vodka glasses, and sighed. Everything she knew and thought of her best friend and roommate was on the table. Could she really share that with the public and use it as a way to further her career? It didn't take Jinx long to answer her own question.

"My gut says I have to write this story," Jinx confessed. "But I don't know if it's the right thing to do."

"Right and wrong isn't always as black and white as the world would like us to think it is," Helen remarked.

"On Wall Street we used to call it the Gray Zone," Joyce said.

"What's that?" Alberta asked.

"If a client wanted to make an investment in a new business without a track record or venture into what we considered to be risky territory, that would fall into the Gray Zone and we'd have to make a judgment call," Joyce explained.

"How'd you advise your clients?" Jinx asked.

Shrugging her shoulders, Joyce replied, "We'd weigh the options, have a junior trader whip up a financial analysis, and use previous deals to forecast the future. Which is a fancy way to say that we guessed."

"Based on your gut impression?" Jinx asked.

"Exactly."

"So you all think that my writing a tell-all exposé about Nola while she's languishing behind bars is something that a friend should do?"

"Absolutely," Helen said, wolfing down her third helping. "Because if you don't do it someone else at the paper will."

"And if someone who doesn't know Nola writes it,

it'll be a smear campaign only focusing on the smutty, sensational bits," Alberta added. "And not the fair and balanced article that her best friend would write."

"Also too, Nola knows how seriously you take your career so she knows that you'll be reporting the facts and will leave innuendo and gossip to those hacks over at *The Millville Penny Saver*," Joyce said. "I don't know why anyone would read the trash printed in that paper."

"I have a subscription," Helen announced.

Shaking her head dismissively, Joyce said, "That settles it, Jinx, you have to write this article to show the world that journalism is more than a trashy read. It can also be news."

Jinx opened up her laptop and punched a few keys on the keyboard to bring her article up on the screen. She held her head on both sides with her hands for a moment and then ran her fingers through her long hair, gathering and tying it into a ponytail with the rubber band that had been doubling as a bracelet. She placed her hands on the table, took a deep breath, and then gulped down her eggnog vodka. Placing the glass down on the table with a thud, she looked at her grandmother and her aunts, and nodded. It was time to get serious. And to show her family that despite her youth and relative inexperience in her field, she truly wanted to be a serious journalist.

"Forgive me, Nola," Jinx whispered, and then began to read from the laptop screen.

Less than three weeks after police uncovered the body of Jonas Harper in Tranquility Park a suspect has been arrested in the murder of the forty-seven-year-old life-long resident. But the arrest of twenty-seven-year-old Nola Kirkpatrick, a celebrated teacher at St. Winifred's

*Academy, raises more questions about the shocking
murder than answers. Could the English and drama
teacher, voted Teacher of the Year three years in a row,
really be responsible for the murder of a man known to
everyone in town? And if so, what could have driven a
young woman with no previous criminal record to kill?
In this tale of the high school teacher and the town custodian it seems there is much more to learn. As Nola's
roommate and best friend, I won't stop investigating
until I uncover the answers.*

"That's very good, lovey!" Alberta exclaimed.

"And a very smart tactic to include yourself in the
article," Helen said. "It's what priests do with their
homilies when they want to create a connection with
their parishioners."

"Thanks, Aunt Helen," Jinx replied. "I know that a
reporter is supposed to remain objective and unbiased,
but most everyone already knows I'm Nola's roommate, anyone can do a search online and find out, so I
thought I should use it before some anonymous online
hater called me out for it. I just hope Wyck likes it."

"If your editor is as smart as you say he is," Helen
said, "I'm sure he'll expect nothing less from you."

Raising a glass filled with vodka, Alberta enthused,
"That's my college girl."

"She's not the only one," Joyce remarked.

"What do you mean, Aunt Joyce?"

Joyce held up a piece of paper from a pile on the
table. "Have you read through all these papers?"

"Most of them," Jinx replied. "I kind of went through
Nola's desk and the little filing cabinet she keeps in her
room. It's mainly work stuff, old tests and papers. I did-
n't want to be a snoop, but I thought I could use it to

build a profile of a caring teacher getting her students to realize their full potential."

"Looks like Nola's still trying to realize *her* full potential," Joyce advised.

Dropping her fork on her plate, Helen folded her arms in front of her and glared at Joyce. "Will you just spill it and tell us what you found?"

"According to this, Nola's still taking college classes," Joyce announced waving the paper in front of the ladies.

"That's not unusual," Jinx said, shaking her head. "Teachers often have to take graduate classes to maintain their license or if they want to get a raise."

"True, but Nola's taking undergraduate courses," Joyce corrected. "In English."

"But isn't she already an English teacher?" Alberta asked. "Why would a teacher take a class in a subject she's already teaching?"

"Because she doesn't have her teaching certificate that's why," Helen declared. "I told you she was a fraud."

Alberta removed the few remaining plates from the table and Joyce immediately spread out the papers to rummage through the pile farther. She flipped through a stack of essays with lots of red markings on them and tossed them aside. She then picked up a thick bunch of pages that were stapled together, which upon closer inspection turned out to be a classroom planning lesson. When she picked up the third stack, she stopped.

"Here we go."

"What is it?" Jinx asked.

"Proof that Helen's right and, unfortunately, Nola's a fraud."

"Score another one for the crotchety ex-nun," Helen declared, raising her vodka glass.

Jinx grabbed the papers out of Joyce's hand and her expression grew grimmer each time she turned a page. "*Dio mio!*"

"That's an even better pronunciation, Jinx," Alberta exclaimed. "Keep it up and you'll sound like a native in no time."

"I can't believe it," Jinx said. "According to this, Nola took an English composition class over the summer."

"What's that say?" Joyce asked, pointing at some scribbling on the top right-hand corner of the paper.

"Only three credits to go," Jinx answered. "I don't know that much about the teaching world, but I do know that you need to be a college graduate and have a teaching certificate to be able to teach in a high school."

"Not always," Helen heeded. "Out of necessity, parochial schools can be less strict in their teacher requirements, which is rather ironic given the rest of the church's beliefs. They don't pay as much nor do they offer a union pension so if they want to attract teachers they have to compromise."

"You are right Helen, but St. Winifred's Academy holds its teachers up to a higher standard," Joyce announced waving her phone around. "According to the school's website, all applicants for teaching positions must hold a degree from a four-year college, and they even say that a graduate degree is preferred."

"So how is Nola teaching if she doesn't have the qualifications to be a teacher?" Alberta asked.

"Do you know how easy it is to forge a diploma?" Helen snapped. "When I was working at the shelter, there was this guy . . . we all called him the Paper Boy because he made a living creating fake documents. He could whip up everything from driver's licenses to birth certificates to social security cards, and you would never know they weren't originals. Right before he was hauled off to jail, he gave me a passport just in case I needed to flee the country and adopt a new identity. If I ever disappear, do a search for Guadalupe Alvarez from Peru and you'll find me."

"Shut up, Lupe," Alberta scolded.

"Don't dismiss it so quickly, Berta, you never know when you'll need me to hook you up."

"No wonder Father Sal calls you the black sheep of the Catholic Church," Alberta remarked.

"I consider that a compliment," Helen said, once again raising her vodka glass.

"Can we focus, please?" Jinx asked. "Do you think Jonas could have found out about this and . . . I don't even want to say it out loud. Aunt Helen, would you mind?"

Draining her glass, Helen swallowed hard and replied, "Nola killed him over it." She scrunched up her face and shook her head. "I don't really like the girl, but that's a bit of a stretch even for me."

"He could've found out and blackmailed her to keep quiet," Joyce suggested. "Maybe that plus the previous stalking incident got to be too much, and Nola decided she needed to get rid of Jonas once and for all."

Jinx abruptly stood and started pacing the small kitchen. The room wasn't quite large enough to contain her energy so she started to walk quickly around the table.

"I don't believe it," she said. "There is absolutely no way that Nola is a murderer. Even if for some crazy reason they were in the tree house together, she might have—*might have*—gotten angry enough to push him out the door, but he was poisoned so his murder was premeditated, and there's no way Nola could've done that."

"I wonder if anyone else knows about Nola's indiscretion?" Alberta asked. "I mean if she's keeping a lie that she isn't Kichiro's girlfriend and only his beard so his real girlfriend doesn't get caught cheating on her husband, then it's very plausible that she hasn't told anyone about her fudged résumé, and the school may not even be aware Nola isn't truly qualified to teach."

"Only one way to find out," Joyce said. "Tomorrow morning we ask the principal."

Waving her finger back and forth in the air, Helen said, "Count me out. I like that one less than I like Nola. Anyway, I took on another shift at the animal shelter so I'm volunteering in the morning."

"I can't go either," Jinx stated. "I have to go all the way to Princeton to interview a woman who lived next door to Nola growing up."

"Nola grew up in Princeton?" Alberta asked.

"No, she grew up in South Jersey, near Asbury Park, but this woman, who used to be her neighbor, now lives in Princeton," Jinx explained. "She's the only person I could find from Nola's past, it's like everyone else disappeared."

"Or the Paper Boy helped them reinvent themselves," Helen declared.

"I'm not talking to you anymore," Alberta said. "Joyce, why don't you pick me up tomorrow morning at 6:45, and we'll drive over to the high school."

"That's a bit early," Jinx advised. "School doesn't start until eight o'clock."

"Perfect, I want to get to the principal before she gets too busy with the students and the craziness of the day," Alberta explained. "This way, we'll catch her with her hair down so to speak."

That wasn't the only thing that was down when they went to see Sharon the next morning.

Alberta and Joyce pulled into the high school parking lot a few minutes before seven o'clock. Luckily, they made all green lights and Joyce drove her Mercedes a bit faster than usual. The only other car in the lot was a four-door silver Subaru that looked to be a few years old. There was a small dent over the passenger side rear tire and some of the paint over the back bumper had been scraped off. Since the Subaru was parked in the spot reserved for St. Winifred's principal, they couldn't take any real credit for figuring out that it belonged to Sharon, but Joyce was impressed with Alberta for knowing that Sharon would be at school early and alone. If only they could get into the school before the rest of the staff and students arrived.

"It's locked," Alberta said, pulling on the front door.

Joyce was about to ring the bell to the right of the door when Alberta reached out and grabbed her hand to stop her. "Let's see if there's an entrance in the back."

"Good thinking."

Leading the way, Joyce walked around the brick building and just as she was about to turn the corner she stepped back causing Alberta to bump into her.

"What are you doing?" Alberta asked, her voice instinctively lowering to a whisper.

"I saw a man go in the back door," Joyce replied.

"*Col cavolo!* I was hoping to catch Sharon alone, not with a colleague."

"This wasn't a colleague," Joyce said. "It was a cop."

Throwing her hands up in the air and shaking her head, Alberta declared, "That's worse. All we need is Vinny to get in the way of our investigation and lecture us again about how we should keep our noses out of police business."

"Should we leave?" Joyce asked.

Alberta thought about it for a moment and while she was thinking she looked around the parking lot. "Wait a second, where's his car?"

Joyce joined in the search and even peered around the corner, but couldn't find another vehicle let alone a police car on the premises. "That's odd," Joyce said. "He could've walked I suppose, but the police station is across town."

"Well, we're here," Alberta declared. "If we can't talk to Sharon alone, we can find out why Vinny thinks it's so important to talk to her this early in the morning and on what they call the down low."

Joyce would have cracked up laughing at Alberta's remark if she didn't see what she saw through the small window next to the back door. The women looked in shock as they saw Sharon standing in the boiler room between two large water heaters with her arms around a policeman. Vinny looked shorter from this angle, but Alberta figured he was squatting down a bit to make it easier for Sharon to kiss him. It was only when the man lifted Sharon up, her legs wrapping around him and he turned to the side to walk over to the wall that she realized the cop wasn't Vinny, but Kichiro.

"Sharon's the married woman Kichiro is having the affair with!" Joyce whispered excitedly.

"*Dove l'allievo è disposto, apparirà l'insegnante,*" Alberta said, her voice hushed.

"The pupil isn't the only one who's willing, Berta,"

Joyce said. "The teacher looks like she's enjoying herself, too."

When Sharon's skirt dropped to the floor of the boiler room, Alberta tugged on Joyce's hand indicating that they had seen enough and should go. They scurried all the way to the car, giggling like two girls who just caught their parents making out.

They closed the Mercedes's doors quietly on the off chance that the lovers could hear the echo of the doors closing. Although Alberta and Joyce doubted Sharon and Kichiro would be able to hear anything other than their own sighs and passionate grunts and groans for at least the next fifteen minutes, give or take.

"So we may not know if Sharon knows that Nola is qualified to be a teacher," Alberta began, "but we do know that Sharon and Kichiro are having an affair."

"And I guess it only makes sense that Nola knows Sharon is the other woman," Joyce added. "I mean why else would she pose as Kichiro's girlfriend? She doesn't have any loyalty to him that we know of so she's probably participating in this sham because of her loyalty to her boss."

"Or because her boss is blackmailing her into doing it," Alberta suggested.

"Holy smokes, Berta, you're right!" Joyce shouted. "Sharon probably knows that Nola is shy of some college credits so she arranged for a little quid pro quo."

Although she spoke fluent Italian, Alberta was rusty on her Latin. "A little what?"

"Quid pro quo," Joyce repeated. "You wash my back and I'll wash yours. Sharon demanded Nola's participation in return for her silence, it's classic blackmail."

"Do you know what else will be classic?" Alberta asked.

"What?"

"My sister's face when she finds out what she missed," Alberta laughed. "She's gonna be pissed she didn't get the chance to see phony Sharon's true colors in all their X-rated glory. And I can't wait to be the one to tell her."

CHAPTER 14

Spazzatoio nuovo spazza ben la casa.

For the tenth time within the past five minutes Alberta looked out her kitchen window. Raindrops lazily plopped onto the surface of Memory Lake, making the sprawling body of water seem to come alive. Feeling ignored, Lola leaped from the kitchen table to the counter and purred loudly in an attempt to capture Alberta's attention and distract her. Even her cat knew that Alberta was exhibiting telltale symptoms of nervous tension.

"*Mi dispiace*, Lola," Alberta said, scooping up the cat in her arms and giving her a few apologetic kisses on the streak of white fur above her left eye. "Mama's had a big shock this morning, and she still hasn't recovered."

Sitting at the kitchen table playing a game of solitaire, Joyce kept her focus on her cards, but without lifting her head added, "Honey, if you thought that was shocking you should've seen some of the things I witnessed on Wall Street in the eighties."

"If I had I would've run from the place screaming and gotten right back on the boat to the mother country," Alberta replied while rocking Lola gently from side to side and stealing yet another glance out the kitchen window, "Like Uncle Nunzio."

Joyce threw down a five of hearts on top of a six of clubs. "I don't think I've ever heard of that one."

"My grandfather's younger brother so technically my great uncle," Alberta clarified. "He came to Hoboken to live with his brother, but the crowds and the smells made him so nervous he hopped on a ship back to Sicily the very next day."

"The rat race isn't for everyone," Joyce reflected.

"No it isn't," Alberta agreed. "I don't know how you survived in that industry and handled being a witness to all those crazy shenanigans."

Refilling her jelly glass with some lemon-flavored vodka, Joyce replied, "I really only had two choices, be a man or be successful. Since I've always been quite fond of my boobs, I chose the latter."

"You always had *budella* . . . guts, and look at me, I'm climbing the walls after what we saw!" Alberta cried, peeking out the kitchen window once more. "I guess I'm just dying to tell Jinx and Helen what we discovered, and both of them are taking their sweet time getting here."

"Don't be so hard on yourself," Joyce said as she turned over the ten of diamonds and subsequently won her fourth game in a row. "It isn't every day you witness a cop and a high school principal doing the vertical tango on Catholic school property."

"I knew there was something wrong with Kichiro ever since we found Jonas's dead body," Alberta announced as she began to pace the kitchen floor. "I don't know if it's coincidence or . . ."

Joyce stopped in mid-shuffle and looked at Alberta. "Or what?"

"If he's more involved in this murder than we origi-
nally thought."

"Berta, what exactly are you trying to say?"

"*Non mi dispiace*," she replied shaking her head in
agitation. "I don't know, but . . . the only thing I do
know is that I don't trust him."

Lola purred either in agreement or to get Alberta
to change the subject to something less morbid, and,
instinctively, Alberta's rocking turned to a bounce.
The sudden movement immediately reminded her of
the first time she caught her daughter, Lisa Marie, in a
lie.

Lisa Marie was four and her brother, Rocco, was almost a year old. Alberta was alone with the kids and
was fighting the stomach flu, but losing the battle. As
she ran to the bathroom she told her daughter to sit
on the bed next to her brother, who was sleeping on
his back and surrounded on all sides by a barricade of
pillows so if he rolled over he'd be protected by cush-
ions. From her position sitting on the toilet bowl, Alberta couldn't see her children but only heard the low
murmuring of the TV, a sound that was soon accompanied by a repetitive squeak.

"Lisa Marie stop jumping on the bed!"

The squeaking only stopped after Alberta heard a
thud.

Running into the bedroom, her panties and slacks
bunched up around her calves, Alberta saw her daughter sitting quietly on the bed while her son lay on the
hardwood floor still sleeping, his head turned to the
right and sliding slowly down the side of a pillow. On
the TV screen Jack LaLanne was showing his audience
how to master the trampoline, bouncing up and down
in a variety of positions. Furious that her daughter
would mimic a TV personality and ignore her mother,

Alberta glared at Lisa Marie, who appeared unfazed by her mother's rage.

"I told you not to jump on the bed!"

Lisa Marie looked away from the TV screen and directly into her mother's eyes. "I wasn't jumping. Rocco rolled over and fell on the floor. I didn't pick him up because I heard you coming, and I didn't want to hurt him."

Alberta hadn't been surprised by the lie, all children lie, but she had been startled by the ease at which the lie formed in her four-year-old daughter's mind. She was frightened that her young child could and would choose to concoct an alibi so effortlessly instead of admitting the truth.

Pressing Lola a little closer to her body, Alberta wondered if she could have prevented her daughter from relying on telling fabrications as an easy escape to avoid handling the truth had she challenged Lisa Marie further or made her understand that her lie wasn't acceptable. Maybe she could've prevented so many mother-daughter arguments and fights had she only trusted her instincts. But Alberta had been too afraid to listen to her own inner voice urging her to guide her daughter down a better path, so she just picked up her son, grateful that he hadn't been injured, and let her daughter get away with her lie. She couldn't make the same mistake again with Kichiro.

For some reason she suspected the cop was concealing more than the fact that he was having an affair with a married woman, but could that other lie, even if it did exist, have something to do with Jonas's murder? As long as there was the possibility that she could be right, Alberta knew she was going to have to act. There was a lot more at stake than a child's broken arm. Several lives and reputations were on the line, a presumably innocent woman was in jail, and a man had been murdered. She wasn't entirely sure how to act, but she was grateful that she wasn't going to repeat the same mistake and remain silent. She would trust her gut and figure out what to do, but for now, she'd settle on trusting her cat.

When Lola squirmed in her arms and tried to break free, Alberta knew that Jinx would walk through the door in less than a minute. She wasn't sure if Lola could hear Jinx's Chevy Cruze from a few blocks away or if she possessed some feline extrasensory perception, but she always sensed when Jinx was about to arrive. Tonight was no exception.

"Lovey, thank God you're back!" Alberta cried as Lola squirmed in her arms.

"What are you talking about, Gram? I'm early," Jinx replied entering the kitchen carrying two large shopping bags. "I told you I probably wasn't going to get back until six and it's only five-thirty."

"Sorry, but do we have news for you."

"So do I, but first things first," Jinx said, hoisting her bags onto the kitchen table as Joyce gathered her cards and put them back into their deck. "I brought dinner for everyone."

Alberta and Joyce remained silent as Jinx pulled out several cardboard boxes each with a sticker on it that read VVV and spread them out onto the table. Alberta wasn't sure what was more confusing: what the initials stood for or what the smell was that emanated from the boxes. She thought she would start by taking the safe route.

"What's VVV?" she asked.

"Very Very Vegan," Jinx replied. "This great little restaurant I found in Princeton. You'll love what I got for us."

Alberta and Joyce glanced at each other and without either of them saying a word knew they had to change the conversation until they could think up an excuse to avoid eating whatever horrible-smelling food was contained in the boxes without hurting Jinx's feelings too badly. Lola came to their rescue by purring loudly.

"I'm sorry, Lola!" Jinx squealed. "I didn't mean to ignore you, come here."

Lola practically jumped from Alberta to Jinx and immediately nuzzled in the crook of Jinx's neck. While Jinx was catering to Lola and making sure the cat was getting the attention she believed she deserved, it gave Joyce enough time to come up with a segue that spoke right to Jinx's journalistic ego and gave them a reprieve from having to succumb to what would inevitably be an indigestible dinner.

"I need an appetizer before dinner in the way of some news," Joyce declared. "What did you find out?"

Bubbling with excitement, Jinx forgot all about eating and instead spewed information. "I interviewed Nola's former neighbor, Crystal Lopez, who's a social worker. She told me about Nola's upbringing, which was not all sunshine and roses as you might say, Gram. Seems that Nola was adopted, which I knew, but by an older couple. They had always wanted to have children, but despite assurances from doctors that they were both capable of reproducing, they never did. So when biology didn't work in their favor, they took matters into their own hands and adopted. Crystal said that Nola's parents were good people, but what do you call them, Gram? The ones who just can't catch a break, but would give you the shirt off their backs."

"Good-hearted slobs," Alberta replied.

"That's it!" Jinx exclaimed. "Nola's dad worked in a

factory, but hurt his leg and couldn't work anymore, and Nola's mother had never had a real job so after the husband was hurt she could only find minimum wage work and waitressing gigs."

"You never knew any of this?" Joyce asked.

"Nola doesn't really talk about her parents," Jinx realized. "I mean, I knew they had passed, but I didn't know that they died within a year of each other when Nola was a freshman in college. She's been on her own ever since."

Alberta made the sign of the cross and whispered, "*Caro signore,* what a sin."

"The poor thing," Joyce added. "Does she have any other family?"

"Doesn't look like it," Jinx said. "According to Crystal, there were very few visitors to Nola's house growing up."

During the silence that followed Jinx's comment, Alberta aimlessly walked around the table until she sat in the chair next to Joyce. "No family," Alberta muttered almost to herself. "How is she supposed to get through this without any family?"

Jinx placed Lola on the floor and the cat immediately stretched, yawned, and pranced over to her bed in the corner of the kitchen to take an early evening nap. Jinx then took a seat next to Alberta and placed her hand over hers. "She has us, Gram," Jinx said softly. "And Crystal said she would absolutely be a character witness for Nola if it came to that."

"That's good to know," Joyce said. "But hopefully this will never get to trial if we can prove that Nola isn't the murderer."

"Which we all know she isn't," Jinx stated firmly. She then patted Alberta's hand just as firmly. "Now what's your news?"

Alberta was so lost in thought thinking about Nola being abandoned by her own mother and then abandoned yet again by the only parents she ever knew, that she almost forgot the news she was aching to share.

"Berta!" Joyce shouted. "Speak up or I'm gonna steal your thunder."

"Oh yes . . . s-sorry," Alberta stuttered, then announced matter-of-factly. "We stumbled on the fact that Kichiro is having an affair with Sharon."

Jinx's jaw dropped. "Sharon? As in *Principal* Sharon?"

"The one and only," Joyce confirmed.

"Are you sure?"

"We, um, caught them in . . . oh, how do you say it?" Alberta questioned. "In fragrance delectablé."

Joyce barely stifled a laugh. "I think you mean in flagrante delicto, which is Latin for getting caught with your pants down."

"You caught them having sex?" Jinx screamed. "Where?"

"In the basement of the high school," Alberta replied.

"Technically the boiler room," Joyce corrected.

Jinx's jaw dropped even farther and she started waving her arms around like she was guiding a 747 as to where to park on a crowded tarmac. "That totally gives new meaning to putting the 'pal' in 'principal,' " she said. "But I mean Sharon is married and the principal of a Catholic high school, isn't she like breaking every single rule in the book? And by book I mean the bible!"

"I think she's breaking most of the rules in both testaments," Joyce agreed. "Which is why she was so desperate to keep it a secret that she must have convinced Nola to act as her surrogate and masquerade as Kichiro's girlfriend so no one, especially her husband, would put two and two together."

Taking advantage of Jinx's preoccupation with the revelation that Kichiro was Sharon's male mistress, Alberta stacked the cardboard boxes of food one on top of the other and pushed them to the side so she could cut a piece of Entenmann's lemon pie and pour some glasses of lemon-flavored vodka. She took a bite of pie and savored the tart citrusy filling before adding, "The main question is, did Sharon convince Nola or did she blackmail her?"

"No, the main question is, How does Jonas fit into this very messy equation?"

The presence of Helen in the kitchen startled all of them so much that Lola very unhappily woke up from her nap, hissed at Helen, and trotted out of the room.

"Holy Benito Mussolini!" Alberta shouted. "Where did you come from?!"

"The front door."

"Nobody uses the front door!"

"I do from time to time," Helen said, taking off the plastic head covering she had been wearing and placing it in the dish drainer to dry.

"Did you drive up?" Joyce asked. "We didn't even hear your car?"

"I had one of the other volunteers drop me off so instead of walking around the house in the rain I came in the front door."

Helen took the empty seat at the table, placed her pocketbook in front of her, and proceeded to cut herself an extra-large piece of pie. "But who cares how I got here? You should just be happy I'm here now so I can bring some reality to this powwow. I overheard everything and it's good, efficient detective work, but ladies it has nothing to do with Jonas or the murder investigation."

The three women wanted to rebut Helen's comment, and Alberta even opened her mouth to speak, but quickly shut it closed. As much as they all wanted to argue with Helen, they couldn't because she was right. Kichiro and Sharon were having an affair and Nola was an accessory to that moral crime, but none of it tied them to Jonas's murder.

"Wait a minute!" Alberta cried. "We're all *stunods.*"

"Why?" was the collective response.

"Jonas worked at the high school and, most damaging, he has a track record of stalking Nola," Alberta reminded them.

"But Nola retracted her restraining order," Jinx said.

"So she had a change of heart," Alberta said dismissively. "It doesn't change the fact that at one point she was scared enough to demand police intervention."

"Okay, that's a link," Helen said, munching loudly on her pie. "But it still doesn't connect Jonas's murder to Kichiro and Sharon's adultery."

"Maybe Jonas was stalking Sharon too, and as a result found out about her affair with Kichiro," Alberta surmised.

"Very possible," Helen replied. "Or he found out that Nola was covering for her boss, saw her as the weak link, and blackmailed her for money or else he would tell Sharon's husband."

"Or maybe Jonas had been stalking Nola because he liked her and when he found out she was dating Kichiro he thought it was for real and he got a bit more aggressive in his stalking," Jinx hypothesized.

"That's at least two 'ors' ladies," Joyce pointed out. "Not that I'm keeping count."

"But each 'or' has one thing in common," Helen said. "Which you're not going to like."

"What's that?" Jinx asked.

"Each one gives Nola motive for killing him," she replied.

The only sounds in the kitchen were the rattling of the blinds in the window stirred up by a rain shower breeze, Helen's chewing, and Jinx's long, deep intakes of breath.

"Whether Jonas was blackmailing Nola about her role in covering up the affair or if he was stalking her more aggressively, which made Nola fear for her life, she might have gotten desperate, decided to take the law in her own hands, and killed him," Helen described. "I've seen women do worse things."

Jinx leaned back in her chair and crossed her arms in front of her chest, textbook body language for when a person was on the defense. Whether it was plausible or not, Jinx did not want to hear any theory that hinged on Nola being a murderer even though she knew her friend was keeping secrets and acting oddly.

"And what if Jonas didn't know Nola was involved in the covering up of the affair?" Jinx speculated. "What reason would she then have for killing him?"

Helen took a long sip of vodka and placed her jelly glass on the table. "I know it sounds strange and you may not understand it, but she could have acted out of loyalty to Sharon."

"Aunt Helen, that's ridiculous. Nola might be indebted to Sharon for her job, but it's hardly worth killing someone over."

"And we don't know for certain that Sharon is aware that Nola isn't truly qualified to be a teacher," Joyce reminded them. "In fact, I hate to say it, but we aren't certain of much of anything."

Another long pause crept its way into the kitchen. The women nibbled on pie, took sips of vodka, and stared into empty space until Helen broke the silence.

"Here's one thing I do know," Helen said.

"What's that?"

"I am not eating any of the junk that's in those boxes."

"Aunt Helen! How can you say that? You don't even know what's in there."

"I can smell it! And whatever is in there is either dead, rancid, or both," Helen wisecracked.

"The veggie burgers aren't rancid, they're delicious. I had them for lunch!" Jinx cried. "So are the tofu fries, the quinoa, kale, and especially the fungi salad."

"Fungi salad?" Alberta shouted. "Oh *mamma mia*, Jinx! You were brought up better than that."

"Also too," Joyce said. "I don't think you can actually use 'delicious' to describe fungi."

"I have an idea," Helen started. "Why don't you bring all this . . . *food* . . . to Nola in prison? It can't be much worse than the slop that poor thing is being forced to eat in there."

"Trust me, if Jinx likes that stuff, it's definitely worse than what they fed me in prison."

"Nola!" Jinx cried. "What are you doing here?!"

"I'm sorry, the front door was open so we came right in," Nola said.

"No, I mean . . . you're like . . . supposed to be behind bars!" Jinx cried again.

"Please don't tell me you broke out of jail!" Alberta said.

"Are you a fugitive?" Helen asked. "In addition to being a bad director."

"I'm out on bail," Nola explained. "And my show

got raves by the way. One reviewer said that New Jersey was never more alive with the sound of music."

"Because Jersey is tone deaf," Helen snapped.

"Ignore her," Alberta instructed and guided Nola to take her seat at the table. "But honey, we were told the judge refused to allow bail because he thought you were a flight risk since you don't have real roots here in Tranquility, otherwise I would've posted your bail."

Nola looked down at the table in the hopes that her tears wouldn't be so obvious. "I know," she replied, her voice soft and thick. "That's why we came here. We went to my apartment first, but Jinx wasn't there so I assumed she'd be here and, well, I didn't want to be alone."

"But you're not alone, honey," Joyce said. "Who's the boy?"

All heads turned to the door leading into the living room and saw a young blond-haired man, who despite his navy pinstripe three-piece suit and bright red power tie, looked to be no more than twenty years old.

"This is my lawyer," Nola said.

"Don't you mean your lawyer's *intern*?" Jinx asked.

"I'm Nola's public defender," the man said, his deep voice an almost comical contrast to his youthful looks. "And before you ask, no this isn't my first case."

"Is it your second?" Helen asked.

"Your third?" Joyce added.

Unable to suppress a smile during the cross-examination, he replied, "It's actually my two hundred and twenty-fourth. And because I know everyone likes to keep score, I've only lost thirty-six of those cases and only fifteen of them have resulted in significant jail time so my track record is rather good."

"When did you start practicing law?" Helen asked. "Kindergarten?"

This time he laughed out loud. "I know I look young, but I've been practicing for over five years," he explained. "I'll be thirty in December, but I inherited my mother's smooth Swedish skin so I'm blessed or cursed, depending on how you look at it, with a baby face."

Alberta grabbed a folding chair from the hall closet and wedged it between where Nola and Helen were sitting. "Here, sit down, and have some vodka and pie," she ordered. "Did you pay Nola's bail?"

"No, I only got the judge to change his mind," he explained.

"So who paid your bail?" Joyce asked.

"I don't know, it was posted anonymously," Nola replied as she began to devour her pie. "This is seriously amazing. I know I was only in prison for a few days, but it felt like an eternity."

Alberta examined Nola's face and had to agree. The girl was about the same age as Jinx, but looked years older thanks to the shadows under her eyes and the tension lines around her mouth. But at least she could still smile.

"Lola!" Nola squealed. "How nice to see you again."

"Ooh, Nola and Lola, it's like a nursery rhyme," Joyce said.

"Looks like Lola's passed her nursery rhyme days and has graduated to more adult material," Helen said.

Elongating her body and purring softly, Lola wove herself in and out of the lawyer's legs and when he picked her up to cradle her, she threw her head back as if in ecstasy.

"As you can see, Bruno is quite the charmer," Nola shared. "If we do have to go to trial, he'll have the jury wrapped around his finger."

"Bruno?" Alberta said. "That's hardly a Swedish name."

"My dad's Sicilian," he explained.

"*Veramente?*" Alberta asked. "You wouldn't just be saying that to get on our good side, would you?"

"From what I've heard about you ladies, I doubt I'd be able to get anything past you," Bruno replied. Transferring Lola to his left hand, he extended his right hand to Alberta for a formal greeting. "The full name's Bruno Bel Bruno."

"You can't get much more Sicilian than that," Alberta observed, shaking Bruno's hand.

She liked his grip, soft, yet strong, like a comfortable cushion on top of concrete. She looked directly into the young man's bright blue eyes and they were staring right back at her, unwavering, but filled with kindness. She felt a sense of calm in his presence and something more, something that reminded her of when she looked into Sloan's eyes, the feeling of being protected. Maybe there was hope for the male species after all, she thought. Helen, however, didn't seem to share her opinion.

"What town is your father from?" Helen quizzed.

"Trapani," Bruno answered.

"We could be neighbors, we're from Tortoli," Helen claimed.

Before Alberta could comment, Bruno corrected Helen, "Only if my family owned a speedboat to cross the Mediterranean. Tortoli is in Sardinia. You're a good cross-examiner."

"I used to be a nun," Helen said. "Kind of the same thing. I just wanted to make sure you weren't luring us into a false sense of security."

"I wouldn't dare. I know all about the wrath of the Sicilian woman," Bruno conveyed. "One year my mother served Swedish meatballs at Christmas and my Sicilian aunts almost ran her back to Örnsköldsvik."

"As they should have!" Helen cried.

"Ornsko-who?" Alberta repeated.

"Her hometown," Bruno clarified. "A few hours north of Stockholm."

Alberta turned to Helen and asked, "Are you going to test him about that, too?"

"No he's passed the Helen test with flying colors."

"Don't worry, I'm in really good hands," Nola confirmed.

"Even if my longshoreman dad always said my hands look like they never did a real man's work in their entire life," Bruno joked.

"I think I can speak for the rest of us when I say that we like you," Joyce announced. "And that we know you'll not stop working until the charges are dropped and Nola can put this whole unfortunate situation behind her."

"That's exactly what I intend to do," Bruno announced. "And, if you're all willing, I'd really like your help."

"*Spazzatoio nuovo spazza ben la casa,*" Alberta said. "Looks like a new broom is looking to sweep the house clean."

"I find a fresh pair of eyes—or a new broom—is always helpful when trying to uncover a mystery," Bruno stated.

"You do know that you're in the presence of the Ferrara Family Detective Agency, right?" Jinx said. "The title's unofficial, but our determination isn't."

"Nola told me," Bruno replied. "And I also know that you and your grandmother were the ones who found Jonas's body."

"Yes, while we were out for our morning jog," Alberta confirmed.

"The rain's passed and there's still an hour or so of light left, how'd you like to take me back to the scene of the crime?" Bruno asked.

"As long as we can drive," Alberta said. "I limit my jogging time for the morning when I'm too tired to come up with an excuse not to exercise."

"Why do you want to go back there?" Jinx asked. "The police have thoroughly searched the area, and it's definitely been contaminated by now. There wouldn't be any clues to pick up."

Flashing a smile of perfectly white teeth that would be the envy of any movie star, Bruno said, "Jinx, you'd be surprised what you could learn by going back to where things all began. If you're game, I'd like us to go back to Tranquility Park and reenact the crime."

"I'm free," Joyce said.

"I love a good reenactment," Alberta concurred.

"As long as we stop at the diner on the way back so I can get some real food and not have to eat this Jinx-approved vegan nightmare of a smorgasbord, I'm game," Helen added.

"You're such a sport, Aunt Helen."

"I know, sweetie."

"Then ladies, please follow me to the tree house," Bruno commanded. "Who knows what secrets we'll uncover."

CHAPTER 15

Siamo ancora morti?

Entering Tranquility Park for the first time since finding Jonas's dead body, Alberta felt her bravado slither away from her like a snake burrowing into a mound of dirt to escape a stronger enemy. She didn't immediately notice her strength had betrayed her, in fact, she had been enjoying the stroll through the park on the crisp autumn evening, the smell of rain still clinging to the breeze, the leaves, not entirely water-logged so they still crackled underneath her feet. But by the time she stood underneath the tree house, she felt exhausted as if she had just run several miles bare-foot and without her sports bra. She felt wounded and bruised, physically ill, and she realized that it was be-cause she was standing on the very spot where Jonas most likely took his last breath. Figuratively and liter-ally, she was standing on the threshold of death. Of course this was all in a day's work for a private detec-tive, but it was definitely an out-of-the-ordinary experi-ence for a grandmother helping out her ambitious granddaughter.

However, if Alberta was going to continue working alongside Jinx as well as Helen and Joyce to solve crimes, she was going to need to learn how to reconcile these types of situations and maintain an emotional distance from murder victims and would-be clients. It was a gratifying and even humbling feeling to help people who were lost and who didn't have family to lean on for support like Nola, but if Alberta wound up losing herself in the process, she wasn't going to be able to help people for very long.

Alberta exhaled deeply and looked around at Jinx, Helen, and Joyce, and wondered how they were feeling. She knew that despite leaving the convent for reasons still unknown to her, Helen had a much stronger spiritual foundation and believed unequivocally in the continuation of life after death. As a Catholic, Alberta technically shared that belief, but privately had doubts and entertained the possibility that upon death all type of life, physical and spiritual, terminated. It was a frightening thought, but one she couldn't escape. Perhaps it was time to get back to church on a regular basis, she thought, or at least say her evening prayers again. She instinctively touched the crucifix and never took it off, which caused her to feel ashamed because even though she wore the religious symbol around her neck, she would be a hypocrite if she labeled herself a true believer.

Although Joyce was raised a Baptist, she converted to Catholicism when she married Alberta's brother, Anthony. Even though Alberta knew Joyce to be an independent woman who rarely strayed from her own convictions to please someone else, she always felt she converted to make life easier for her husband. Having a black wife was one thing, but having a black wife who wasn't Catholic was almost blasphemous. Regardless of the reason, Joyce's conversion was hardly a gesture as both her boys were baptized, received their First Holy Communion, their confirmation, and graduated from a parochial high school. Joyce had clocked in as many hours kneeling in pews as Alberta did and probably many more hours in the last few years. It didn't matter if the core of her belief was Baptist or Catholic, either way it was unshakable.

As part of a new generation, Jinx had a much different take on organized religion, and her participation in church came a distant second to her own personal spirituality. Alberta and Jinx had yet to have an in-depth conversation about Jinx's beliefs so Alberta didn't know the strength of her granddaughter's foundation, but she hoped it was built on firmer ground than hers. It was not easy to deal with death, murder, and criminal activity on a constant basis without having the knowledge of some greater good lurking just beyond your own shadow and within your own breath. Alberta made a mental note to strike up a conversation with Jinx to find out her thoughts on religion and spirituality right after they proved who really killed Jonas. At the rate they were going, however, that conversation wasn't going to take place anytime soon.

"So this is where you found Jonas's body?" Bruno asked, standing underneath the tree house.

"Yes, on our way back from the other side of the park," Jinx replied.

"And when you found him did you see anyone nearby or running from the scene?" Bruno followed up.

"No, it was very early and the park was deserted that morning," Jinx replied. "But Gram did see something inside the tree house when we ran past it the first time."

Bruno's blue eyes lit up. "What did you see, Mrs. Scaglione?"

"First, call me Alberta," she replied. "Second, I'm not exactly sure what I saw. Vinny thought it was a bird, but I believe it was a person though I can't prove it."

Bruno pondered Alberta's comment, nodding his head and surveying the area. A wild breeze stirred up out of nowhere rustling the leaves and mussing up his hair so his bangs fell onto his forehead giving him an even more youthful look. He held his hands behind his back and started to walk around the area as if he was in a courtroom presenting a case to a jury, which gave the women some insight into how the combination of his deep voice and boyish charm could captivate his audience.

"So let me set up one possible timeline," Bruno said. "Someone was in the tree house along with Jonas when you entered the park, you and Jinx jogged past, that person pushed Jonas to his death, then jumped out of the tree house himself, or herself for that matter, ran off, and was out of sight by the time the two of you returned to find Jonas's dead body."

"That sounds right to me," Alberta concurred.

"Which means that whoever was in the tree house with Jonas probably saw the two of you run by," Bruno said.

"Why do you say that?" Jinx asked.

"Because the person was working under a strict deadline, pardon the pun," Bruno began. "The sun had already started to rise so our murderer wasn't working in complete darkness and he—or she—didn't know how quickly the two of you would return, so the moment you ran by, the clock started ticking and he or she had to act quickly in order to get out of there unseen."

While the rest of the group continued to talk and recount the details and timeline of what happened the morning Jonas's body was found, Nola was standing by herself, a few feet from the group, looking up at the tree house as if it was an alien structure. Her face resembled a mask worn to hide what lay just underneath. Despite her attempt to conceal her emotions, Alberta could sense that Nola was utterly confused and deeply wounded by her current situation. She moved closer to the young woman as quietly and inconspicuously as possible until she was standing next to Nola, who didn't alter her gaze and appeared not to notice Alberta's presence.

"You're awfully quiet, honey," Alberta whispered. "Are you okay?"

Nola shook her head almost imperceptibly before speaking. "No, I'm not," she replied, her voice even quieter than Alberta's. "People think I actually killed a man." After a moment, she turned to face Alberta. "How could that be possible?"

"Remember you're innocent until proven guilty," Alberta replied.

Smiling broadly, Nola looked like she was going to burst into laughter. But when she spoke, her voice was rich with sarcasm, fear, even panic. "You know that's a lie. I know I'm innocent, but to the rest of this community I'm guilty as sin because that's much easier to comprehend. Why is evil so much easier to accept than goodness?"

Alberta wasn't sure if she was more stunned by the question or the tone of Nola's voice, which was childlike and reeking of innocence. She didn't know Nola very well, but she had never heard her speak so despondently. She had even less gumption than when she was in prison, and it broke her heart. Alberta wanted to reach out and hug her, take her in her arms, and tell her that everything was going to be alright, but she didn't want to lie. She didn't want to make a promise that she couldn't keep. So instead, she answered the question as honestly as she could.

"Maybe it's because people want to think someone else is bad so they can feel good about themselves," Alberta replied.

Nola looked at Alberta with such intensity that even though they were a few feet from a group of people still chattering and debating clues, she felt as if they were the only two people on the planet. "I'm not perfect, Mrs. Scaglione, but I'm not a murderer," Nola said. "Do you believe me?"

The question was so simple, yet so complicated that it made Alberta smile involuntarily as if she had stumbled on a new recipe to make lasagna that was obvious and revolutionary at the same time. It was something she should have known all along, but something that had somehow eluded her. All this time Alberta had taken for granted that Nola was innocent because she was Jinx's friend. How could her granddaughter be friends with a coldhearted criminal? Why would Jinx defend a ruthless killer? But Alberta had never really taken a moment to ask herself what she truly thought. Did she agree with Jinx's proclamation that Nola couldn't be guilty of premeditated murder? Was she as certain as her granddaughter seemed to be? Until the moment Nola asked her question, she didn't know. But the answer came to her quickly and decisively.

"Yes, Nola, I believe you," Alberta stated.

Relief crept across Nola's face slowly, yet steadily, her face brightening like the end of an eclipse, and gratitude filled her eyes. Just when she looked like she was about to cry, she turned her gaze back toward the tree house and spoke in a much louder voice so as to bring the rest of the group into their conversation.

"What I really want to know is how in the world could anyone even get up there without a ladder?"

Turning around to face Nola, Jinx shouted, "I was about to ask the same question. I mean seriously, are you psychic or something?"

"Nope," Nola replied. "Merely curious."

"That makes all of us," Joyce added. "I mean there was no ladder found inside the tree house and when Vinny tried to climb the tree, he fell flat on his back. He had to have Kichiro bring a ladder for him to climb so he could get inside."

"You're all going to laugh at me, but I'll say it anyway," Alberta forewarned. "The only thing that makes sense is if there was some kind of portable, retractable ladder that extended up when you placed it on the ground so you could climb it, get into the tree house, and then retract it once again. It would be the opposite of one of those ladders that roll down like on a fire escape or a helicopter."

"That's not laughable at all," Bruno said.

"It isn't?" Alberta asked.

"No, it's brilliant," he replied.

"But pure fiction," Helen added.

"Not at all," Bruno said. "There is such a thing as a retractable ladder and it's something that the police would have access to."

"Seriously?" Alberta cried, shocked that she intuitively stumbled on a real clue that could help their investigation.

"And in case anyone's forgotten," Bruno said before taking a dramatic pause, "Nola's fake boyfriend is a cop."

The comment created the hushed silence its speaker intended. If Kichiro had access to such a ladder, he could gain entry to the tree house at any time without anyone knowing he was up there. It also meant, most notably and more frighteningly, that it could've been his shadow Alberta noticed inside the tree house.

"You think Kichiro could've been the person Alberta saw?" Joyce asked.

"It's very possible," Bruno replied. "More than possible actually. Those ladders aren't that easy to come by and they're much more expensive than the traditional kind so you'd want to have a ladder that was not only easily transportable, but also easy to hide."

"An adulterer is very good at hiding things," Helen said not realizing exactly what she had said.

Alberta, Joyce, and Jinx quickly glanced at each other and then over at Nola whose face was starting to turn even paler than normal. Quickly, Alberta decided she needed to put a verbal Band-Aid on the leak that was about to hemorrhage thanks to Helen's slip of the tongue.

"Technically Kichiro isn't committing adultery," Alberta corrected. "Only his, um, lady friend is."

"You know about that?" Nola asked.

"Yes," Jinx replied. "Kichiro kind of confessed it to us."

"That is a huge relief actually," Nola said. "Jinx knows that I have a tendency to ramble, and keeping that secret from everyone was making me a little crazy."

"Now that's one less thing you have to keep hidden," Alberta rationalized.

The women fought the urge to look at each other because they had agreed, for the time being anyway, not to disclose to Nola that they knew the other woman was Sharon. They were rather certain Nola had to know this information, but on the off chance it was also a secret they thought it best to keep the knowledge among the four of them only. Knowledge that thanks once again to Helen was about to be spilled.

"Vinny did say the tree house was used as a lover's hideout," Helen said. "So maybe Kichiro went to rendezvous with Sharon at the tree house and found Jonas there instead."

Nola reached out to hold onto the tree to steady herself. The women weren't sure if she was stunned that Sharon was Kichiro's married girlfriend or shocked that Helen would announce the truth so cavalierly. Not that it really mattered because once the words had been spoken there was no taking them back.

"Helen . . . sometimes, *Giuro su Dio!*" Alberta seethed.

"Knock it off, all of you!" Helen cried. "We know Kichiro was shacking up with Sharon, and Nola knows Kichiro was shacking up with Sharon. The only one who probably didn't know about the affair was Bruno."

Clearing his throat, Bruno replied, "You are, um, right about that, ma'am."

Letting go of the tree, Nola was stronger now. She didn't look very happy, but she was definitely more in control of her emotions. "Bruno doesn't know about Sharon because I didn't want him to know."

"Why not, Nola?" Bruno asked. "This is incredibly useful information."

"No, it isn't!" Nola shouted. "All it proves is that I'm a liar and a really good one. How is that supposed to help me beat a murder charge?"

She had a point, Alberta thought. If Nola could willingly walk around as Kichiro's girlfriend all the while knowing that his real girlfriend was her married boss who may or may not know that Nola was also not qualified to be a teacher, it could destroy her character in the eyes of the court. No one felt good about keeping the information hidden, but exposing it could do irreparable damage.

"I'll make a deal with you, Nola," Bruno started. "We'll keep Sharon's name out of this unless it becomes apparent that she is somehow involved in Jonas's murder."

"Sharon has absolutely nothing to do with Jonas's death," Nola stated. "So we have a deal."

"Good," Bruno replied. "Now, can we please continue with our reenactment? If Kichiro is the one with the ladder—allegedly of course—he couldn't have found Jonas inside the tree house, it would've had to be the other way around."

"Right," Jinx huffed. "It's all about that dumb ladder."

Standing back from the tree house, Alberta looked up and tried to imagine a scenario that would include the two men inside the small space. "Just suppose that Jonas somehow was hiding up there since it was his personal tree house in the first place that his father built for him and Kichiro climbed up thinking that he was going to meet Sharon."

"That would've been awkward," Joyce said.

"Exactly!" Alberta agreed. "Maybe Jonas saw Sharon and Kichiro in there once before and he was waiting for them."

"To blackmail them?" Joyce asked.

"Yes," Alberta said. "If Kichiro thought that Jonas was going to reveal the truth about their affair, he might do anything to prevent him from exposing the truth knowing that it would destroy Sharon's marriage as well as her career."

"A Catholic high school principal having an affair with a much younger cop isn't what you'd label the good kind of publicity," Bruno added.

"I can't believe this is happening!" Nola screamed.

The young woman's outburst disrupted not only the peaceful surroundings but the hypothetical speculations as well. The time for ruminating over possible ways that Jonas might have met his untimely death were over and it was time to deal with the reality Nola was having to endure.

"All I was trying to do was help my . . . my friend . . . you know?" Nola explained. "I wanted to help Sharon and now I'm being charged with murder and have to defend myself against a crime I didn't commit."

"Don't worry, Nola," Jinx consoled, hugging her friend. "We're going to find out who really did this."

Alberta was delighted to see Jinx's maternal instinct kick in and embrace Nola the way she wanted to only moments ago, but she realized a mother also had to dispense tough love.

"Is Sharon really your friend, Nola?" Alberta asked.

"What?"

"You said that all you were trying to do was help your friend," Alberta repeated. "I didn't think the two of you were that close, more like employer and employee."

"We're . . . both," Nola replied.

She jabbed at the tears still falling from her eyes and Helen grabbed a handkerchief from her pocketbook and offered it to her. Alberta watched her go through the motions of wiping away her tears, but thought she looked odd. Not scared by her circumstance or embarrassed to have virtual strangers witness her vulnerability, but nervous. When Nola resumed speaking, she punctuated her explanation with sniffles, stuttering, twitches, and pauses. Alberta felt like she was making up her speech on the spot.

"It's a . . . a small school you know? And since we're a Catholic high school . . . parochial . . . we're working with a much smaller b-budget than p-public schools so . . . so, you know, we all have to pitch in where we can and, well, that . . . that kind of um . . . um . . . work environment makes you get closer to each other."

Alberta wanted to look around to see if anyone else was alarmed by Nola's dismal effort at public speaking, but she couldn't take her eyes off of Nola. "I just find it strange, not to mention disappointing, that neither Kichiro nor Sharon have come to your aid since you've been arrested."

"I'm sure they're just . . . trying to, um, distance themselves from me so they d-don't accidentally out themselves and reveal their affair," Nola stammered.

"After all you've done for them, I think it's time they returned the favor and came forward, don't you?" Alberta asked.

"No!"

The word echoed throughout the park, hovering overhead like a steel dome, its power and conviction as strong as the sturdy oak trees that dotted the immense landscape. The authority and command of Nola's voice even surprised Bruno, who up until then had exuded an air of unflappability.

When Nola spoke again, the volume of her voice wasn't as loud, but her tone was just as unwavering. "Absolutely not. We just agreed. I do not want Sharon brought into this. You all promised me that you wouldn't say anything, and you can't go back on your promise! Her affair has nothing to do with Jonas's murder."

An image of Alberta's deceased husband, Sammy, yelling at her flashed through her mind. Alberta had rarely talked back to Sammy when he sounded like that, but Sammy was dead and so were those fears. She could speak her mind, she had earned that right, and often what she had to say needed to be heard.

"You don't know that, Nola, and we don't either," Alberta replied. "All we really know about Sharon is that she's a liar and a cheater."

It could have been the cool weather, but Nola's neck and ears started to turn a light shade of red. She didn't appear to like what Alberta said.

"Mrs. Scaglione, you have to promise me that you're not going to do anything that will implicate Sharon," Nola demanded. "Swear to me!"

"I can't do that, honey," Alberta replied. "All I can do is promise that I won't say a word unless I feel I have to. The first thing we need to do is speak with Kichiro and find out exactly what he knows about this whole situation and if he really does have access to some kind of retractable ladder."

Nola looked up at the sky that had turned into a blend of dark blues and pinks like an unfinished abstract painting. Its visual beauty seemed to soothe her spirit and help her understand that Alberta, Bruno, and everyone gathered were all on her side.

"Okay fine, that sounds like a good plan," Nola said.

"I agree, Gram, Kichiro's been acting strange since this whole thing began."

"It could be that he feels guilty for sleeping with another man's wife," Helen suggested.

"Or he's feeling guilty for taking another man's life," Alberta proposed.

"You really think he could've killed Jonas?" Jinx asked.

"It's a very real possibility and one we need to explore," Alberta declared. "First thing tomorrow I'll speak with Vinny and pick his brain to find out what he truly thinks about his detective's peculiar attitude lately."

"I have a better idea, Gram."

"What's that, lovey?"

"We might have more luck if I ask Freddy to talk to Kichiro," Jinx said. "You know, guy to guy."

"As the only guy represented here," Bruno remarked, "I think that's a smart idea."

Blushing slightly, Jinx replied, "Thank you, Bruno."

"Whoa, look at the time," Bruno said, glancing at his watch. "Nola, I have to get you back home."

"She's a little old for a curfew, don't you think?" Helen asked.

"It has nothing to do with my age," Nola said. "But everything to do with this."

Lifting up her pants leg she revealed that she was wearing an ankle monitor that tracked her every step. She explained that the terms of her bail insisted that she not leave the state and that she had to be home by eight o'clock every night. Since it was seven forty-five, Nola only had fifteen minutes before she would get into trouble the first night she was out on bail.

"You two go ahead," Jinx said. "I'll get a lift home."

"Thanks again, everyone," Nola said, smiling and tearing up at the same time. "Despite my little outburst, I really am very grateful."

They all exchanged quick good-nights and Bruno

and Nola raced to his Volvo that was parked near the entrance of the park. By the time the women were standing under the metal arch, the Volvo had already made a right turn at the end of the block.

"Who's in the mood for some potato pancakes?" Helen asked. "My treat."

"That's one of my favorites," Alberta cooed. "Is this a special occasion?"

"Alberta Marie Teresa, you are a worse actress than Nola," Helen barked.

"What are you talking about?" Alberta asked.

"Berta, it doesn't happen a lot, but I have to agree with Helen," Joyce added.

Perplexed, Alberta stared at the women and saw that only Jinx looked as confused as she did. "Seriously, I have no idea what you're talking about."

"It's your birthday, Berta!" Helen shouted.

"Today?" Alberta exclaimed.

"Gram, I can't believe I forgot. I'm so sorry!"

"Oh please, lovey, I didn't even remember," Alberta said with a laugh. "Well, happy sixty-fifth to me! Let's celebrate with some potato pancakes!"

"I might even allow myself some real dairy sour cream," Jinx said.

"Also too, some applesauce," Joyce added.

"Berta, take us to Veronica's Diner," Helen ordered. "Unless you forgot how to drive, too."

"I have to drive on my birthday?" Alberta joked.

"Even though you've taken up the crazy sport of jogging, you're still too old to walk all the way to the diner," Helen said. "So yes, you have to drive."

"Yes ma'am."

The four women walked to Alberta's BMW having a bizarre conversation that continued as they drove to the diner. They were marveling at how Alberta could have forgotten her birthday, comparing silver dollar pancakes to the conventional size, and wondering if Kichiro really could have committed premeditated murder by poisoning and tossing Jonas out of the tree house. All thoughts about birthdays, pancakes, and poison were forgotten when Alberta ran a red light.

"Gram, you didn't even slow down."

"I tried."

"Try harder, birthday girl," Helen shouted from the backseat. "I'd like to get to the diner in one piece."

"I'm not doing it deliberately," Alberta said, a trace of fear creeping into her voice. "The brakes aren't working."

"What?!" Helen shouted.

"They were working fine on the ride over here," Joyce said, leaning forward from behind the driver's seat.

"Well, they're not now," Alberta said.

"This is not funny, Berta!" Helen shouted.

Alberta pumped the brakes several times, pressing her foot all the way down on the brake pedal, but the car didn't slow down, in fact, it started to go faster.

"Somebody cut the brake lines!" Jinx screamed.

"What?" Helen and Joyce screamed simultaneously.

"Oh my God!" Alberta shouted. "Who would do such a thing?"

"Somebody who doesn't want us helping Nola," Jinx answered.

Thinking quickly, Alberta swerved to make a left-hand turn and barely avoided colliding with an oncoming car. She breathed a sigh of relief for not crashing into another vehicle, but when she saw what lay ahead she immediately regretted her decision.

"Berta! What are you doing?" Helen cried. "This is Crimson Lake Road."

"I know!"

"It's all downhill!"

"I forgot!"

"And do you know why they call it Crimson Lake Road?"

"No!"

"Because people crash here all the time and leave blood stains on the road!" Helen screamed.

"Gram, are the brakes seriously not working?"

"If they were I wouldn't be going eighty miles per hour down a dirt road."

"Use the emergency brake!" Joyce screamed.

Both Jinx and Joyce reached for the emergency brake at the same time and pulled it back, but all they heard was a loud screeching sound coming from somewhere inside the car. Looking out the windows they saw the scenery whizzing by on both sides. On the left was a very narrow patch of land with a low, barbed wire fence that was built to keep cars from falling into a ditch and on the right was Crimson Lake, which was about half the size of Memory Lake. Alberta thought she could steer the car into the lake, but there were stone barriers built to prevent such a thing from happening. She looked to the left and tried to see how deep the ditch was, but at the speed the car was going she couldn't tell how severely they would be hurt if they careened off the side of the road. She looked straight ahead and saw their only option.

About a hundred feet in front of them the road curved to the right and followed the circumference of the lake, but just before the curve was a huge enclave of bushes. Alberta had no idea what was on the other side of the bushes, but she thought if she could turn the car to the left, the bushes might cushion the blow, and allow the car to continue driving up the hill and eventually lose momentum. If they kept driving to the right where the road continued to dip for at least another mile and sped into a more congested area, they could do a lot more damage to themselves and to other unsuspecting cars. Alberta had never taken a defensive driving class, but how hard could it be to turn a wheel?

"Hold on!"

Out of reflex and not necessity, Alberta pressed both feet onto the brake and turned the wheel sharply to the left just as the passenger side of the car slammed into the thick barricade of bushes. Since the shoulder of the road was unpaved dirt, the wheels on the passenger side lost their grip and started to spin around, which drastically slowed down their speed. Just as Alberta felt the car start to get back onto the road, she turned off the ignition in a last ditch attempt to get the car to stop moving. It lurched forward a few feet and then rolled back into the bushes where it finally stopped.

"*Siamo ancora morti?*" Helen asked.

"I don't think we're dead," Alberta replied. "Are we?"

"It looks like we all survived," Joyce confirmed.

"Is everyone okay?"

"Yes, thanks to you, Gram."

"Some happy birthday," Alberta muttered.

"It would've been very unhappy if it weren't for your expert skills behind the wheel," Jinx proclaimed.

Joyce jumped out of the BMW and ordered Alberta to release the hood of the car. The rest of the women slowly followed while Joyce surveyed the engine and the surrounding area. By the time the rest were out of the car, Joyce slammed the hood back down. "Someone cut your brakes, alright," Joyce announced.

"Seriously?" Jinx shouted.

"Dead serious."

"Don't use that word, Joyce," Helen said, leaning against the car and using another handkerchief to wipe some nervous perspiration from her forehead. "Not on an empty stomach."

"I can't believe someone would do that!" Jinx exclaimed. "We were only a few hundred feet away."

"You don't think Kichiro could've done this, do you?" Alberta asked.

"Right now I don't know what to believe," Joyce replied. "I can't even believe we're all alive and unharmed. That was some fancy driving, Berta."

"If we're done praising Mrs. Mario Andretti," Helen said. "Would someone mind calling the police so we can get out of this ditch?"

"We should leave the police out of this for the time being until we know exactly what happened," Jinx said.

"I don't know," Alberta hedged. "This has gotten dangerous."

"Plus, super fabulous!" Jinx squealed.

The three women looked at Jinx as if she was certifiably insane.

"I'm serious," Jinx protested. "Somebody is so afraid of us that they want us dead or, you know, seriously injured."

"And that's super fabulous?" Alberta shouted.

"Yes!" Jinx shouted in reply. "It means we're legit. A Ferrara force to be reckoned with."

The women contemplated Jinx's reasoning for a

moment and realized that her thought process, though warped, was correct.

"Not for nothing, lovey, but you're right," Alberta said.

"Maybe we're getting closer to the truth," Joyce commented.

"Then we can't call the fuzz 'cause that'll take away our street cred," Helen added.

"Then what do you suggest?" Alberta asked. "That we hitchhike home?"

"I have a better idea," Jinx said typing into her cell phone. She paused until the person on the other end picked up. "Hi, Freddy! I hope you're not busy because I need you to do me a *really* big favor."

CHAPTER 16

Odi, veti et tace, se voi vivir in pace.

Before the dinner party even started, Jinx knew that she should have cancelled it. One bad omen could be overlooked, but five?

After Freddy came to their rescue and picked them up, he arranged for his cousin, Dino, who owned his own mechanic shop in nearby Newton, to fix Alberta's car. Dino confirmed that the brake lines were deliberately cut, and it was only after Alberta agreed to cook him several pans of homemade eggplant rollatini, and bracciole, Joyce agreed to give him advice on which stocks to invest in, and Helen agreed to pray that his ex-wife would grow tired of living in Costa Rica with her new boyfriend and return to him that Dino agreed not to share the information with the police. Freddy was a bit more reluctant.

"Jinx, I know you enjoy solving crimes with your grandma and your aunts, and Nola's your best friend, but this is getting serious," Freddy said while they were snuggled on the couch watching an old rerun. "You could've been killed."

"I'm touched that you're so concerned," Jinx replied, trying to make a joke out of it. She failed.

"Hey, I'm not kidding around," Freddy said. To prove his point he pressed a button on the remote control and the TV screen faded to black.

"I was watching that," Jinx protested.

"Stop joking, all four of you could have been killed," Freddy said.

Jinx looked at her boyfriend, concern and fear shaping his features, and she never thought she saw a more beautiful face. "I know and to be honest it scared the life out of me," Jinx confessed. "After I got over being really excited about it."

"Excited?"

"Yes! Somebody went to a whole lot of trouble to silence us, which means we're on the right track and Nola is definitely innocent."

"Of course she's innocent," Freddy confirmed. "And, well, I guess it's kind of exciting in a freakishly weird way. But Jinx, it's still really scary."

Smiling, Freddy kissed Jinx tenderly. "At least we're on the same page."

Jinx threw her arms around her boyfriend and said, "Freddy Frangelico, I think you and I have been on the same page for quite a while now."

After several more minutes of kissing, Freddy finally broke away and stroked Jinx's long black hair, running his fingers through it, feeling the shape of her skull, brushing it away from her face and around her ears. "I know I'm not going to get you to stop investigating and I am not trying to change you," Freddy said. "But please promise me that you'll be careful and if you won't go to the police for help, you'll at least come to me."

An unexpected heat rose up from her belly to her

throat, and Jinx felt a little short of breath. She thought it was the most wonderful feeling in the world. "That I can promise," she whispered. "Now I think we should get back to doing what we were doing before you so rudely interrupted us."

"Watching TV?" Freddy asked.

Smiling devilishly, Jinx replied, "We can do that after."

That was the night before the Friday night dinner party when the world seemed perfect and nothing could possibly go wrong.

The day of the party was another story entirely.

First, Jinx woke up and discovered that she was having her period. And, of course, it wasn't a light, carefree kind of day, it was the worst kind of period complete with a heavy flow, cramps, and mood swings. Second, she caught Nola cleaning out her closet and saw that she had all her shoeboxes strewn out over her bed, which is a well-known way to invite bad luck to visit. Third, while dressing in her bedroom, Jinx pulled the chunky Bakelite necklace that used to be her mother's and was hanging on the mirror over her vanity, and the entire mirror fell to the floor and crashed at her feet ensuring that from that moment on she would suffer seven years of bad luck. Fourth, while scribbling notes about the investigation she realized that adding up the letters in Kichiro and Sharon's names added up to the dreaded number thirteen. And finally, Kichiro showed up to the party drunk.

Most people would have ignored these events and probably wouldn't have even linked them together as coincidences. But as someone who was born on Friday the 13th and whose nickname was based on a series of bad luck incidents, Jinx was hypersensitive to omens of misfortune, and she knew the evening was going to be the beginning of a disaster. Eerily, she was right.

To guarantee that whatever transpired at the party would be memorialized and not forgotten or misinterpreted, Joyce suggested that they tape the evening. After several discussions as to the best way to go about it and the emptying of one full bottle of kiwi-flavored vodka—which no one thought they'd like, but everyone loved—it was decided that Jinx would plant a bug in her apartment that would be connected to a wiretap machine in Alberta's kitchen. It was a simple enough plan, but it got off to a rough start when Alberta forgot to mute the volume on her end so everyone in Jinx's apartment could hear the conversation taking place around Alberta's kitchen table.

"Lola! *Scendi dal tavolo o sarai cena!*" Alberta yelled.

"What was that?" Kichiro asked, looking around the living room.

"Me," Freddy answered.

"You?" Kichiro replied, hardly believing the comment. "It sounded Italian, I think."

"Because I am taking lessons so I can speak my native tongue," Freddy lied.

Nola quickly entered the living room from the kitchen with a tray of hors d'oeuvres. "That's terrific, Freddy, what did you say?"

Startled by Nola's comment and stunned that she didn't understand Freddy was lying, Jinx kicked Nola in the shins so she lurched forward and the tray landed right in Kichiro's lap. "Sorry, but dig in," Nola said. "And don't worry, this is all real food, none of Jinx's fake vegan, gluten-free nonsense. Those pigs in the blanket are made with real pig."

Popping one in his mouth, Kichiro chewed happily,

thoroughly enjoying the food. It wasn't enough, however, to make him forget Nola's question. "So what was it you were saying in Italian?"

"What?" Freddy said. "Nothing, nada, just a little Italian slang that's kind of hard to translate. I'm sure there are a lot of similar phrases in Japanese."

Nodding and chewing at the same time, Kichiro replied, "*Karite kita neko.*"

Sitting next to Kichiro on the couch, Freddy turned to him and asked, "What does that mean?"

"People act better when they're not in their own home," Kichiro explained. "Literally it means a borrowed cat."

"Cat?" Freddy shouted.

"Lola!" Alberta screamed, her voice once again echoing through Jinx and Nola's living room.

"You know you sound like a girl when you speak in Italian," Kichiro commented. "So what were you saying before? What does it translate to?"

Jinx took Kichiro's glass and poured it full of red wine. "It's a very old saying that doesn't really make any sense in English."

"But the, um, literal translation is something like turn off the volume on the cat because it's waking up the neighborhood," Freddy said.

"It reminds me of another Italian saying my grandma would always say," Jinx started. "*Odi, veti et tace, se voi vivir in pace.*"

Finally, Alberta understood that the machine's volume was turned on, but of course didn't know how to solve the problem. She nudged Sloan, who was sitting next to her, and pointed to the wiretap device and through a series of very elaborate hand gestures got him to realize the sound was still on. Quickly, Sloan pressed the mute button on the machine so the rest of the talking around Alberta's kitchen table would be confined to that room and not be transmitted across town.

"Jinx is getting so good at her Italian," Alberta commented.

"What did she say?" Sloan asked.

Alberta was getting ready to translate, but Bruno, who was sitting across from Sloan, answered first, "Keep your mouth shut and your ears open."

"She's a quick learner, that one," Helen remarked.

Not everyone caught on so quickly.

"That's hilarious!" Kichiro shouted and then proceeded to laugh loudly and long.

"What is?" Freddy asked.

"The saying about the cat!"

Every time Kichiro's laughter subsided he would mumble something to himself, throw another mini hot dog into his mouth, and start laughing hysterically all over again. "Two different languages, both preoccupied with cats. I hate cats."

In two separate locations, Jinx and Alberta made the same comment at the same time. "How can you hate cats?"

"Ignore what you hear, Lola," Alberta said to Lola, who was napping contentedly in Sloan's lap. "That one doesn't know what he's saying."

"You don't know what you're saying, Kichiro," Jinx repeated. "Cats are wonderful."

"They're sneaky, they shed tons of fur all over the place, and they've got long nails that'll gouge your eyes out in your sleep."

Shaking her head, Nola walked into the kitchen to open up another bottle of wine, mumbling along the way, "I'm glad I don't have to pretend to be your fake girlfriend anymore, I love cats."

"Whatcha say?" Kichiro asked.

"I said I'm glad I didn't get us tickets to see *Cats*, the musical," she yelled from the kitchen counter.

"Is that why you're wearing that bandage on your finger?" Jinx asked.

Kichiro lifted up his right hand to look at his index finger, "This?"

"Yes, that," Jinx confirmed.

"Dog bite from a lost poodle, almost as vicious as a stray cat," he replied. "Way deeper than I thought."

Jinx recalled the last two conversations she had with Kichiro about his bandaged finger and realized each time he offered a different excuse. "First you said you cut yourself, then it was a splinter, and now it's a bite from a rabid poodle."

"He never said the poodle was rabid," Freddy injected.

"Freddy!"

Freddy knew from Jinx's tone that she wanted him to keep his mouth shut and stay out of the conversation. The way Kichiro stared at Jinx, sober as a prohibitionist, he knew that Jinx wasn't going to stop until he ended the conversation. "I'm accident-prone."

Jinx felt that his stare was meant to intimidate, but she wasn't going to give in so she maintained the stare until he looked away. "You need to take better care of yourself."

Following Nola's earlier lead, Jinx took the platter of food from Kichiro, and started for the kitchen. "I'll replenish the snacks and give you boys a chance to talk man to man." She punctuated her comment with a death glare to Freddy just in case he didn't get the very obvious hint that he should start to pump Kichiro for information before the evening was over.

"So dude," Freddy started.

"Yup," Kichiro grunted.

"You and I should go scuba diving, you know, now that you're not working," Freddy suggested.

"I'm still working," Kichiro corrected. "Just on administrative leave until, you know, this whole thing blows over."

"Oh right, sorry. Well, still . . . maybe it'll help get your mind off of things," Freddy suggested. "Being underwater, separated from all the crazy stuff on land, always makes me calm and kind of Zen."

Looking into the distance and seeing nothing and probably everything all at once, Kichiro's head bobbed up and down. "I could use some Zen."

"Cool then, we'll plan on it," Freddy said. "How about next weekend? Saturday, before it gets too cold."

"Saturday?" Kichiro repeated. "Yeah, I'd like that. I could use a little time underwater."

"It's a date then," Freddy blurted out. "Well, you know, not a date, Jinx is my girl and all, but you know a bro-date thing." Freddy gulped down half a glass of his wine to stop himself from rambling any further and swallowed hard. "Hey, you know what I've been looking for to bring on an ocean expedition I have coming up, but just can't seem to find, is a ladder."

"I have a ladder," Kichiro said, then bellowed, "Hey Jinx, come back with that food!"

"I'll be right there," Jinx shouted from behind the kitchen door.

Freddy poured himself some more wine and leaned over to fill up Kichiro's glass as well. "I don't mean a regular ladder, I have one of those, what I need and I don't know if you've even heard of it, is one of those fancy retractable ladders. They're a lot sturdier than a rope ladder and way easier to carry around than a regular metal ladder."

"Sure, I know what you mean," Kichiro said. "I've got one of those at home."

Luckily, Kichiro couldn't hear the commotion that arose in Alberta's kitchen.

"*Santa madre di misericordia!* Did you hear him?" Alberta shrieked.

"I can't believe he just admitted to having a retractable ladder," Joyce said.

"Are you writing this down, Bruno?" Helen asked. "This is evidence. Irrefutable evidence."

"I don't have to write it down," Bruno replied. "We're, um, recording it on tape."

"This is incredible," Sloan declared. "He practically confessed."

"It's solid information but hardly a confession," Bruno cautioned.

"You have to say that because you're the lawyer," Sloan said. "But as the boyfriend I can say that I'm quite impressed, Alberta."

"Boyfriend?" Helen shrieked. "It's like I'm listening to an episode of *The Romance of Mary Trent.*"

Before anyone could comment, the episode turned from a single girl's romantic entanglements to the fury of a single girl scorned.

"You have a what?" Nola screamed, running into the living room.

"Nola, babe, why are you yelling?" Kichiro asked, holding his hands over his ears.

"Don't Nola *babe* me! I'm not your babe! Now answer me, you have a retractable ladder?"

"Yeah, so what?"

"Of all the selfish, stupid things you could say," Nola seethed.

She started speed walking around the apartment and circled the couch where Kichiro and Freddy were sitting. Kichiro twisted his body to follow Nola's movements, but soon grew too dizzy to keep up.

"Nola, please stop, you're making me sick."

"I'm making you sick! Do you know how you make me feel?"

"This is starting to sound really bad," Bruno said. "Maybe we should turn off the machine."

"Not on your life," Alberta scolded. "We need to hear what else Kichiro has to say."

"I'm not concerned with what he has to say," Bruno advised. "I'm worried about what else Nola's going to say. She was supposed to keep quiet and play along, that was the plan."

"After everything I've done for you this is how you repay me?" Nola screeched. "I spend time in jail, I'm up for murder, and you have a retractable ladder!"

Done with words as her weapon, Nola decided to use her body next and lunged for Kichiro. She pushed him back on the couch and her hands went right around his neck. His wineglass flew out of his hand, splattering on the floor. Even though he was at least fifty pounds heavier than Nola, her rage and his inebriation meant they were on equal footing, and he wasn't able to pry her fingers from around his throat.

"Help me," he gurgled.

"What's happening?" Alberta cried.

"Sounds like Nola's finally standing up for herself," Helen guessed, munching on a cranberry muffin.

"Or setting herself up for an even bigger fall," Bruno said.

"Nola, stop!" Jinx cried, grabbing her friend by the waist and pulling her off of Kichiro.

Freddy was able to wedge his fingers between her grasp and Kichiro's skin and finally separate the two. But even apart, Nola was still enraged.

"Get out! Get out of here Kichiro, and I don't ever want to see you again!"

Coughing and clutching his throat, Kichiro looked like a wounded child. He couldn't comprehend why Nola had gotten so violent or what had prompted the attack.

"Look, everybody knows we're not really a couple," Kichiro admitted. "But we're still friends."

"Wait a second!" Freddy ordered. "You broke up with her 'cause she got arrested for murder? Dude, that is so not cool."

"She isn't my girlfriend," Kichiro insisted.

"Because dude . . . *you broke up with her!*"

"Freddy, I'll explain everything later," Jinx interrupted.

"There's nothing to explain. No wonder Nola's ticked off," Freddy realized. "Jinx, I want you to know right here and now that I would never break up with you if you got arrested for murder and had to spend a few nights in jail. Even, you know, if you had to spend like a whole week behind bars."

"*Dio mio*, I like that boy," Alberta gushed.

"He's a keeper," Joyce claimed.

"Also too," Helen said, stealing Joyce's catchphrase. "Jinx better not screw this one up."

"Thank you, Freddy, that's really, really sweet," Jinx implored. "But seriously, I will explain everything later. Right now, we need to deal with Nola and Kichiro."

"There is no Nola and Kichiro! We're nothing!"

Nola finished. "Now get out of here before I call the police."

Looking around seemingly confused by his surroundings, it took Kichiro a few moments to gather his strength to respond. "I am the police!"

"Not for long!" Nola spat. "When I'm through with you, you're gonna be nothing! Now get out!"

"Come on, Kich," Freddy said, grabbing his arm and leading him to the door. "I'll take you home."

"I don't understand, Freddy," he mumbled. "What's going on?"

"It'll all make sense in the morning," Freddy said. "Let's go."

The second the door shut behind Freddy and Kichiro, Nola started to cry. "I can't believe he's been lying all this time. He has the only kind of ladder that could be used to get into the tree house. Jinx, do you know what that means?"

"I know what it *could* mean," she said, trying to bring a sense of calm to the conversation. "We can't jump to conclusions though."

"And the whole lying about the bandage on his finger," Nola said. "It's very easy to get a splinter when you're hanging out in a tree house you know."

Jinx could see the fire in Nola's eyes was not diminishing, and she was starting to get worried that she wouldn't be able to contain her friend before she exploded. "Nola, listen, now that we have Kichiro's confession, we can present it to the police and let them use it in their investigation. That information plus his affair with Sharon."

"How many times do I have to tell you that we're keeping Sharon out of this?" Nola exploded. "I know you're my friend and you want to help me, but this is my life and for once I'm going to take control of it."

"What exactly does that mean?" Jinx asked.

"It's better if I didn't tell you."

Without saying another word, Nola marched into her bedroom and slammed the door behind her leaving Jinx to wonder what her roommate was planning to do.

The next morning Jinx knew exactly what she was going to do. She was going to reintroduce a bit of normalcy to her life and resume her weekly early morning jog with her grandmother. She was at Alberta's house at six thirty and they were entering Tranquility Park fifteen minutes later with every intention of running to the other end of the park and back, but when they reached the tree house their jog was abruptly interrupted.

Lying exactly where Jonas Harper was found was the body of another man. Alberta and Jinx gasped in horror and grabbed each other tightly as they stood over the dead body of Kichiro lying on the grass. Trembling, they saw that his dress shirt, the same one he was wearing the night before, was almost completely covered in blood.

CHAPTER 17

Chi non ha figliuoli, non sa che cosa sia amore.

The tiny bird walked to the very end of the thin branch and stopped unsure of how to continue. Should it retrace its steps back to the trunk of the tree? Should it jump a few inches to the right to land on a thicker, sturdier branch? Should it descend to the grass below and explore the land underneath? Or should it take to the skies and see what adventures and mysteries lay beyond the morning's horizon?

Alberta looked up at the majestic oak, the one Jonas's father selected as the cradle from which he built his son a tree house as an escape route from the stress and ugly realities of the world, a haven to retreat to when life became unbearable, and saw the purple finch perched at the very end of one of the skinniest branches on the tree. The bird was still, not sure of which direction to take, but Alberta could see underneath its plumage, that its tiny heart was beating rapidly. It so desperately wanted to make a decision, it so fervently wanted to make a move, but the creature was confused and uncertain as to where to go.

There were no other birds around to offer companionship, there were no distant bird calls to serve as an invitation, there wasn't even wind to create an involuntary push behind the bird's wings to get him to move. The finch was on its own.

Alberta wondered if she was watching some kind of physical incarnation of Kichiro's soul. A fancy thought yes and possibly a selfish one too because she wasn't entirely certain the soul wasn't just a convenient myth to help humans keep living while death loomed in the distance, inching closer with each passing day. She so desperately wanted to believe without any doubt that the physical body of every man, woman, and animal on earth was equipped with a soul that would continue to live in some altered state after death, and in theory she succeeded. But when faced with reality like when she was forced to look down and see Kichiro's dead, bloodied body on a patch of lush green grass, her conviction wavered and wonder crept in. What if what she witnessed was final? The unmoving body was nothing more than that, dead flesh, and not the former house of a soul that was now traveling to its new home, intermingling with the souls of family members, friends, and even acquaintances the human being knew when it was alive. What if no spiritual reunions took place? What if there was truly an ending to life and absolutely no form of rebirth?

Shivering, Alberta clasped Jinx's waist tighter and put her arm around her shoulder so her granddaughter could bury her face in Alberta's neck and continue to cry. Alberta would cry later. Right now she had to be strong so Jinx didn't have to be.

Alberta rubbed Jinx's back and felt her tears fall on

her cheek and neck reminding her of when she would hold her as a baby. Jinx was a woman now, but she still needed her grandma, and that filled Alberta with such pride, strength, and joy she thought she would burst. She thought she would rise up from the ground and spread wings powerful enough to let her fly to the heavens. When she looked up she saw that the bird was doing what was in her heart.

The purple finch had spread its wings so they were flat and tilted against the air and able to carry the little body higher and higher and farther away from the tree and from reality toward something unseen and, from Alberta's vantage point, unreachable. But the finch had begun the journey.

When she looked back down at Kichiro's unmoving body she noticed that the swirl of red blood had momentarily changed color, and it appeared to be drenched in lighter shades of violet, lilac, and deep pink, like the multicolored feathers of the finch. She blinked her eyes and the colors faded back to bloodstained red. Alberta knew what she saw was nothing more than an optical illusion created by looking up into the morning sun, but she took it as a sign of hope. And that would do for now.

She felt Jinx's sobbing subside and pushed her away, but still held Jinx's shoulders firmly. "You have to pull yourself together, Jinx."

Nodding her head quickly, Jinx replied, "I know. But, Gram, this is all our fault."

Stunned by the accusation, Alberta didn't quite know how to respond; however, she did know that Jinx was wrong. "What are you talking about? We had nothing to do with this?"

"If we hadn't set last night's plan into motion, if we had just stayed out of it, Kichiro wouldn't have been killed."

Hugging her granddaughter tightly once more, Alberta recognized the reflex, or maybe it was the need, to take responsibility for dire consequences. Sometimes it was admirable, but in this instance it was simply wrong.

Pushing her away once again, Alberta grabbed Jinx by the shoulders, but this time squeezed her tightly to command her full attention. "You listen to me and you listen to me good. We had nothing to do with Kichiro's death. This is a tragedy and we will find out who is responsible, but Kichiro is the one who set his journey into motion, not us. All we're trying to do is help Nola and get to the truth."

"I hear what you're saying, Gram, but if we hadn't pushed . . ."

"This would still have happened, maybe not today, but most likely tomorrow or next week. Secrets don't stay buried for long, lovey, and when they're revealed bad things can happen."

When Vinny arrived and saw his detective's dead body, his face turned gray and it was clear that he had never thought something this bad would happen on his watch. Standing behind him, Lori bowed her head and touched Vinny's arm either selfishly as an anchor or selflessly as an offering. Whatever its intent, Vinny hardly seemed to notice and didn't acknowledge the gesture, but Alberta was glad to see it because Vinny needed to know that he wasn't alone at a time like this.

"When I got your call, Alfie, and you told me there had been another murder and it was Kichiro I thought you had made a mistake. . . . I prayed that it was. I never imagined . . . this could really happen to him," Vinny said.

"I'm so sorry, Vinny," Alberta said. "I didn't want to tell you on the phone, but I knew you'd have to prepare yourself."

"I know," Vinny nodded. "Thank you."

Alberta waited for him to continue talking, but he remained silent and just stared at Kichiro's body. She turned to look at Lori for help, who seemed to be more interested in what time it was. Alberta saw her turn her wrist over to look at the face of her watch and was going to question her, but then realized that as the medical examiner she was probably checking the time to use it later on when trying to determine the time of death. When Lori caught Alberta looking at her, she finally spoke.

"The rest of the team will be here shortly," Lori conveyed. "We were at a breakfast meeting with the Police Benevolent Society when you called, so I thought it best to come along."

"I'm glad you did," Alberta agreed.

She patted Vinny's shoulder with more strength than before, and Alberta marveled at the human need to make physical contact with others in times of shock. Once again, even though her immediate family was fractured, she was grateful to be living so close to members of her family and good friends.

"Alberta, could you tell us exactly what happened?" Lori asked.

"Not yet," Vinny interjected.

"We need to get as much information as we can," Lori protested.

"That can wait," Vinny ordered. "First, we need to say a prayer."

Vinny extended his hand to Alberta and she willingly took his. Jinx grabbed Alberta's other hand and the three of them stood over Kichiro's body as one connected line mourning the loss of a friend. Alberta felt bad for Lori who stood behind them and wondered why she didn't move to Vinny's other side and hold his hand to join in their group prayer, but she realized again with some humility that each person approaches religious participation in their own way and just because Lori was Italian it shouldn't be assumed that she was automatically Catholic. And even if she was, not all Catholics believe in prayer, and she should know. Still, she felt bad for the woman as she was left out of the spontaneous ceremony. But she felt worse for Vinny.

An old Italian phrase came to her mind—*Chi non ha figliuoli, non sa che cosa sia amore*—and she realized her ancestors had no idea what they were talking about. It meant that he who has no children doesn't know what love is. Looking at the raw pain and heartache on Vinny's face, no one could say that this fatherless man hadn't loved Kichiro like his own son.

Vinny took a deep breath and clasped Alberta's hand tightly. "Lord, please embrace Kichiro's soul into your heart. He was a good man and, trust me, you'll enjoy his company. Please tell him . . ."

A few seconds passed and Alberta wasn't sure if Vinny would be able to continue. She pressed her hand against his flesh in the hopes that he would use some of her strength since his was faltering. It worked.

"Please tell him that he will be missed and that . . . we love him. Amen."

Alberta and Jinx repeated the word, but Lori remained silent. She didn't speak nor could she even look at Kichiro's body. Alberta thought it odd that a medical examiner would be so distraught that it would prohibit her being able to gaze upon a dead man, but seeing a corpse in its natural setting was far different than seeing one under a white sheet on a cold metal slab. As a doctor and a scientist, it was quite possible that Lori was not in tune with her emotions or learned early on to ignore her feelings in order for her to do her job. The result made her look distant and incapable of speaking. Vinny, however, had more to say.

"Now, tell me everything you know about what happened here."

"We really don't know much at all," Alberta started. "We came for our morning jog, but didn't get very far because we saw . . . this."

"Two morning jogs and two dead bodies," Lori remarked. "That's some track record, ladies."

"Nothing more than a terrible coincidence," Alberta replied.

"You didn't hear or see anything else?" Vinny asked.

"No, nothing," Jinx answered and then realized that she needed to share as much information as she could with Vinny before he heard it elsewhere. "Kichiro was at my place last night with Nola and Freddy. He was drinking quite a bit, but Freddy drove him home."

"Are you sure of that?" Vinny asked.

"Yes," Jinx answered. "Freddy called me last night and said he had to help Kichiro into his apartment. When he left, Kichiro was passed out on the couch."

"What is going on with you?"

No one answered Vinny's question because the person he was addressing was dead and couldn't respond. Alberta knew that Vinny was disturbed by Kichiro's recent unprofessional and erratic behavior, and she could sense that he was now angry that he had been unable to prevent the current outcome. There was nothing else to do except figure out why and how Kichiro's life ended so violently.

Lori provided the answer to the latter part of that question.

"He was shot," she said, kneeling over the corpse. "Right through the heart."

"Dammit!" Vinny cried.

Fists clenched, Vinny started to walk aimlessly near and around Kichiro's body, and Alberta and Jinx thought that he was about to grab Kichiro by the shoulders and shake him until he explained why he let himself get shot. If the rest of the police and medical team hadn't arrived, he might have done just that, he looked so desperate. But when backup arrived, Vinny had no choice but to contain his wild emotions and act like the chief of police.

When Alberta's cell phone rang, it gave her and Jinx the opportunity to act like amateur detectives.

"Helen, this isn't a good time," Alberta barked into the phone.

"You need to come home now," Helen said.

"What's wrong?"

"Everything's fine," Helen assured. "But you and Jinx need to come home right now. Nola may have done something we're all going to regret."

Immediately, Alberta looked at Kichiro and wondered if Helen's ominous warning had already come true. As always, she regretted not informing Vinny of what she knew, such as Kichiro's affair with Sharon, but she had learned it was always best to get the facts straightened out before sharing them with the authorities. It could be a total misunderstanding and Helen could simply be the nun who cried wolf. When Alberta and Jinx got back to her house she realized the only misunderstanding had to do with thinking Nola was innocent and not capable of violence as everyone asserted.

The moment Alberta and Jinx entered the kitchen, Jinx blurted out that Kichiro had been murdered and they found the body under the tree house. Alberta had every intention of sharing the information with Helen but wanted to wait until Helen told them what she knew so at least one person on the team could remain objective. Too late for that.

"Jinx, you really need to learn patience," Alberta chided.

Helen made the sign of the cross and then declared, "This is worse than I thought."

"What could be worse than Kichiro being murdered?" Jinx asked.

"Nola being the murderer?" Helen replied. "Sit down."

The wiretap machine was still on the kitchen table and Helen explained that they must have forgotten to turn it off or did so incorrectly because the tape kept recording all through the night.

"When I realized what happened I made myself a pot of coffee and started listening," Helen explained. "Less than an hour after Kichiro left your apartment and you two girls presumably went to bed, I heard more voices."

"Somebody broke into my apartment?" Jinx asked, visibly frightened.

"No," Helen said. "One voice was muffled, but the other . . . I'm sorry, but the other was Nola."

Nervous, but not yet connecting the dots, Jinx replied, "That's hardly unusual, I mean she does live there."

"She was on the phone and I heard her tell Kichiro that she needed to see him immediately," Helen said and then added as gently as she could. "And that he should meet her at the tree house."

"In the middle of the night?" Jinx asked. "That . . . that doesn't make any sense."

"Unfortunately, in light of what we just saw, lovey, it makes perfect sense," Alberta said.

"A few minutes later, there's the sound of a door opening and closing," Helen conveyed. "I didn't hear anything else, but I'm sure at some point there will be the sound of Nola reentering the apartment."

Before anyone could stop her, Jinx had taken out her cell phone, touched the screen a few times, and placed a call to Nola. "We need to talk."

"I'll be home in a bit," Nola replied. "I came into the school early before the students arrived to bring home a few more things."

"Stay there," Jinx ordered. "We'll be right over."

"Jinx, I'm not sure if this is the wisest thing to do," Alberta said.

"I don't want to be wise," Jinx snapped. "I want to know why my best friend keeps lying to me."

When they pulled into the parking lot of St. Winifred's Academy it was filled with more cars than the last time Alberta had visited. Most worrisome was the presence of a police car parked illegally outside the front entrance. No one took that as a good sign.

"What in the world are the police doing here?" Alberta asked.

"Maybe they've come to the same conclusion," Helen replied.

Jinx raced ahead toward the school and when she flung open the front door, Nola's screams hurled out into the air.

"I didn't do this! You have to believe me!"

Alberta and Helen followed Jinx, who was running in the direction of Nola's terrified voice, and they all wound up in Sharon's office. Nola was standing in the middle of the room, her hands handcuffed behind her back, and Tambra was trying to get her to leave. Nola, however, didn't want to go anywhere.

"Nola Kirkpatrick, you're under arrest for the murder of Kichiro Miyahara," Tambra said.

Tambra grabbed Nola by the elbow, but Nola twisted her body away, stumbling a few feet to the right. "I'm innocent! Please, you've got to believe me. I didn't kill anybody!"

Vinny and Sharon stood on opposite sides of the room wearing contradictory expressions. While Sharon looked devastated by Nola's arrest for the murder of her secret lover, Vinny looked enraged, his hulking frame hunched over as if he was about to spring forward and pounce on Nola. Alberta had never seen her old friend so furiously angry, not even when they were teenagers and hormones were flying at an accelerated and unstoppable rate.

"Your blood was found on Kichiro's body, Nola," Vinny seethed. "How do you explain that?"

"That's . . . that's impossible," Nola stammered. "I didn't do this!"

"Vinny, how did you find that out so quickly?" Alberta asked.

"We had Nola's blood on file when she killed Jonas Harper, so Lori did a quick blood test, and it was a match!" Vinny shrieked. "Tambra, lift up Nola's pants."

All the women in the room were stunned by Vinny's order except Tambra, who carried out the command without question. Before Nola could even struggle or refuse, Tambra lifted her left pants leg to reveal a bloody cut on her calf.

Everyone gasped, but they were quickly drowned out by Nola's screams.

"I cut myself shaving," Nola explained. Once she realized Vinny didn't believe her, panic took over. "Help me! Tell them the truth!"

Alberta and Jinx would have shared every piece of information they knew except Nola wasn't shouting at them, she was shouting at Sharon. The principal backed up a few steps until her body was pressed against the wall as if Nola's voice was propelling her backward. And if her voice didn't do it, Nola was ready to use even greater force.

The same thought raged through Alberta's and Jinx's mind at the same time—thank God they didn't share the fact that Kichiro and Sharon were having an affair with Vinny because it could only be used as further incriminating evidence against Nola. At some point they may be forced to reveal that information, but for now they were grateful they had remained silent.

Nola ran toward Sharon, but only made it a few steps before Tambra grabbed her arm and pulled her back. Nola's body jerked forward in a futile attempt to break free, and when she was pulled back again, Nola hit a vase filled with roses that was on Sharon's desk causing it to fall to the floor and scatter shards of blue and white porcelain as well as the roses throughout the room.

"That's enough!" Vinny bellowed. "Get her out of here."

Vinny stomped out of the office passing by Alberta, Jinx, and Helen without saying a word. He was quickly followed by Tambra and Nola, who continued to beg Sharon for help.

"Please! Tell them the truth!"

Sharon buried her face in her hands and started to sob, she was barely able to help herself, there was no way that she was going to help Nola. Someone else was going to help her.

"Gram, let's go," Jinx said. "I'll call Bruno on the way."

"You go," Alberta replied. She then hugged Jinx and whispered in her ear, "We'll stay here and see if Sharon is ready to confess anything."

"Good idea. I'll call Aunt Joyce and have her pick you up."

Sharon was still crying so she didn't even notice Jinx leave or Alberta and Helen picking up the broken pieces of the vase from the floor. When she finally pulled herself together and looked up, she was startled to find that she wasn't alone.

"What are you doing here?" Sharon asked.

"We thought you could use some help," Alberta said, standing up and tossing a handful of jagged bits of the vase into the garbage can next to her desk.

"Thank you," Sharon muttered, standing in the middle of the room helpless.

Alberta then gathered up the roses and handed them to Sharon, who accepted them as if they were a precious gift. "I'm so sorry for your loss."

A flicker of recognition passed over Sharon's face, and for a moment Alberta thought she was going to confide in her. The woman looked desperate to rid herself of a secret. But the moment passed as quickly as it came and Sharon once again started to cry. "I'm sorry, you'll have to excuse me," she said, just before running out of the room.

Well, Alberta thought, *so much for that.*

When she turned around to see Helen reading a book, she thought her sister had lost her mind. "This isn't a library, Helen."

Helen clutched the book to her chest and said, "You will never believe what I just found out."

CHAPTER 18

Un'immagine vale più di mille parole.

"**A**s much as I love to see you, Alberta, I have to admit this isn't my idea of a date."

Even though Sloan was in his small office at the library where he'd worked for the past thirty years, he looked incredibly out of place. He was wearing a chestnut brown velvet sports jacket, an orange ribbed turtleneck, dark navy jeans, and Timberland hiking boots—hardly his usual work attire. He was dressed that way because he and Alberta had planned on going on a late afternoon hike on Tranquility Trail, the five-mile stretch of low mountains and woods that started on the far western end of Tranquility Park and continued into the neighboring town, as a belated birthday celebration. But just before Sloan was about to pick Alberta up, she called him and altered their plans.

"Sloan, don't be mad," she said.

"I could never be mad at you," he replied.

"You say that now, but I need to cancel our date."

"Are you feeling okay?"

"I'm fine, but I stumbled on some information that I think is pertinent to the Jonas Harper murder case and I need your help."

There was silence on the other end of the telephone line.

"Sloan? Are you still there?"

"Yes. I'm just wondering if angry is the same thing as mad."

"Don't be so dramatic!"

"You were the one who planted the seed," Sloan teased.

"You know you love doing research and I can definitely use your help to dig a tiny bit deeper, *un pochino*."

"I guess you have me on that, my favorite thing is spending time with you, but a very close second is doing research."

"So now you get to combine the two!"

"You're a sly one, Alberta Scaglione."

"I can be when I want to, Sloan McLelland," Alberta replied. "So meet us at the library in half an hour?"

"Us?"

Sloan never got an answer to his question because Alberta had hung up. When she arrived at the library with Helen in tow, Sloan realized why.

"I know sixty-five is the new forty," Sloan remarked. "But you really don't need a chaperone."

"Guess again, Sloanie," Helen corrected.

"Sloanie?" Alberta asked.

"Yes, I'm warming up to your fella so I figured it's time to give him a nickname," Helen explained.

Smiling, Sloan replied, "I can only imagine what you called me beforehand, Helen, so I'll gladly accept the moniker."

"You see, Berta," Helen said. "If Sloanie approves, so should you."

As Alberta shook her head and mouthed the words "I'm sorry" to Sloan, Helen looked out into the hallway like a mafioso's bodyguard casing a joint. When she was satisfied that no one had been eavesdropping on their conversation, she shut the door and sat in the burgundy upholstered chair opposite Sloan's desk. "Now, people, can we get down to business?"

Amused by Helen's brusque formality, Sloan walked behind his desk and sat in his own chair, which was a larger version of the guest chair Helen occupied. Since there were no other chairs in the office, Alberta perched herself on the edge of Sloan's desk and felt a bit like Rosalind Russell in a 1940s black-and-white film where she was always dressed impeccably and spat out her dialogue like bullets shooting out of a machine gun. Her chance to speak would have to wait as Helen had the floor.

"This is exhibit A," Helen announced as she placed the oversized hardcover book on Sloan's desk.

"St. Winifred's Academy Yearbook?" Sloan said, reciting the title of the book.

"Not just any yearbook," Helen countered. "This is Sharon Basco's yearbook."

Sloan looked from Helen to Alberta and saw that they were wearing matching grins and nodding their heads up and down like twin Cheshire Cats who were trying to choose between feasting on a dinner of canaries or mice.

"I'm sorry, ladies," Sloan began. "But if there's some significance about the year Sharon graduated, it escapes me."

"I guess we should give him some more info," Alberta suggested.

Helen propped the book up on Sloan's desk and continued. "We found this while we were in Sharon's office at the high school, and when she ran out of the room crying . . ."

"Because of poor Kichiro being killed?" Sloan asked.

"Undoubtedly," Alberta answered.

"I looked through the yearbook to find her picture and found something else that was even more alarming than her hairdo," Helen said.

She opened the book to the page that had been bookmarked and pointed to the photo of a young woman with powder-blue eye shadow, red lipstick, draped in a swath of cleavage-baring navy blue material, accented by a gold satin honor stole that she wore around her neck. She was holding her graduation cap with her left hand, her long fingernails painted the same shade as her eye shadow. The most startling characteristic, however, was the mane of blonde hair that was teased so high and on all sides of her face that it almost bled out of the frame. "Sharon Rose Inchiosa, she of the outrageously high hair."

"To her credit, padded shoulders, neon colors, and poofy hair were all the rage at the time," Alberta offered.

"I remember it well," Sloan said with a smirk.

Inspecting her photo further he remarked, "Looks like her signature underneath her photo is as big as her hair, at least her initials anyway."

"Clearly she likes attention, then and now," Alberta added.

"I'm not sure I understand why Sharon's dated photograph should arouse such curiosity and interest in the both of you," Sloan said.

Once again Alberta and Helen looked at each other and shared identical grins. Sloan relished their impishness but still had no idea why the uncovering of Sharon's yearbook photo had resulted in Alberta's canceling their date. Until Helen pointed to the photograph of a boy in the upper left-hand corner on the opposite page.

"Well, I'll be," Sloan remarked, exhaling a long, slow breath. "That's Jonas Harper."

"The one and only," Alberta replied. "He and Sharon were classmates and graduated high school together."

Sloan grabbed the yearbook from Helen and began looking from one photo to the other, his own interest growing with each glance. "I can understand how this would have piqued your curiosity, ladies. I mean, I have no idea what it means other than the fact that they both knew each other, but it is quite a coincidence."

"It's more than a coincidence," Alberta stated.

"How can you be so sure?" Sloan asked.

Looking at Helen, Alberta said, "May I take over?"

"Be my guest," Helen said magnanimously, clutching her pocketbook in her lap.

Alberta grabbed the yearbook from Sloan and opened it up to another bookmarked page toward the back. The two pages didn't have any pictures on them, but were filled with handwritten notes under the heading "St. Winifredoodling."

"I thought it was odd that there were so few comments written underneath the photographs like there are in a typical yearbook," Alberta explained. "But it looks like they relegated most of that to the back of the book in a special section."

"Show him the note Jonas wrote," Helen said impatiently.

"I'm getting to that, *Dio mio*!" Alberta replied. "You really can be a scootch."

Almost as impatient as Helen, Sloan asked, "Now I am curious. What did Jonas write?"

Pointing to some writing in the bottom left corner of the right page that could only be described as chicken scratch, Alberta read out loud, "Sharon, I've watched you from afar since kindergarten, and no matter what happens after graduation I'll never be able to take my eyes off of you. Yours, forever and always, Jonas."

Whistling softly, Sloan leaned back in his chair and replied, "Sounds like teenaged Jonas was smitten."

"And by all accounts he never grew out of it, but only turned into Stalker Jonas," Helen said.

"You think that Jonas was stalking Sharon and not Nola all those years ago when Nola put the restraining order on him?" Sloan asked.

"That's what we think," Alberta replied. "At least that way it makes sense that Nola would drop the restraining order once she found out Jonas wasn't interested in her, but rather her boss."

Sloan scrunched up his mouth and nodded several times in deep thought. "So why do you think I can help investigate their connection further?"

Alberta practically bounced onto the edge of Sloan's desk, not noticing that the action made her skirt rise up a few inches above her knee. It was something, however, that Sloan was very conscious of especially in the presence of Alberta's sister. He did his best to ignore the appearance of Alberta's thigh and focused on her face.

"Sharon was class valedictorian so I was thinking that there may have been some mention of her in the papers that link her to Jonas," Alberta conveyed. "And since you did all that research recently for the town's centennial, I thought you could check your files and see what you find."

Impressed, Sloan replied, "It's definitely worth a try."

Alberta scurried around the desk and sat on the arm of Helen's chair, the two of them looking as excited as they did when they were toddlers on Christmas morning. While Sloan typed on his keyboard to bring up his research files on the computer screen, Alberta looked at her sister and loved seeing how soft her features could become when she smiled. She touched her arm gently, warmed by the sight of her sister so happy. She really didn't care the reason why, but it was nice to see.

Sloan's eyes were moving from side to side and his lips were silently reading words from the screen, but he hadn't yet found something worth sharing. He did, however, find something interesting enough to mumble about.

"What did you find?" Alberta asked.

"Nothing about Sharon, just St. Winifred's," Sloan said, still silently reading the article. "Some girl . . . they only mention her first name because she's a minor I guess, but she was expelled from school for, and I quote, 'inexcusable and aggressive behavior in the biology lab.' "

"Aren't the frogs usually dead before they cut them up?" Helen pondered.

"How I hated biology," Alberta said, crossing herself. "I didn't care if they were dead, the poor things, their tiny legs stretched out and pinned down."

Sloan smiled at Alberta, "You have a good heart, that's why. This Loretta kid, not so much. Not sure what she did, but it got her expelled from school." Sighing deeply, he continued to scroll through his files. "Let me see if I can find something that can actually help Nola's case." It took another full minute for him to finally speak. "Here's something."

"What?" Alberta and Helen shouted at the same time.

"Don't get too excited," Sloan warned. "When I was compiling all my research for the articles I wrote in *The Herald* for the centennial, I kept a chronological list of events that I found. Luckily I included even the most mundane items just in case I needed to reference them later on in an article about something more compelling and vital to the town's history."

"Not for nothing, Sloan, but you are thorough," Alberta said.

"Thank you," he replied, slightly blushing.

"Continue please," Helen interrupted.

"Yes, of course," Sloan stammered. "It seems that after graduation Sharon was set to go to Ramapo College in Mahwah to become a teacher."

"That would make sense," Alberta commented. "She has had a career in education. But there has to be something more. What else do you got?"

Sloan did a quick search for Sharon's name and when the results came in he looked much more interested than he did before. "Here's a reference to an article that stated Sharon married David Basco when she was twenty years old."

"Wouldn't that be before she graduated college?" Helen asked.

"Yes it would," Sloan confirmed. "Let me see if I can find the article itself."

The women watched Sloan search through the tall, four-drawer filing cabinet in the corner of his office. When he bent over to pull out a file from the bottom drawer, Helen whispered to Alberta, "I will say that he's got a nice tush."

"Helen!" Alberta gasped, slapping her sister's wrist. "Even a former nun isn't supposed to notice such things."

"I wasn't a *blind* nun, Berta."

Shaking her head, Alberta said, "For as long as I live, Helen, I will never understand you."

Turning around, Sloan pulled out a photograph and handed it to the women. Helen reached out and snapped it from his hand.

"According to that article, Sharon was set to study in Europe for her last semester at college, and she and David wanted to tie the knot before she left," Sloan explained.

"Why?" Helen asked. "Was she going off to war?"

"Sometimes when you're young you think every day is going to be your last and you rush into things too quickly," Alberta mused.

"Even though she was having an affair, she and David are still married," Sloan observed. "Marriages come in all different shapes and sizes."

"Don't I know it," Alberta muttered under her breath.

"Sorry I couldn't be more help, but I can keep looking to see what else I can find."

Helen's "good" was almost as loud as Alberta's "no."

"No?" Sloan repeated. "I thought you wanted me to do some research?"

"And you did," Alberta replied. "And now it's time for my birthday date. It's still light out if you want to go on that hike."

Grinning broadly, Sloan nodded his head and, looking at the threadbare gray carpet, resembled an awkward teenager right out of the pages of Sharon's yearbook. "I'd love that."

Clearing her throat, Helen said, "Don't mind me I'll just go home and starve."

"*Sta' zitto!*" Alberta shouted and handed her keys to Helen. "Take my car back to my house, I have sausage and peppers in the fridge, and you know there's always a lasagna in the freezer."

"You always keep a lasagna in your freezer?" Sloan asked incredulously.

"Doesn't everybody?" Alberta replied. "Now c'mon Sloan, let's go hiking."

Six hours later when Sloan dropped Alberta off at her house, she found not only Helen waiting up for her, but Jinx, too.

"It's ten o'clock, Berta," Helen announced the second Alberta walked through the kitchen door. "The sun set hours ago."

"Sloan took me to dinner after our hike."

"Did you go to Veronica's?" Helen asked. "This week's special is a very nice meatloaf."

Rolling her eyes and kissing Jinx on the cheek at the same time, Alberta replied, "No, Sloan did not take me to the diner for dinner, we went to a new Japanese place in Lafayette."

"You went to Sushi Sushiwa?" Jinx asked.

"That's the one."

"You ate sushi?" Helen asked, picking apart her Danish.

"Yes."

"I can't believe you ate sushi, Gram, that's so cool."

"And it was also disgusting," Alberta said opening up the fridge. "Is there any sausage left?"

"There's a bowl in the back," Helen replied.

"Thank God! I need real food after that *scarsa scusa* . . . that poor excuse for a meal."

While Alberta took the aluminum foil off the bowl filled with the rest of her sausage and peppers and placed it into the microwave to heat it up for a few minutes, Jinx poured Alberta a glass of jalapeno vodka, which she thought would be a perfect complement to her meal.

"Speaking of a poor excuse, Gram, Aunt Helen filled me in on what Sloan uncovered today, and I have to say I can't understand why a twenty-year-old woman still in college would want to get married and then go to Europe without her husband. What kind of honeymoon is that?"

"The relaxing kind," Helen quipped.

The microwave beeped four times and Alberta opened the door greeted by a wave of steam and the smell of a home-cooked meal. Alberta inhaled deeply and thought without any ego that she was quite a good cook. Much better than Chef Sushi. Or even Sous Chef Sushiwa.

"You have to remember it was a different time, lovey," Alberta said, pouring the contents of the bowl onto a plate. "Even when Sharon was in school, women were still conditioned that the most important thing in the world was to get married. Maybe she wanted to seal the deal before she went away to Europe and David met someone else."

"I guess so," Jinx reluctantly agreed. "But if my fiancé can't wait a few months for me to get back from a trip overseas before moving on to someone else, he doesn't deserve me."

"I hope you remember that when Freddy proposes," Alberta replied, chewing ravenously.

"Gram! Freddy's not going to propose!"

"Maybe not tomorrow, but trust me he will," she said. "I can tell when a man is interested, and Freddy is very interested."

"What do you think, Aunt Helen?"

"Don't look at me, I was a nun for most of my life."

Alberta replied so quickly she practically choked on

her food, "Why do you only hide behind the nun card when it's convenient for you to avoid answering a question?"

"Because if the Lord can work in mysterious ways, so can I."

Laughing, Jinx replied, "I have no idea if I even want Freddy to propose, but if he and I can have as much fun as the two of you, I'll gladly accept."

"Marriage can be a beautiful thing, Jinx," Alberta said, her tone becoming very serious. "Make sure it's the right decision and you'll only have to do it once."

"Unlike Sharon," Jinx replied. "I just can't help but think there's more to why she got married when she did."

Even though it was Sunday, Jinx couldn't push the idea of Sharon and David Basco getting married right before she left the country to finish her studies out of her head so she went into work for a few hours to see if she could uncover any more clues in an old copy of *The Herald*. The chronology leading up to Sharon's marriage just didn't make sense to her, and it had more to do with the fact that she and Sharon were from different generations. They were still both women, after all, and even if they were separated by a few decades there should still be a common denominator connecting them to help Jinx understand why she would have made what Jinx considered to be such an inappropriate decision.

When she found an old issue from the time right before Sharon was to embark on her trip to study abroad, Jinx found the link. She immediately called Alberta on her cell phone and asked her if she was with Helen.

"Yes, we're in the ShopRite doing some grocery

shopping," Alberta said. "I got a craving for shrimp parmigiana, and I used up all the mozzarella making an omelet for breakfast this morning."

"We'll discuss better eating habits later, Gram, for now look at the photo I just texted you."

"Okay, hold on."

Alberta pressed a few buttons on her phone and suddenly a photo from a newspaper clipping popped up on the screen. Immediately, Alberta recognized the young woman as Sharon. She looked very similar to how she appeared in her high school yearbook photo except that she had adopted a less radical hairstyle and was wearing less garish makeup.

"She looks so much prettier in this picture," Alberta said.

"Maybe it's because she's glowing," Jinx replied.

It took Alberta a moment to realize what Jinx was referring to, but when she looked at the photo closer she saw a slight bulge in Sharon's belly, the unmistakable beginning of a baby bump.

"*Ah Madon*, of course!" Alberta cried. "She left town because she was pregnant."

"Exactly!" Jinx shouted on the other end. "I knew there had to be a reason for why she got married so quickly and then hightailed it to Europe. She didn't want anyone to know she got knocked up before her wedding."

Alberta enlarged the photo slightly causing it to get a little blurry and asked, "Who's the woman in the background?"

"I don't know," Jinx said. "Could be a teacher, but she could've just been standing around and got caught in the photo by mistake."

Helen grabbed the phone from Alberta's hand to look at the photo herself. She didn't know who the woman was, but she immediately knew who the other person was in the photo standing next to Sharon.

"Don't you recognize who the man is standing next to Sharon?" Helen asked.

"No, Aunt Helen, who is it?"

Alberta looked at the photo one more time and she made the sign of the cross when she realized who it was. *"Un'immagine vale più di mille parole."*

"A picture might be worth a thousand words, Berta," Helen corrected. "But this one is worth two: Father Sal."

"The young priest in the photo is Father Sal?" Jinx screamed.

Staring back at them from the photograph standing next to a visibly pregnant Sharon was a young priest who was the spitting image of Father Sal.

"Do you know anyone else who can look so smug wearing a priest's collar?" Helen asked. She handed the phone back to Helen. Jinx was still jabbering excitedly on the other end of the line. "And tell her that I already know what she's going to say. It's time for Sister Helen to go back to church."

CHAPTER 19

Le mani inattive sono il giocattolo del diavolo.

Sitting in the last pew of St. Winifred's Church next to Helen, Jinx was happy she had decided to retire playing the role of Sister Maria to hoodwink Father Sal into being more cooperative when disclosing confidential information. Masquerading as a novitiate in a priest's private office was one thing, doing it in a real church was borderline sacrilegious. And what a church it was.

St. Winifred's Church was a large structure, built in 1932 during the Great Depression when money was scarce, but it was also a time of need when people craved answers, and religious institutions were never more popular than during times of natural or man-made disasters when the world seemed to be imploding all around. Somehow money was found to build an impressive house of worship.

Twenty white steps about thirty feet wide led up to the entrance to the church flanked on both sides by a sturdy gold railing. Double walnut-stained doors opened up to the church foyer, a small, enclosed space that housed a community bulletin board, various other marketing materials extoling the virtues of the Vatican, a bathroom, and a stairwell leading downstairs to the basement where bingo and various other functions were held.

Separating the foyer from the church proper was a panel of floor-to-ceiling soundproof windows with two glass doors on both sides. This allowed for the grandeur of the church to be witnessed from the foyer—or even the steps outside if the double doors were opened—without the outside world interfering with the inside ceremony.

The church itself was simple, yet majestic. Two long rows of pews, made from the same walnut as the doors, took up most of the interior space. They were beautifully crafted but without ornament or detail; their presence like the church itself was to serve. Their beauty, however, was enhanced by the ornate quality of the marble floor, a swirl of grays, whites, and blacks that created the image of a whirlpool or clouds in the heavens moments before an apocalyptic storm. The strong, sturdy pews among such a turbulent landscape served as a metaphor for the Catholic Church—that even during the most trying of times, when salvation seemed futile, hope was never lost.

Large stained glass windows depicting the stations of the cross decorated both sides of the church allowing for light to flicker in, but to create serenity, rather than sight. Who needed to see when God's light was leading the way?

The platform that housed the altar was about a foot above the marble floor, stained a lighter shade than the pews, and the paneling around the curved walls behind the altar were even lighter in color, almost blending into the pale gray ceiling. This was perhaps to indicate an ethereal quality, the closer to the heavens, the less burdened by earthly goods.

The altar itself, however, was a pure example of man's talent. A thick slab of ivory resting on legs of twisted gold that appeared to drill themselves right into the platform and down into the earth below. The ivory surface was bare except in its center where it was split by a long red cloth that fell to the floor on both sides and cascaded down a few steps leading to the audience. On top of the cloth lay the traditional accouterments, the chalice, bowl, bell, all made out of gold and polished to shine. Three standing gold candelabras in descending height adorned the edges of the altar with tall, thin white candles gracing their tops. It was a magnificent display and made even more dramatic given that the body of the church was more utilitarian than ostentatious.

Completing the church were two hollowed out enclaves on each side of the platform that housed white marble sculptures of the Pietà and St. Winifred, who was depicted as having a long narrow face; high, flat cheekbones; and swathed in a royal blue head covering. Fresh flowers in an array of bright colors were laid at the feet of both carvings as a sign of devotion.

And in the center of it all was Father Sal.

His jet black hair was a beautiful complement to his green vestments, his outstretched arms gave his physical appearance both an embracing and a foreboding quality, but it was his voice that kept his parishioners enthralled. His deep baritone boomed throughout the church, and Jinx was surprised to find that she felt compelled to listen and, most shockingly, to agree with his words. She was hardly a devout Catholic, but hearing Father Sal speak outside of his office and in his more natural setting she wanted to become one.

Looking over at her Aunt Helen, Jinx realized she did not feel the same way.

Mouthing the words of the responsorial psalm, "The Lord is compassion and love," Jinx got the distinct impression that her aunt no longer believed that sentiment to be true. Unlike Alberta, Jinx hadn't spent much time wondering why Helen had left the convent she spent so much of her life in, and like most young women was more astonished that a young woman would devote herself to such a life of subservience. Bowing her head in shame, Jinx realized that she had been quite narcissistic in her thoughts and hadn't truly considered how difficult a decision it must have been for Helen to, in essence, turn her back on the church, or the depth of pain her aunt could be feeling returning to a place she once revered in order to play amateur detective.

"Aunt Helen, do you want to leave?" Jinx whispered.

Helen turned to Jinx and even the thick lenses of her glasses couldn't hide her gratitude. "No," she replied, "but thank you for asking."

The mass continued and Jinx listened intently, though for the life of her she couldn't remember who the Corinthians were that Paul had written a letter to; she made a mental note to google that later on. Right after Father Sal wrapped things up because she didn't want to miss a word he had to say.

He stood up from the wooden chair he was sitting on against the back wall behind the altar and walked to the pulpit, the sleeves of his robe flowing behind him.

Standing in front of the podium Sal stood still for a moment. It looked as if he was collecting his thoughts and surveying his domain, but Jinx knew that it was to allow his domain to survey him. People flocked to church during times of crisis, and with two murders in less than a month the townsfolk of Tranquility were suffering. It was Father Sal's job to help them heal.

"Death becomes him. And he becomes death," Sal said. The cryptic opening lines of his homily resulted in the exact response he was hoping for, stunned silence. "It doesn't matter if you capitalize the *h* in 'he' or keep it lowercase, the result is the same. Human beings or Jesus Christ, we all become death and death becomes us. No matter how hard we try to avoid it, we fail because death is inevitable. We can fight it, rail against it, ignore it, curse it, court it, but nothing will change and the only thing we can do is accept it. Death is part of life. Just as life is part of death.

"What's the old saying? Resistance is futile. We all know that and yet we continue to try. We try because we often don't understand why a good man like Jonas Harper—quiet, gentle, harmless—who lived his whole life here in Tranquility, would be killed. What did he ever do in his lifetime to deserve an exit like that? Or Kichiro Miyahara. Who was even younger, a policeman, a defender of the people in this town, how could God possibly allow him to be shot down in his youth? It makes no sense. To us. But it makes Godsense if you try to stop thinking like yourself and think like Him. We have given death power. We have allowed it to be synonymous with an ending, the end of life, the disruption of everything good, everything we desire and need and want instead of what it really is: a gift from God. God giveth and God shall taketh away. He gives each and every one of us life, stands back so we can freely live that life, and then returns to offer us death, which is just another way to say everlasting life. So turn death on its head, look at it from a different angle, and instead of looking at it through angry, tear-stained eyes, you might look at it and smile and see it for what it truly is: God's love and his promise of a life unbroken and eternal."

When Father Sal finished, the only sound that could be heard was the click of his heels against the floor until the clapping began. Jinx was stunned at first to realize that the applause was started by Helen, then mortified when several members of the congregation turned to gape at Helen for her blatant display of public disrespect, but finally a feeling of pride came over Jinx when the rest of the parishioners joined in and kept the clapping going for a full minute.

Ten minutes after mass, Helen knocked on Father Sal's office door with Jinx by her side.

"Come in," he shouted from the other side of the closed door.

When they entered they saw that Sal had already changed out of his robes and was wearing a normal outfit of black pants, black long-sleeved shirt, and white priest collar. The only indication that Sal was not a typical priest was the burgundy bedroom slippers with a lamb's wool lining he was sporting. What was even weirder to Sal, though, was seeing Jinx once again not dressed in her Sister Maria garb. But only because he had enjoyed the charade.

"Jinx," Sal said. "I have to say I am disappointed in your attire."

Quickly surveying her outfit, Jinx didn't think there was anything wrong with wearing jeans, a mohair sweater, and ankle boots to church, but maybe today was a special occasion that she had forgotten about. "I'm sorry Father Sal, are jeans not really allowed?"

"Jeans are fine for Jinx," Sal said. "But Sister Maria normally adopts a more conservative wardrobe."

Startled, Jinx didn't immediately realize Sal had called her by her fake ecclesiastical name until Helen pointed it out.

"Looks like the gig is up, sis."

"Holy Stefani Germanotta!" Jinx cried.

"Who?" Helen asked.

Before Jinx could explain, Father Sal interrupted, "Lady Gaga, of course. Helen, you may be old, but you really need to get with the times."

"There is absolutely no reason why a priest should know who Lady Gaga is," Helen retorted.

"And there is absolutely no reason why a former nun should be in cahoots with Sister Fraudulenta here."

"Oh . . . oh my . . ." Jinx stammered, her cheeks flushing and growing a deep red. "I'm so sorry, Father, I never meant you or the church any disrespect."

"No offense was taken," Sal assured, chuckling. "On the contrary, I'm flattered you'd go to the trouble of impersonating one of us merely to acquire information. It speaks of your dedication to uncovering the injustices of the world."

"Did you know it was me when I saw you in Nola's cell without my disguise?"

"Yes, but that wasn't what gave you away," Sal confessed. "I had already figured out Sister Maria wasn't a real Sister."

"Really?" Jinx asked, severely disappointed.

"Absolutely."

"So how did you figure out Sister Maria was nothing more than a religious ruse?" Helen asked.

"The last time you were here in my office, Jinx forgot to change into a sensible black pump," Father Sal described. "And while I appreciate a brown patent leather ankle boot, flashy footwear isn't something our bishop condones." Sal waved a slipper-clad foot in the air. "Which is why I only wear these in private."

"I can't believe my footwear gave me away!" Jinx cried.

"Our luck we'd be saddled with a priest who's got a shoe fetish," Helen added.

Laughing, Sal poured three glasses of white wine into much fancier glasses than those that ever graced Alberta's kitchen table and asked, "To what do I owe the honor of your company this time?"

Sal sat back in the black leather chair behind his desk, his feet propped up on a stack of old newspapers, giving the appearance of being in a production of a Noël Coward play instead of the spiritual leader he proved he could be.

Helen and Jinx sat side by side in the chesterfield sofa across from Sal's desk.

"*Le mani inattive sono il giocattolo del diavolo.*"

"Idle hands *are* the devil's plaything," Sal translated Helen's comment. "But that doesn't answer my question, which is why have you two *forced* your way into my office?"

"Because we suspect you've been playing God," Helen explained. "And that's something only the devil would approve of."

Sal's expression changed slightly as he contemplated the cryptic nature of Helen's words. It changed even more drastically when she placed a copy of the photo of a young Sal standing next to a twenty-year-old Sharon onto his desk. While the photo might be old, the memory was still fresh in Sal's mind.

"There's an unwritten rule in the priesthood," Sal began. "Sometimes revealing priest-parishioner confidentiality is unavoidable especially when the priest is growing weary of keeping secrets."

"What secrets?" Jinx asked. "About Sharon's baby?"

Raising an eyebrow, Sal replied, "So you know Sharon was pregnant when this photo was taken?"

"The baby bump is pretty obvious," she confirmed.

"If you're looking for such a thing," Sal muttered.

"The photo was taken right after Sharon married David Basco and right before she left to study in Europe," Helen explained.

"Yes and no," Sal replied.

"Spill it, Sal," Helen said. "What do you know about this?"

"Yes, this photo was taken after Sharon and David's wedding, but she was never going to study in Europe," Sal divulged. "That was just a ploy to get her out of the country."

"Why?" Jinx asked.

"So she could have her baby overseas," Sal replied.

"To ensure the baby could have dual citizenship?" Jinx questioned. "That doesn't make sense."

"Oh dear," Helen whispered. "The baby wasn't David's."

Shaking his head sadly, Sal confirmed, "No, it wasn't. And even though you could tell she was pregnant from this photo, David didn't notice or maybe he ignored the fact, but as far as I know he was clueless that she was having another man's child."

"Whose child?" Jinx asked. "Who was the baby's father?"

Sighing, Sal rubbed his forehead with his hands, clearly this trip down memory lane was not a leisurely stroll. "I will deny this if this information ever leaks out, do you understand me, Helen?"

"I understand."

"Sharon didn't know who the father was," Sal explained. "She wasn't what could be described back then as a 'good girl.' Despite the fact that she was class valedictorian and had a college scholarship, inner beauty is sometimes only skin deep."

"No one else knew she was pregnant except you?" Jinx asked.

Fidgeting in his chair, Sal was suddenly upset and looked like he might bolt from his own office. "The young girl came to me for help, she was pregnant with another man's child, her new husband had already told her that he didn't want children, he was vehemently against it and since he was wealthy and came from a good family Sharon, whose own family life was less than ideal, felt that her future was guaranteed if she remained his wife. If the truth were revealed, she would lose everything."

"Exactly what kind of help did she want from you?" Helen questioned warily.

"Absolution because she was planning on having an abortion," Sal replied. "Thankfully I was able to get her to understand there were other options and I concocted a plan that got her out of the country to study in Europe for a semester."

"But that isn't what happened," Jinx said.

"No," Sal confirmed. "What really happened was I arranged for her to meet with Catholic Charities in Ireland, who would help her give birth and put the baby up for adoption."

"You did all of that?" Helen asked.

"I know you don't approve of me, Helen, and I know you have your . . . doubts about the Catholic Church, et al., but we are not all bad people," Sal said, visibly moved by his words. "You do remember all the work I did for St. Joe's?"

Helen rolled her eyes, but by the looks of her pout it was obvious that she not only knew of Sal's work, but approved of it. "Yes, I remember."

"What's St. Joe's?" Jinx asked.

"A mental institution," Helen replied.

"Please don't call it that," Father Sal urged. "We referred to it as a therapeutic facility. Even though those of us who worked and volunteered there did put our lives on the line dealing with such violent, wayward, and out-of-control youth."

Throwing up her hands, Helen barked, "Even when you've done something good you still have to pat yourself on the back."

"There is nothing wrong with honesty, Helen," Sal countered. "And the truth is I did what I thought was best for the girl and her unborn child. And by all accounts everything worked out the way that God and I planned."

"Until Sharon started having an affair with Kichiro to escape her loveless marriage that literally began on lies and betrayal," Jinx reminded.

"Young girl, there are some personal demons that you can never run from," Sal commented. "Just ask your aunt."

The air immediately turned thick and Jinx, not knowing what else to do, grabbed her aunt by the hand and squeezed it. Helen didn't return the gesture. Instead, she stood up, took the copy of the photo, returned it to her pocketbook, and left the office without saying a word.

"Thank you," Jinx said. "I mean it, you really have given us quite a lot to think about."

Jinx waved goodbye to Sal. When he returned the gesture, in spite of the unborn child he had saved, all she could think of was that the priest had blood on his hands.

CHAPTER 20

Una rosa da qualsiasi altro nome.

The ladies' black wardrobe perfectly matched their mood.

Alberta, Jinx, Helen, and Joyce were sitting around Alberta's kitchen table along with Bruno, Sloan, and Freddy, sitting on mismatched chairs brought into the kitchen from the rest of the house. Even though Alberta had put in the extension to the table to make it larger, it was still overflowing with food and there was barely space for each person's plate. There were trays of lasagna, baked ziti, and stuffed peppers; two cold-cut platters with prosciutto, soppresata, and capicola rolled into thin meat cylinders; several small dishes with mozzarella floating in a river of watery milk; platters stacked with sliced cheeses and sprinkled with olives; bowls of peppers in a variety of colors; little dishes filled with artichoke hearts; a bowl of broccoli rabe; in between all the trays and platters were scattered loaves of hard, crusty bread; and in the center of the table there was a huge bowl filled with meatballs, sausage, and bracciole. It was a feast fit for several kings, plus their entourages, but hardly anyone was eating and no one looked festive. Lola, whose shiny black fur with her chic white stripe over her left eye made her appropriately dressed for the occasion, sauntered into the kitchen enticed by the cavalcade of smells, but took one look at the dismal-looking crowd, let out a disdainful purr, and returned to her bed in the living room. At least in there an Eydie Gormé record was playing so the room might be empty, but the atmosphere, at least, was festive.

The humans, however, had a reason to be somber, they had just returned from Kichiro's burial, which was a much sadder affair than the service that was held for Jonas Harper. Jonas's death was no less a surprise, but even though he had lived his entire life in Tranquility he had become something of an outsider. He was someone who was familiar to everyone, but almost too familiar, and Jonas had become like one of those signs seen on the side of the road every day that after a while aren't noticed. While he was part of the community, like Lori had noted, he had become *persone invisibile*.

On the other hand, Kichiro's death had a much greater impact and had shaken up the community. When it was divulged that Jonas had been murdered, there was interest and speculation. But now that there was a second murder victim, who was a police detective, there was outrage. No one wanted to do anything but talk about vengeance and making sure the culprit was tried, convicted, and served a full life sentence. Since that culprit was Nola and she was their friend, they believed—or desperately hoped to believe—that she was innocent so none of them thought it appropriate to attend the repast held at the police station. Making matters worse, Kichiro's parents had flown in from Minnesota, where they lived, and they were justifiably devastated by the loss of their only son.

"I wanted to say something to Kichiro's mother," Alberta said, breaking the silence in the room. "But for once in my life I didn't know what to say."

"Vinny was with her for quite a bit so she wasn't alone," Jinx replied. "And Lori spent a lot of time with her and Kichiro's father, too."

"Yeah, I overheard her telling some stories about Kich to them, which made them smile, even laugh a bit," Freddy added. "I didn't realize she knew him so well."

"All aspects of the police force work very closely together," Sloan said. "Detectives, cops, medical examiner, judges, district attorneys, they're a close-knit family. Which is why when they lose one of their own it's sometimes more devastating than when they lose a relative."

"Family isn't only made up of blood relations," Alberta said. "It's filled with the people we meet along the way and choose to love. Like Nola."

At the mention of the young woman's name the room once again went silent. Eydie could be overheard blaming it on the bossa nova, and each person thought how wonderful it would be to cast blame for the murders of Jonas and Kichiro on someone else, but the unfortunate reality was that the blame for both of those murders was put on only one person—Nola Kirkpatrick. And since one of those murder victims was a police officer, the case against Nola had become high profile. People were interested and people wanted justice. They also wanted it swiftly.

"I was waiting for a good time to share this with the

rest of you, but since the information isn't very good I've just been stalling," Bruno announced.

"Make believe you ate one of Jinx's concoctions and spit it out," Helen ordered.

"I take umbrage with that description, but I agree with the advice," Jinx said. "And yes, I'm a reporter so I can use words like 'umbrage.' "

"The district attorney is putting Nola's trial on the fast track and it's scheduled for two weeks from today," Bruno shared.

The entire table erupted, each person responding to Bruno's statement with a shout, a groan, a hand slap on the table, overpowering Eydie's singing and each other's words. The volume grew and the disjointed conversation continued until Alberta's shrill voice quieted the group. "What did you expect would happen?"

"I, for one, thought that we'd have some more time to investigate and find the real killer," Jinx offered.

"Why?" Alberta asked. "The police believe they've found her and from all the evidence so far I honestly don't blame them for thinking they have an ironclad case and don't need to look any further."

"Gram! I thought you believed Nola is innocent?"

"I do, lovey, but it doesn't matter what I think or what any one of us thinks," Alberta replied. "The only thing that matters is what the police think the DA can prove. And let's face it, the cards are stacked pretty high against the poor girl."

"I'm afraid Alberta's right, Jinx," Bruno said, almost sheepishly. "The police have a really good case against her."

"Is this how a public defender is supposed to talk?" Jinx cried. "You're Nola's lawyer. You're supposed to proclaim her innocence every chance you get, not bend to the power of the mob."

Visibly angered by Jinx's accusation, Bruno proved that he had inherited not only his mother's looks, but also her Swedish temperament. When he spoke, his voice didn't possess a hint of the Sicilian rage that was more than likely bubbling just underneath his skin. He was professional, articulate, and, unfortunately, honest.

"I completely believe in Nola's innocence, please don't question that, Jinx. In fact, I hope none of you question it, but as her lawyer it's my job to accept reality and not gamble with my client's life. That's why I urged Nola to accept a plea bargain and take a lesser sentence."

"You did what?"

Jinx's outburst led the group into another round of screaming, bickering, fist pounding, and arm raising. The little mob was definitely getting restless, and all of their anger, frustration, and fear was being directed at the one man who was in a position to help Nola the most.

"Don't worry, Nola refused."

"Good!" Jinx cried. "She shouldn't confess to something she didn't do."

"But, lovey," Alberta started, "things might get a lot worse for Nola if this really does go to trial."

"Which it most definitely will," Bruno assured.

"How can things get worse when she's innocent?" Jinx said.

Alberta gave Jinx a look as if to say that she should know better, and Jinx immediately understood that her comment sounded like a foolish child's wish. "I know I sound like a spoiled brat who doesn't understand why she can't have a golden goose, but you can't throw in the towel before the fight's even begun."

"Do you really think that Nola's going to get a fair trial in this town?" Bruno asked, then continued on without waiting for a reply. "Thanksgiving is right around the corner and there are statistics to prove that juries will rush to a decision just so they don't have to deliberate over a holiday. And worse, the court of public opinion has already ruled that the allegedly prim and proper Catholic high school teacher is really a double murderess who killed both Jonas and Kichiro."

"But isn't all the evidence against her kind of circumstantial?" Freddy asked.

"Not really," Sloan said, shaking his head. He turned to Bruno and asked, "Would you like to lay it out or shall I?"

"Why don't you go ahead," Bruno replied, then continued sarcastically. "No one wants to hear the truth from a lawyer, maybe they'll believe it if it comes from the kindly librarian."

"I usually love to hear the things you have to say, Sloan," Alberta said. "But I don't think I want to hear this."

Patting Alberta's hand, Sloan said, "Don't hold it against me, but you know I'm a man who deals with facts and research and, well, the facts are not being kind to Nola's case." He took a deep breath and continued to detail the case against Nola and just how guilty it made the young woman look.

"Nola doesn't have an alibi for the times of the murders. She was allegedly with Kichiro when Jonas was killed, and we have the tape recording of her asking Kichiro to meet her the night he was killed. She had a restraining order out against Jonas for stalking her that she subsequently withdrew, but still something happened to make her file for it in the first place. The final toxicology report identified the pesticide that was found in Jonas's system and was the actual cause of his death as parathion, the same pesticide found in the dirt outside of Nola's classroom and that was hidden in the toilet bowl in her bathroom. Her blood was found on the bodies of both the murder victims. And worst of all she has motive for both murders." Sloan finally took a breath before summing things up. "The stalking incident gives her motive to kill Jonas, and the fact that her boyfriend was cheating on her gives her a reason to want Kichiro dead, too."

"But Kichiro wasn't really her boyfriend!" Jinx cried.

"That's hearsay!" Bruno interjected. "Her word against the court's. And Kichiro's not here to corroborate her story."

"But Sharon is!" Jinx cried.

"And what makes you think she would do such a selfless thing as to come forward and exonerate Nola?" Bruno asked. "You're just being naïve and stupid."

"Hey! Watch your mouth!" Freddy yelled, defending his girlfriend.

"No, I'm not going to watch my mouth because it's the truth," Bruno said, not backing down. "Sharon might be the principal of St. Winifred's Academy, but she's hardly saintly herself. She was cheating on her husband with a town cop and instead of trying to keep it on the down low she enlisted an employee to act as her lover's girlfriend to thwart any suspicion from herself. Her actions are the definition of a narcissist, and a narcissist is never going to help someone else especially if that help is going to expose their crime."

"I have to agree with you," Helen said. "You could

put that woman under oath, ask her point blank, and she'd still lie on the stand to save her own backside. And our silence has only made matters worse."

Shaking her head, Alberta agreed, "We should've told Vinny the moment we knew. Now it would sound like we're making it up to help Nola."

"If only we had proof that Sharon was a liar," Jinx said. "Maybe not about the affair, but something else to chip away at her credibility and plant doubt in a jury's mind."

"I've thought about that, but I've come up empty," Bruno said. "Sharon's the link that connects Nola to at least one of the murdered victims, maybe both for all we know, but I've found nothing that depicts Sharon as a liar."

"We stumbled on something that might be helpful," Alberta said.

"What?" the men in the room replied.

"When she was barely twenty years old, Sharon gave up a child for adoption."

"*Per amore di Dio!*" Bruno cried. "How long have you known about this?"

"We just found out," Helen answered. "And except for the word of a shady priest and a compromising photo in a very old edition of *The Herald* we don't have any proof."

"I can get proof."

Since this was the first time Joyce had spoken all evening her words had a greater impact than they normally would have. But it wasn't just her words that gripped everyone's attention, it was also her behavior.

Even before they had returned to Alberta's after attending the funeral service, Joyce had been quiet and reflective. She hadn't engaged in any conversation on the drive home nor had she participated in the debate about Nola's innocence or commented on her predicament. It was as if she was on autopilot and silently set the table, reheated some of the food, unwrapped platters, all the while living in her own world and not joining in the rowdy discussion surrounding her.

Alberta had assumed she was tired or not feeling well or the death of the young detective hit her harder than she had expected and she was grappling with her own feelings. With so many people around and so much to do and think about, she had gotten distracted. Now she realized that something was wrong with her sister-in-law and she wanted to know what it was.

"Joyce, what's going on with you?" Alberta asked.

"Me?" Joyce replied. "Nothing."

"Don't *nothing* me, something's wrong," Alberta pushed. "And what do you mean you can get proof. How?"

"The same way I found out the name of Nola's birth mother."

Yet again the table erupted in shouts, gasps, cutlery that jumped when hands were slammed against the table's surface and only quieted down when one voice cut through all the noise.

"You went back to Catholic Charities?" Helen asked.

Joyce didn't answer verbally but simply nodded her head.

Confused, Alberta looked at her sister-in-law, then at her sister, then back at her sister-in-law. "What do you mean you went *back* to Catholic Charities?"

Taking a deep breath, Joyce looked distraught, not upset by the question but the memories it ignited. Her finger traced the inside of her gold hoop earrings the way it always did when she was nervous. Alberta knew this was one of Joyce's tics, but she also knew that Joyce was having a difficult time speaking so she allowed her sister-in-law the time to gather her thoughts and control her emotions. After a few moments she was prepared to speak.

"When Anthony and I first got married, no I'm a liar, even when we were dating behind everyone's back, we knew we loved each other and we knew that no matter how much grief the family and the world would give us we were still going to get married," Joyce shared. "The Italian man and the black woman weren't going to let society dictate how we were going to live our lives."

"*Grazie mille.* We're all so glad the two of you were so brave," Alberta said.

"But when the idea of children arose, we lost some of our courage," Joyce said. "And we weren't sure how wise it was to bring mixed-race children into the world so we considered adoption and with Helen's help got an appointment with Catholic Charities."

Shocked, Alberta once again gawked at Joyce, then Helen, then back at Joyce. "I had no idea."

"Because I can keep my mouth shut," Helen said. "Go on Joyce, tell them what else I did for you and my brother."

Smiling for the first time all day, Joyce continued, "Helen pulled some major strings and got us placed at the top of the list. A difficult feat normally since so many couples were hoping to adopt, but a downright miracle to get an interracial couple in the top spot."

"What can I say, I had a lot of power back then," Helen said, shrugging her shoulders.

"I'll never forget what you did and what you did after that, too," Joyce said, placing her hand on top of Helen's.

After a few seconds of silence, Jinx erupted like a dormant volcano desperate to see some action. "*Ah madon!* Do not leave us hanging, Aunt Joyce! What did Aunt Helen do next?"

Joyce took a deep breath and accepted the handkerchief Helen offered her to wipe away some tears. "She convinced your brother and me that if we wanted to bring our own children into the world God would welcome them with open arms," she said, clearly moved by the memory. "A few months later I got pregnant with the twins."

"*Dio mio,* I had no idea," Alberta said, visibly moved. "I guess Bobby and Billy owe their life to their aunt Helen."

Searching for another handkerchief in her pocketbook to wipe away her own tears, Helen scoffed and said, "I was only the messenger."

"That's a lovely story, Joyce," Sloan said. "But I'm sorry, what does that have to do with getting proof about Sharon giving up her own child?"

"When I heard about the adoption and Father Sal hooking Sharon up with Catholic Charities, it got me thinking about my own past with them and it dawned on me that I'm still connected to them," Joyce explained.

"In what way?" Sloan asked.

"I donate to them every year and I correspond with a few of the nuns who I met when Ant and I interviewed there, especially Sister Clare," Joyce continued. "She was incredibly gracious and always helpful so I thought I'd call in a marker."

"So you found out the name of Sharon's baby?" Sloan questioned.

"No, Sister Clare didn't have that information because Sharon had her baby overseas, but . . . she was able to give me the name of Nola's birth mother."

Stunned, Bruno looked at Joyce with amazement and admiration. "You got a nun at Catholic Charities to give you sealed information about the name of someone's birth mother?"

"When you say it like that, you make it sound like it was a hard thing for me to do."

"It was," Bruno corrected. "How in the world did you do it?"

"I brought over some homemade apple pie, and while I was writing out a check I asked."

"Joyce Ferrara," Bruno said. "I think I'm in love with you."

"Well, don't get too excited," she cautioned. "I found out the name of Nola's mother, but it doesn't mean I found the woman. I've done an extensive on-line search, called in a few more favors from former colleagues, and still came up empty."

"What's the woman's name?" Alberta asked.

"Rose Wood."

"Sounds like a made up name to me," Freddy replied, giving voice to what everyone else was thinking.

"That's what I think, too," Joyce agreed. "I doubt we'll ever find out who Nola's mother is, but we might be able to find out who Sharon's baby is."

"And how in heaven's name can we do that?" Alberta asked.

"I got the name of a nun who still runs the Catholic Charities office in Dublin, Ireland, where Father Sal said Sharon went to have her baby. So all hope might not be lost after all."

Hope might not have been lost, but Eydie Gormé suddenly got a case of laryngitis and lost her voice.

There was an earsplitting screeching sound heard from the living room, immediately followed by the sound of a loud crash, and topped off by a triumphant meow.

"Lola!" Alberta cried. "What have you gotten into now?"

Alberta ran into the living room followed by the rest of the group to find Lola standing on top of Eydie Gormé's album and spinning around the record player purring contentedly and clearly enjoying herself. A brown wicker cornucopia and wooden pieces of fruit were strewn all over the hardwood floor, obviously the cause of the loud crash. Mesmerized, Jinx bent down and picked up a fallen banana as if she had just found the proverbial needle in a haystack and found out the needle was encrusted with diamonds and precious jewels.

"It's made of wood," Jinx announced.

Amused by his girlfriend's comment, but a tiny bit concerned, Freddy asked, "Jinx, are you okay?"

"Gram! Where's that yearbook?"

"Right over there on the cocktail table," Alberta replied. "Why?"

Instead of answering, Jinx picked up the yearbook and opened it up to the page containing Sharon's high school photo. Raising the banana over her head triumphantly, she exclaimed, "*Una rosa da qualsiasi altro nome.*"

"Why are you and that banana quoting Shakespeare at a time like this?" Helen asked.

"Because a rose by any other name is still a rose," Jinx replied not at all answering her aunt's question.

"It's really cool that you're smart and all, Jinx," Freddy started. "But I don't think anyone knows what you're trying to say."

Pointing to Sharon's photo, Jinx said, "Read her name."

"Sharon Rose Inchiosa," Alberta said.

"Her middle name is Rose!" Jinx cried.

"Oh lovey, that's a very common middle name," Alberta corrected. "Helen's middle name is Rose."

"Named after my grandmother, I am," Helen confirmed.

"And her last name," Jinx said.

"Inchiosa?"

"No! Her married last name is Basco," Jinx said, shaking the banana wildly in her hand. "And Basco means wood in Italian."

"Oh my God, you're right!" Freddy shouted.

"She is!" Alberta agreed. "That means Rose Wood is really Sharon Basco."

"It's too much of a coincidence not to be!" Jinx exclaimed. "Nola's adopted parents are Irish so they must've went to Catholic Charities in Ireland to adopt her."

"Well, what do you know? I did find out who Sharon's baby is after all," Joyce said.

"It's Nola!" Alberta cried. "Good job, lovey!"

"And Nola has to know the truth," Freddy exclaimed.

"I think you're right about that," Jinx agreed.

"At least that would explain why Nola agreed to act as Kichiro's girlfriend," Freddy continued. "You know, in order to save her mother's marriage and reputation."

"And also why Nola's adamant that Sharon be kept out of the whole investigation," Sloan added.

"Do you know what all this means, Aunt Joyce?"

"I would like to say that I do, but honestly, I have no idea."

"Nola isn't being blackmailed by Sharon because she's shy of a few teaching credits," Jinx said. "Nola's being blackmailed to take the fall because Sharon is the real killer."

"Yes!" Alberta cried. "That has to be it."

"Nola isn't guilty of double homicide," Jinx declared. "The only thing Nola's guilty of is protecting her own mother from going to prison for life!"

CHAPTER 21

Il sangue non è acqua.

"**A**re you sure we're doing the right thing, Gram?" Alberta looked out the passenger side window of Jinx's Chevy Cruze and was one hundred percent certain in her reply. "Not at all."

Tranquility Park passed by on their right and in the distance they could see the tree house where their journey began, and now they were en route to a location where the whole thing could end or, as Jinx was starting to fear, could blow up in their face and destroy the life of her best friend.

"Then maybe we should let Vinny and the police handle this," Jinx said. "Or I could write an exposé and have Wyck publish it as an online exclusive."

Alberta noticed how different the park looked from the other day. The lawn was practically covered in brown and orange leaves. Just last month when they stumbled on the body of Jonas Harper, the grass was still green in some areas, with the leaves only beginning to turn color, at the time the whole park looked as if it was valiantly holding onto its beauty despite the fact that another impending winter was on its way. And now it looked like it had given in to the inevitable.

The park was empty and lifeless, no doubt a result of its new reputation as the site of not one, but two homicides. A reputation given momentum and strength thanks to Wyck dubbing it in print Tran-Kill-ity Park. It was a clever moniker, but it was no wonder the townspeople had stayed away from the place in droves ever since. The park had developed the popularity status of a leper colony. And Alberta and Jinx were on their way to meet with the head leper.

"Sharon holds the key to this whole mystery, Jinx, I just know it."

"I agree with you, Gram, but if she's gone to such great lengths to keep her secrets hidden, and I'm talking about killing two innocent men, then what's going to prevent her from killing us?"

Logically, Alberta knew that her granddaughter had a point; emotionally she knew she was wrong. Kichiro was killed in the middle of the night, and Jonas was killed in the very early hours of the morning when there was no chance of witnesses interfering with the murders or finger-pointing the culprit. In the bright sunshine of day, Sharon wouldn't take the chance of killing two more women who were merely trying to tie up some loose ends. Once those loose ends had a pretty bow on them, then it would be time to call in the troops with badges and guns. Knowing that she had Vinny's cell phone number on speed dial made her feel a bit better in case things didn't go exactly as she had planned.

And then there was Alberta's gut instinct kicking in. She believed they had uncovered the mystery that Nola was Sharon's daughter, but there was something else she wasn't getting. There was another piece of the puzzle that had to be discovered, she just felt it in her bones. And it wasn't her arthritis acting up again like it did whenever the temperature dropped. There was something about the principal that made her feel as if there was much more to her story, and Alberta wanted to find that out before allowing Vinny to take over. Plus, ever since Kichiro's death, Vinny hadn't been acting like himself.

"I don't think we have anything to worry about from Sharon, lovey, but I did instruct Helen to call the police if she doesn't hear back from us within the hour."

Making another right onto Mill Creek Road, the street that led directly into the parking lot of St. Winifred's Academy, Jinx wasn't relieved by Alberta's comment. "A lot of damage can be done in an hour, Gram."

"Agreed, but Vinny has been rather emotional since Kichiro's death and he's taken his murder very hard. I think in many ways he was like a father to the young man," Alberta said. "He, like the DA and even Lori, are hellbent on making Nola pay for killing two of Tranquility's favorite sons so if we're going to offer up another suspect for them to pin their hopes on we better make sure we're right."

Parking the Cruze in one of the many empty spots, Jinx turned off the engine and turned to her grandmother. "How did you get to be so smart?"

Alberta turned to her granddaughter and for a moment she was taken back decades to when her own daughter, Lisa Marie, was pregnant and full of life, when their ongoing feud was in one of its lulls and their relationship was filled with hope, encouragement, and love instead of the usual insults, putdowns, and hate.

Swallowing hard so Jinx didn't see how emotional she had gotten just by looking at her face because it resembled her mother's, Alberta replied, "Because I've made quite a few mistakes."

She didn't wait for Jinx to ask a follow-up question or admonish her for exaggerating past history. She didn't want to discuss or defend her remark. It was the truth, she knew it, and Jinx knew it as well even though her youthful spirit and her love for her grandmother would instinctively make her want to assure Alberta that she was being too hard on herself and judging herself too harshly. So Alberta quickly got out of the car and started walking toward the front doors of the school causing Jinx, who was fumbling with her purse, to do a little jog to catch up with her grandmother so they could make their entrance together.

Just as Alberta was going to ring the buzzer in order to have Sharon open up the front door, Jinx pushed it open with ease. "Someone must've forgotten to lock it."

"That's weird," Alberta said. "The last time Joyce and I were here this early the door was locked, which is why we went around the back and saw her and Kichiro doing what they, um, really shouldn't have been doing on school property."

Shrugging her shoulders, Jinx replied, "I guess without Kichiro, Sharon has no reason to lock the doors any longer. It's not like she's going to have a clandestine romp in the boiler room with her husband."

Only slightly shocked by her granddaughter's racy comment, Alberta waved a finger at Jinx nonetheless just to keep her on her toes. She didn't mind that Jinx was all grown up, but she did like to remind her that no matter the age it was still appropriate to act like a lady. Especially when they were kind of breaking into a

Catholic high school to accuse its principal of being a murderess.

Walking down the corridor, Alberta was glad that she and Jinx were wearing rubber-soled shoes, Jinx was sporting a pair of flat ballet slippers in a color that Alberta could only describe as pistachio, while she was wearing a simple brown leather slip-on with a wedge heel. Neither shoe caused any sound while they walked down the hall toward the principal's office, but even if they were wearing stilettos with a metal heel they probably wouldn't have been heard because in the distance all they could hear was Sharon's shouting.

"What is she yelling about?" Jinx asked.

"And who is she yelling at?" Alberta asked in reply.

They couldn't make out exactly what Sharon was saying nor could they hear anyone shouting back at her, but her cries carried down the hall quicker than the latest teenage gossip.

Alberta and Jinx huddled close together as they tiptoed down the hall making sure that they made as little sound as possible so as not to interfere or stop Sharon and her unseen sparring partner end their verbal scuffle prematurely.

"Maybe her husband, David, finally found out about her affair and they're having it out," Jinx whispered.

"Possibly," Alberta replied in the same hushed tone. "Or maybe Vinny found out what we found out and he's beaten us to the punch."

"I didn't see a police car in the parking lot, did you?"

"No, but he could've parked out back," Alberta said, silently cursing herself for not checking the back parking lot before entering. Oh well, she thought, if Sharon already had company, what's two more?

But when they opened the door to the principal's

office, holding on to each other like two frightened freshmen, they were dumbfounded to find Sharon was alone. And on her hands and knees looking through the bottom drawer of her desk. Sharon didn't even look up when they entered, but continued to mutter to herself and rummage through the confines of the drawer, pulling out files and tossing them to the side. It was only when Alberta spoke that she noticed she wasn't alone in her office.

"Hello, Sharon."

Still consumed with her search, Sharon didn't look up instantly, but mumbled, "Be right with you."

Alberta and Jinx ventured a little farther into the room and looked around to make sure the office truly was empty. Could the woman have been shouting at an unseen person? The empty air? The vision of the two dead men that she murdered?

"Sorry to bother you, Sharon," Alberta said again. "But the front door was unlocked."

This time, Sharon acquiesced to her company and stood up, running her hands down her black and tan plaid pencil skirt to smooth out any wrinkles her previous position might have imposed on the fabric. She was wearing a tan silk blouse and a vest that matched her skirt, and she finished off the outfit with classic black patent leather pumps. Her outfit, combined with the fact that her blonde curls had been straightened into a classic pageboy, reminded Alberta of one of her grade school teachers. It was a much more refined look than her usual wardrobe. Possibly without a young lover to tease and arouse, Sharon no longer felt the need to dress so alluringly. This outfit made her look like she had stepped out of a memory or an episode of an early 1970s sitcom, perhaps playing the role of guest teacher in *Room 222*. Nothing about her appearance resembled the colorful girl from her year-book portrait or for that matter a woman who was able to kill two men in cold blood. Even though she was clearly a bit frazzled, she looked professional, chaste, and, unfortunately, innocent.

But when Alberta looked closer she detected something in her face that made her realize the woman wasn't as innocent as she liked to pretend. She had seen the look before, but she wasn't quite sure if she was creating fiction or had finally landed on fact. She would have to choose her words carefully in order to find out which it was.

"We didn't mean to interrupt you," Alberta said.

"No, you're not interrupting anything," Sharon replied. She opened her mouth as if she wanted to continue speaking, but instead she ran her finger along the rim of a blue and white porcelain vase that was identical to the one that crashed to the floor the last time Alberta was in Sharon's office. It was exactly the clue that Alberta was looking for. Suppressing a smile and trying very hard to be inconspicuous, Alberta stretched her left foot to the left until it tapped Jinx's right shoe to let her know that she should follow her lead. She wasn't sure if Jinx understood her unspoken order, but Jinx didn't respond in any way so at least she wasn't going to interfere.

"It sounded like you were having an argument with someone when we first entered the school," Alberta continued. "Is anyone else here?"

"No," Sharon replied quickly. "I was just looking for something, still am, and what you heard was me yelling at myself for being so absentminded."

Laughing, Alberta inched a bit closer to the woman. "Wait until you get to be my age, you'll start losing things on a daily basis. Trust me, you'll get used to it."

Looking around the room, Sharon shook her head and was obviously not yet at the stage in her life where she would accept forgetfulness as part of her daily regime. "It makes me crazy though because it was right here on my desk and now I can't find it." Her annoyance at her inability to find what she was looking for was starting to grow in intensity. Luckily, Alberta was able to put her out of her misery.

"Is this what you're looking for?"

Alberta took the yearbook out of her pocketbook and placed it onto Sharon's desk but didn't take her eyes off the woman's face. She wanted to see her expression and how it changed when she realized that the reason she couldn't find what she was looking for was that it had been stolen. Sharon didn't disappoint.

Her soft, feminine features slowly took on a flattened, menacing glow. This was not a woman who was used to being duped, nor was it a woman who was used to being put in a position where she was caught off guard. She also turned out to be a woman who did not like to mince words.

"I hope you have a good reason for having stolen my property," Sharon stated, her voice suddenly shifting to an authoritative tone.

"Actually my sister Helen was the thief," Alberta said, smiling and allowing her eyes to twinkle. "Which really is so unlike her because she used to be a nun."

Sharon smiled back at Alberta, but there was absolutely no twinkle in her eyes, only malice. "I know your sister and I know she can be quite the thorn in someone's side if she chooses to be."

"You know sisters," Alberta replied. "They do what they want to do and we're left to pick up the pieces."

"Luckily I don't know what that's like," Sharon said, her words practically seething out of her mouth. "Now why don't you tell me why your sister felt compelled to take something that belongs to me since she of all people should be familiar with the phrase, Thou shall not steal."

Feeling more at ease knowing that she was making Sharon incredibly uncomfortable, Alberta started to walk around the room stopping only when she got to the window and looked outside. She had an unobstructed view of Nola's classroom and could still see the brown patch of grass just outside her window. There were two school chairs in the corner of Sharon's office, there either because the school didn't have sufficient storage space or because they were used by students if they had detention, but Alberta realized she hadn't sat in one of those chairs in decades. It would be fun to give one a try now.

She placed her purse on the desk and sat in the chair, and was immediately flooded with memories from her own high school days. She enjoyed those days, but wouldn't relive them if her life depended on it. The thought snapped her out of her reverie because she realized Nola's life could very well depend on her next comments.

"I asked you a question, Mrs. Scaglione," Sharon barked, sounding very much like a stereotypical harsh schoolmarm.

"Please don't take that tone with my grandmother," Jinx replied, sitting in the seat next to Alberta.

Sharon clenched her fist and shook it at Jinx. "Don't you get all self-righteous with me! I know why the both of you are here!"

A bit startled by Sharon's outburst, but hardly undeterred, Jinx spat back, "Then why don't you share that piece of information with us instead of trying to be all holier-than-thou?"

"You're here to try and save your friend!"

"Don't you mean your daughter?"

Alberta's question, quietly asked, seemed to suck all the air out of the room. Sharon's fist fell to her side, her hand limp, and it looked for a second as if her body was going to continue on and fall to the ground, but she found the strength to remain standing. She wasn't yet ready to reply though.

"Thanks, in part, to my sister swiping your yearbook when we were last here," Alberta explained. "We were able to deduce that Sharon Rose Inchiosa, Rose Wood, and Sharon Basco are all one and the same: Nola's mother."

Pressing her fingers onto the edge of her desk to steady herself, Sharon seemed to be fighting against the energy swarming throughout her body. She looked like she wanted to run from the room, but something kept her stationary. "You have no idea what you're talking about."

"We have proof, Sharon," Jinx said. "We know that you gave up your baby to Catholic Charities in Ireland and we know that your child was then adopted by the Kirkpatricks in New Jersey. Nola is your daughter."

Sharon's face went white and she opened her mouth to speak, but Alberta beat her to it.

"Don't try to deny it," Alberta said. "The date of your baby's birth and Nola's line up so it's really easy to connect the dots."

"Even if that were true," Sharon said, each word sounding as if it were pulled out of her mouth against her will. "That information is classified."

"You are right about that," Alberta agreed. "And we don't plan on sharing it with anyone. As long as you agree to admit to your crimes so your daughter can be set free. You don't have to reveal that you're Nola's

mother if you'd prefer not to, you can keep your secret, but you need to tell the police that you killed
Jonah and Kichiro."

Suddenly, Sharon let go of any remaining professional or proper façade and lunged at Alberta like an
animal who had finally been uncaged and was ready to
confront its malicious captor. She slammed her hands
down on the student desk with such force that Alberta's purse toppled to the floor. Despite her attempt
at remaining stalwart and tough, Alberta leaned back
as far as she could to put distance between herself and
the rage that was emanating from Sharon's eyes.

"Are you insane?" Sharon screeched.

Against her better judgment, Alberta toyed with the
tigress. "No, but you're a murderer."

Infuriated, Sharon grabbed the desk and actually
lifted it and the seat containing Alberta about an inch
off the ground before letting it crash down back onto
the floor. Alberta had to hold on to the side of the chair
or risk falling onto the floor. Just when she thought the
altercation was about to get physical, Sharon retreated
back to her desk. Alberta thought it was because Jinx
had gotten up and was about to join in the fight, but it
was because Sharon was trying to control her frenzied
anger.

"The two of you need to leave now."

"We're not going anywhere," Jinx asserted. "You're
not getting off that easy after what you've done."

"The only thing I've done . . . look, you should both
go now before it's too late," Sharon ordered omi-
nously.

"Are you threatening us?" Jinx asked.

Sharon's eyes hardened and lost any sign of life almost as if rigor mortis had set in on only one part of
her body. "I'm warning you."

"Sorry to tell you, Sharon, but we're Sicilian so we don't scare that easily," Alberta scoffed.

"And we're not leaving until you confess," Jinx retorted.

"The only thing I'm guilty of is . . . having an affair," Sharon said, choking on her own emotion. "Of loving Kichiro and being a coward not to leave my husband. That's it, nothing more!"

"And making your daughter cover up for you!" Jinx shouted. "How disgusting is that? How evil are you?"

"If you know what's good for you . . . leave!"

"Your daughter is rotting in a jail cell and will probably be convicted for life for killing two people that you murdered!" Jinx bellowed, unable to contain her own fury.

"I told you I didn't kill anyone!"

"And we believe you."

In response to Alberta's unexpected comment, both Sharon and Jinx looked at Alberta wild-eyed and suspicious. Jinx took a step back from Alberta as if afraid to become contaminated by whatever spell she must be under to give voice to such an absurd thought. Sharon stood behind her desk clutching the vase as if she were getting ready to throw it at Alberta's face.

"Gram, what are you saying?"

"Trust me, lovey, no mother would let her daughter rot in jail if she were able to change things even if the mother never held her child a day in her life."

Appalled by her grandmother's change of heart, Jinx was reluctant to agree. "Gram, I know that you wouldn't allow your daughter or any member of your family to take the fall for you, but that doesn't mean everyone's like that."

"*Il sangue non è acqua*," Alberta said. "Do you know what that means, Sharon?"

Before answering, Sharon quickly glanced to her right, and Jinx thought she was looking for a way out of the room, but Alberta knew exactly what she was doing.

"Yes, Alberta, blood is thicker than water," Sharon replied. "And if you understand that, you'll understand that it's best that you leave. Right . . . now!"

"Do not try to bully us the way you bullied Nola," Jinx seethed.

"She's not bullying anyone, Jinx, she's protecting someone," Alberta said as calmly as possible.

"Yeah, herself!"

"No, she's protecting her sister," Alberta replied.

"Her what?"

Jinx couldn't believe what Alberta was saying and thought for sure that her grandmother was joking, but she looked deadly serious. She sounded as serious as she looked.

"Why don't you come out of the closet now?"

Sharon and Jinx looked at Alberta like she had officially gone crazy, but when the closet door opened, it revealed Lori looking at Alberta like she was the smartest woman she had ever met.

Unfortunately, when Alberta saw that Lori was aiming a gun directly at her, she felt like the dumbest.

CHAPTER 22

Per nascondersi a vista.

"Sisters?" Jinx shrieked.

Sharon looked almost as stunned by Alberta's proclamation as Jinx did, but her silence was all Alberta needed to confirm her assumption. That and the bemused expression on Lori's face. But even though Lori appeared to be impressed with Alberta's clever deduction, she was curious that the woman was able to discover her secret.

"I guess you're not the dumb old broad I thought you were," Lori remarked.

Alberta wasn't sure if she should be slightly insulted or slightly appreciative. "Thank you . . . I think."

"I mean it," Lori added. "How did you figure it out when the rest of the *stunods* in this town, cops included, don't have an inkling?"

"Yeah, Gram, I'd like to know that, too."

"There were a few clues along the way that by themselves meant nothing, but together they started to create a picture that was filled with one too many coincidences," Alberta explained.

Moving into the room and closing the closet door shut behind her with her foot, Lori sat behind Sharon's desk, leaned back, and propped her feet up on the desk, never dropping the gun from its aim, which was directly at Alberta's chest. "We have some time, why don't you elucidate?" Lori said. "You do know what 'elucidate' means, don't you?"

"There's no reason to be a bitch, Lori," Sharon admonished.

"Why not, she's already a murderer!" Jinx cried. "Twice!"

"And you're a lousy investigative reporter," Lori snapped. "Let's hear how Grandma Moses figured out I'm Sharon's sister and maybe you'll learn something."

Waving the gun in Alberta's direction, Lori gave the floor to her so she could describe how she uncovered a secret the two women clearly wanted to keep buried.

"First, I noticed that you both wear your watches facedown, with the face of the watch on the inside of your wrist and not on top," Alberta started. "It's uncommon in women so when I saw that both of you wore your watches that way it stuck out in my mind."

"Good eye," Lori said. "Continue."

"Then, I noticed that you both have the same blue and white porcelain design in your offices," Alberta resumed. "Lori had a vase filled with roses and so did you, Sharon. You even have an identical replacement vase with the same kind of flowers. And Nola also had a porcelain bowl in her office that she said was a gift; I assume it was from you, Sharon."

"So what if it was?" the woman replied.

"The design itself isn't unusual and can be bought at any home decorator store, but it stuck out in both your offices and seemed to go against the rest of the design," Alberta elaborated. "I'm guessing that the blue and white design holds some sentimental value for you both."

"Our mother collected Chinese porcelain," Sharon offered. "Both those pieces were from our mother's large, but far from expensive, collection."

"I knew it," Alberta said. "You were very upset, Lori, when the vase almost broke in your office and when yours broke, Sharon, you burst into tears and had to leave the room."

"Our mother didn't leave us very much when she died," Sharon said.

"Except a mountain of debt," Lori added.

"That wasn't her fault, Lori, and you know it," Sharon spat.

"She allowed Daddy to live beyond their means, cash in his insurance policy, get a reverse mortgage," Lori rattled on. "It's entirely her fault. I don't want to talk about her, I want smarty-pants to continue. And I'm not being arbitrary, Alberta, you really are much smarter than I gave you credit for."

"Even though the two of you really don't look anything alike, there are some minor similarities that can't be missed," Alberta said. "Like some characteristics that my sister Helen and I share."

"Such as?" Lori asked.

"You both have the odd habit of signing your name by writing out the first letter in cursive, but printing the rest, I noticed that when you signed the toxicology report and it's how Sharon signed her name underneath her picture in her yearbook," Alberta pointed out. "Like I said, physically you really don't resemble each other, but you share some identical characteristics like your noses. They're both quite small. On Sharon it isn't so noticeable, but on Lori it stands out against the rest of her features."

"I do consider my nose to be the highlight of my face," Lori remarked.

"And then there are the lines around your necks," Alberta said.

Grabbing her throat, Sharon exclaimed, "I do not have lines around my neck!"

"Yes you do," Lori corrected.

"I do not!"

"Stop being so vain!" Lori shouted. "We both do and there's not a thing we can do about it. It's just something else we inherited from our mother."

"A lot of women have neck wrinkles," Alberta added. "But both of yours are those crepe paper wrinkles that continue down to your, um, cleavage."

"I'm flattered you noticed," Lori said with a wink.

"But what put it all together for me was the photo we found from the old issue of *The Herald*," Alberta said. "The one with Sharon, Father Sal, and an unidentified young woman behind them. That was you, Lori."

"It is?" Jinx shrieked. "How'd you figure that out, Gram? I saw that photo and it doesn't look anything like Lori."

"Sure it does," Alberta corrected. "She's much younger, but she still has the small forehead and low hairline and the same blemish on her right cheek. I thought it was part of the photo at first since it was quite old, but when I saw you at the park when we found Kichiro's body, I noticed it again because you kept turning away and couldn't look at the body. That and the fact that Sharon is wearing almost the same outfit you wore in that photograph. I knew it was familiar, but I thought it was just the style. Is it the same by any chance?"

Stunned, Sharon looked at Lori, who just smiled

and shrugged her shoulders. "Yes, it is actually," Sharon said. "And I worked damn hard to fit into it."

Swinging her legs over the desk, Lori plopped her feet on the floor and with an exaggerated sigh stood up. "Alberta, I am sincerely impressed that you noticed all those little details and added them up to come up with the fact that Sharon and I are sisters," Lori said. "I don't think anyone else has a clue that we're related. Not even that idiot, Father Sal, and he and I were the only ones who knew Sharon wasn't going to Europe to study, but to give birth."

"You mean give Nola up for adoption," Jinx corrected.

"Which was my only choice!" Sharon exclaimed.

Outraged, Jinx took a step toward Sharon, but before she could turn that step into any further action, Lori raised her gun and aimed it directly at Jinx's face. Alberta grabbed her granddaughter by the arm and pulled her back so she was standing behind her.

"Looks like Grandma understands the desire to protect the ones she loves," Lori remarked.

"I think we're very much alike when it comes to protecting our family," Alberta said.

Relaxing a bit, Lori let the gun hang at her side, her eyes, however, never looked away from Alberta and Jinx. "Sharon always found herself in trouble, ever since she was a kid," Lori divulged. "And ever since we were kids, I was the one bailing her out."

"I never asked for your help!" Sharon screamed.

"Because you knew you didn't have to!" Lori screamed even louder. "You knew that every time you screwed up I was going to come to your rescue to clean up your mess."

"Like when she found herself pregnant with one

man's baby when she was engaged to someone else," Alberta stated.

"Exactly!" Lori confirmed. "If David ever found out you were pregnant, he would've called off the engagement right then and there. He was going to give you everything, set you up to live the life you had always dreamed about. His only condition was that he didn't want children."

"I thought he would change his mind if he knew I was pregnant," Sharon said.

"So you slept with another man just so you could get pregnant?" Jinx asked.

"I didn't know the real reason David didn't want to have a child," Sharon said.

"Which was?" Alberta asked.

"He carried a gene that almost certainly would've caused any child of his to go blind by the age of five, and he refused to take that risk," Lori explained. "I was a candy striper at the time and saw David in the hospital. I did a little investigating, talked to a chatty nurse, and found out the truth. I also found out that David had a vasectomy so once Sharon told me the delightful news that she was pregnant I knew that it wasn't David's child and I knew that David would dump her and she'd be left alone to raise a child as a single mother. That's when I convinced her to talk to Father Sal. I knew he had helped a few other girls who had found themselves in . . . the family way . . . so I knew he'd be able to help Sharon. And he did."

"I didn't want to go along with it at first," Sharon said. "I really thought David would want to raise my child as his own."

"That's because you were an idiot!" Lori shouted. "And you still are! No matter how old you are you still act as if you're this ignorant teenager. No wonder you work in a high school."

"I have a very important position here!" Sharon cried defiantly.

"That you were willing to risk by having an affair with a man half your age!" Lori screamed.

"So that's why you killed Kichiro?" Alberta asked rhetorically. "To save your sister's reputation."

"He left me no choice," Lori revealed. "He was going to ruin Sharon's life. He was going to finish what Jonas had started."

"*Per nascondersi a vista,*" Alberta muttered to herself. "All this time the truth was right in front of our noses."

"You killed Jonas, too?" Jinx asked. "But why?"

"Because Jonas was the other man from Sharon's past," Alberta answered. "But he also wanted to be the man in Sharon's present and future."

"I told you not to move back to this stupid town, Sharon, but no, you wouldn't listen to me," Lori ranted. "Because none of the advice I ever gave you was any good!"

"David wanted to move back," Sharon protested. "And when I was offered this job how could I say no?"

"In a million different ways!" Lori screamed. "But no, you had to move to the one town where your ex-lover just happened to live. It was like you were deliberately looking for trouble. And guess what? You found it!"

"So Jonas wanted to rekindle your romance with you, Sharon?" Jinx asked.

"Yes," she admitted. "I told him that I was happily married, and for a while he believed it."

"Until he caught you fooling around with Kichiro," Alberta added. "And then he blackmailed you."

"Which is when I moved back to town," Lori said. "It

was obvious that someone had to put a stop to all this nonsense before Jonas blabbed the truth and then Sharon's life would really spin out of control. It was bad enough that she was having an affair with a cop who was barely out of high school himself."

"I loved Kichiro!"

"No you didn't!" Lori replied. "You just liked having sex with a much younger man because your husband hasn't touched you in years."

"I thought you said you had a good marriage?" Alberta asked.

"Alberta, don't be so naïve," Lori said. "You should recognize a sham marriage, you had your own."

"What?"

"Don't look so shocked, research—forensic and otherwise—is my job," Lori reminded her. "I've done my research on you and if you haven't noticed, our friend Vinny likes to talk."

Embarrassed, Alberta kept her focus on Lori, refusing to look over at Jinx, who she knew was doing her best to remain silent. Alberta knew the kind of marriage she had and to herself never embellished, romanticized, or lied. But hearing the truth spoken out loud by a virtual stranger was a completely different story and left her feeling vulnerable and ashamed. She hated the feeling and hated that her negative, self-destructive emotions were linked to her dead husband, who had brought her so many years of agita while he was alive.

"At least I stood by my husband," Alberta finally said, knowing that such a decision could not be considered a major accomplishment. "And didn't wind up being the reason that two men were killed."

"Why don't you fill in the few remaining blanks left, Sharon?" Jinx asked. "Just so we can all be on the same page."

"I made the mistake of telling Lori that I saw Jonas watching me and Kichiro using the tree house to . . . to . . ."

"Have sex," Lori finished. "We're all adults here, isn't that right, Berta?"

Alberta winced at hearing Lori pronounce the word "adult" the same affected way Sharon did and flashed back to when they were all badmouthing and making fun of Sharon at her kitchen table when Lori was their dinner guest. Alberta knew that she would be furious if she overheard people mocking Helen, so she knew how angry Lori must be.

"Jonas told me that he had waited long enough for me and that if I didn't meet him in the tree house, he was going to tell David all about my affair," Sharon explained.

"So I dressed up like Sharon, used Kichiro's retractable ladder, which is really one helluva clever invention, got into the tree house, and waited for Jonas to take the bait, which of course he did," Lori added.

"So poor Jonas climbed up the ladder thinking he was finally going to have the rendezvous with Sharon that he had been dreaming about for decades," Alberta said.

"And instead he found a cheap imitation," Jinx finished.

Lori flicked her gun in Alberta's direction. "You might want to teach your granddaughter some manners."

Ignoring the taunt, Alberta wanted to focus on getting all the details of the story while Lori and Sharon were willing to do their very fine impersonation of the Chatterbox Sisters. "What did Jonas do when he found out he'd been set up?"

"He did what men always do. He turned into a coward and wanted to run away," Lori said. "He acted indignant and pathetic and vowed to make me pay for playing him for the fool. He was already a fool wasting his life pining after my sister!"

"Then how did you convince him to stay?" Alberta asked.

"By playing to his strength or in this case his weakness," Lori replied. "He was already a little drunk, guess he had to work up his courage with a few nips from the bottle, so I offered to share my bottle of white wine with him. Pitiful excuse for a man that he was, Jonas jumped at the chance."

"That's when you gave him the wine laced with the pesticide," Alberta said.

"The idiot didn't even notice any difference," Lori moaned. "And the pesticide does have quite a strong odor, but after a lifetime of heavy drinking your senses dull so he didn't suspect a thing. He just kept drinking and blabbering on about how Sharon was the only woman he ever loved and he was the only man who could ever make her happy. Such a stupid romantic I almost took a drink of wine so I didn't have to listen to him any longer."

"Then you pushed him out of the tree house to make it look like an accident," Jinx said.

"You didn't have to do that, Lori," Sharon whined. "Jonas would never have gone to David or the police. He was too much in love with me."

Lori lunged at her sister with such speed and ferocity that Sharon stumbled into the wall trying to get out of the way. "You were always such a bleeding heart! Thinking the best of people! Haven't I always told you that, down deep, people are no good?"

Thinking that this was a chance to turn the table of power, Jinx stepped forward and reached her arms out to try and grab Lori's wrist and wrestle the gun away from her. But Lori's peripheral vision was on red alert and she noticed the movement. At the last second, she whirled her arm back and the gun whacked Jinx on her temple.

"Jinx!" Alberta cried.

Jinx lay on the floor for a few seconds while a thin stream of blood ran down the side of her face.

"Jinx? *Mi nipotina*?" Alberta whispered. "Wake up, lovey."

It took a few seconds for Jinx to respond to Alberta's command, but finally she did and it was clear that she was stunned and would be bruised, but she wasn't fatally harmed.

"Thank God," Alberta gushed, hugging Jinx close to her body.

"Seriously, Lori?" Sharon shouted. "Is violence always the answer with you? I thought you would've learned your lesson after getting expelled from here."

"Shut up!" Lori yelled, her black eyes widening like the centers of two bull's-eyes.

Ignoring her sister, Sharon continued to reminisce about Lori's stormy past. "You always thought you'd get away with everything, no matter how vicious you were. The nuns proved too smart an enemy and they tossed you out of here after that incident in the lab with the frog and that boy."

Turning on Sharon, Lori shouted viciously in her face, "I told you to shut up!"

"What you did to that boy ... it was horrible!" Sharon screamed. "You deserved to be sent away!"

"You shouldn't talk like that to Loretta," Alberta chastised.

"Gram, her name is Lori, not Loretta."

"Lori's her nickname, a shortened version, isn't that right, Loretta?" Alberta asked.

The long thin line that was Lori's lips soon curved into a malicious smile. "You really are quite smart for an old lady, I must say. My elders have never given me much reason to demand my respect, but you're different."

"So are you," Alberta said, trying to keep her own smile on her face. "That's why you were forced to leave St. Winifred's."

Suddenly Lori's smile vanished and her jaw clenched and the rest of her face began to be gripped with fear. "You know about that?"

"I told you that these two know everything!" Sharon barked. "Nola said they were trying to become amateur detectives. I thought she was just bragging and exaggerating like she usually does, but she was right, they stick their noses in every place where they don't belong, like your past."

"Really?" Lori asked, trying desperately to control her mounting fear. "What else do you know of my past?"

"In Sloan's research he found an article that a young girl named Loretta was expelled from St. Winifred's for some lab experiment that went wrong," Alberta started. "And they made her go to another high school. You were the girl they sent to St. Joe's."

Jinx's face looked more frightened than Lori's. "Oh no!"

"What's wrong Jinx?" Alberta asked.

"St. Joe's isn't a high school, Gram, it's a mental institution."

"It is not a mental institution!" Lori cried. "It's . . . a . . . therapeutic . . . facility!"

Alberta and Jinx both stepped back by the sheer

force of Lori's outburst and grabbed each other's hands. "How do you know that, lovey?" Alberta asked.

"Father Sal told us that he counseled kids who were sent there, putting his own life at risk because some of them were violent and beyond reach."

Giggling and tilting her head from side to side, Lori confirmed Jinx's explanation, "Well, yeah, some of us were."

"Looks like some of you still are," Jinx replied.

Slumping in her chair behind her desk, Sharon looked deflated. "I tried to warn you. I told you both to leave."

"And now it's too late," Lori stated. "The only thing left to teach the two of you is what I learned at St. Joe's."

Alberta and Jinx looked at each other, one face whiter than the other. Alberta found the strength to speak first. "And what lesson would that be?"

"That once you've killed two people, what's two more?"

CHAPTER 23

Bambina vestita come una donna.

"**Y**ou don't have to do this, Lori," Alberta said. "We can help you."

A huge gale of laughter erupted from Lori's body. "You think I need help?" Lori asked. "I'm the one with the gun, Alberta, and you and your granddaughter are the ones with about fifteen minutes left to live. I think the HELP sign needs to be hung around your necks and not mine."

"Lori, we can get you the help you need, trust me," Alberta said, meaning every word she said. "What you did to Jonas and Kichiro, it wasn't your fault."

"So this is all my fault?" Sharon said, responding to Alberta's comment as if she were talking about ruining a recipe by using too much garlic instead of double homicide.

"Shut up, Sharon!" Lori snapped, giving voice to what Alberta was thinking. "This isn't about you, not every single thing in the world is about you! This is about me and what I've done. And sorry, Alberta, but premeditated murder is pretty hard to reconcile even for a nice old lady like you so save your postmortem sympathy spiel because I don't believe a word of what you're trying to sell."

Before Alberta could continue to try and appease Lori and speak to whatever portion of sanity and logic still resided within her brain, Jinx piped up. "One thing I don't understand is why you didn't just fake the toxicology report? You're the medical examiner, all you had to do was say that there were no drugs found in Jonas's system and he died from the accident. End of story."

"Because of the two of you, that's why!" Lori yelled. "My original plan was to falsify the report, but ever since you, your grandmother, and the rest of the old ladies in your family decided you wanted to be amateur sleuths, Vinny knows he's got to cover all his bases so he had two toxicology reports done, one by me and one by an outside service. I had no choice but to tell the truth because of your meddling."

Looking up toward heaven, Alberta said, "Thank you, Bocce."

"It is good to know that we're helping improve the police department," Jinx added.

"At the expense of your own life," Lori replied.

Sharon pounded her fist on her desk as if she was trying to corral an unruly classroom. "You didn't have to kill Jonas! I was handling him just fine."

"Like you were handling your cop boyfriend?" Lori asked. "Or your daughter."

Alberta still couldn't believe that Sharon knew Nola was her daughter all this time and allowed her to suffer in jail and with the possibility of spending her life behind bars for murders she didn't commit.

"Sharon, how could you let this happen to your own daughter?" Alberta asked.

"I gave Nola up over a quarter of a century ago so

she could have a better life, and she did," Sharon replied. "She was adopted by a lovely family so she isn't my daughter and I'm not her mother."

"*Incredible!*" Alberta exclaimed. "Just because you gave your child up for adoption doesn't change anything, she's still your child!"

"And in the end she's going to beat this, I know she will," Sharon declared, though neither Alberta nor Jinx was certain she believed what she was saying. "So why should I have to have some sentimental Lifetime TV reconciliation and uproot both our lives? There's no reason for it except to satisfy your twisted sense of morality."

"Don't you talk to my grandmother like that!"

"I will if she keeps judging me! I haven't done anything wrong."

"But you're the reason all of this is happening!" Alberta shouted. "Two men are dead because of you, an innocent woman is in jail, doesn't that mean anything to you?"

"Of course it does! But there isn't anything I can do to change things."

"If you can't change things, help us make sense of them. Why did your sister have to kill Kichiro?" Jinx disclosed. "He was in love with you, he might not have been happy about keeping the affair secret, but he knew that if he exposed your lie, he would destroy his own career and reputation, too."

"You know what you are Jinx?" Lori said. "*Bambina vestita come una donna.*"

Jinx didn't know what Lori said, but she had the distinct impression it wasn't praiseworthy. "Gram, can you translate?"

"She thinks because you're a good girl, you're naïve," Alberta said, clearly whitewashing the comment.

"No, I think you're a little girl who needs to grow the hell up," Lori corrected.

"Just because I'm not cheating on my husband or killing anyone who I think stands in my way, doesn't mean I'm a child!" Jinx shouted, defending herself.

"And just because you're standing next to your grandmother doesn't mean I won't shoot a bullet through your face!"

Instinctively, Alberta stood in front of Jinx. She knew it wouldn't prevent Lori from shooting them, but she wanted Lori to know that she wasn't the only one who would defend her flesh and blood with her last breath. By the way Lori smiled at Alberta, it was clear that she understood.

"You need to pay attention to your Grandma, Jinx," Lori announced. "She seriously knows more than most of us. In fact, maybe she can answer your question. Alberta, do you know why I had to kill Kichiro?"

Alberta didn't have to think very long to come up with an answer. "Because he was going to betray your sister."

"Give the old lady a gold star! And seriously, there has got to be one around here someplace," Lori said, cracking herself up. "But you're right, Kichiro was a cop first and a secret boyfriend second, isn't that right, Sharon?"

Shaking her head and waving her hands in front of her face as if to push away the truth from getting too close to her, Sharon replied, "No, that isn't right! He loved me too much to have ever done that."

"And *I'm* insane?" Lori screamed and asked the universe rhetorically. "He came over to your place and said that he was convinced you killed Jonas and he had to do the right thing and turn you in."

"He said that?" Alberta asked.

"He was drunk!" Sharon protested.

"That must've been the night he died, the night we taped him while he was at my apartment," Jinx said, not realizing she slipped and gave away a fact that should have remained buried.

"What do you mean you taped him?" Lori asked.

After Jinx reluctantly explained what they had done and that Nola was heard on the tape calling Kichiro and telling him to come meet her, she and Alberta thought Lori was going to go ballistic and possibly shoot them right there, but instead she thanked them.

"You're thanking us," Jinx said.

"You've put the nail in Nola's coffin," Lori said. "Or at least her prison cell. Here, I thought the police might figure out that I was the one who lured Kichiro back to the tree house and shot him, but now I can tell them that you have proof that Nola set a trap for him. That and the fact that they found her blood on his dead body will convince any jury that she was nothing more than a jilted girlfriend who shot her cheating lover."

"I hate to sound like a broken record," Jinx said. "But that's another thing I don't understand. How did Nola's blood get on Kichiro?"

"You should've paid a little more attention in biology," Lori said. "I cut Sharon's leg so her blood would get onto Kichiro's body, blood that contains the same DNA that's coursing through Nola's veins."

Alberta had heard enough. She had tried to find some shred of goodness in Lori's heart, she had tried to reason with her, and even play the complacent and willing hostage, but she had had it. She didn't love her sister, all she wanted to do was control her sister's life out of some morbidly obsessive desire to be powerful.

"You're like the sister from hell!" Alberta cried.

"You should know!" Lori cried back. "Sister Helen is hardly Rebecca of Sunnybrook Farm."

"You know you're never going to get away with this, right?" Jinx said. "It's going to be awfully hard to convince the police that Nola killed Jonas and Kichiro when we wind up dead."

"It'll be awfully hard for the police to know that the two of you are dead when they never find your bodies," Lori said. "It's a little chilly in here don't you think? Time to put a few more coals on the fire in the basement."

"Lori, no!" Sharon shouted.

"Sharon, yes! We need to get rid of these two so there's no trace of them for the police to find," Lori explained. "Now shut up and lead us downstairs to the boiler room so we can all get on with our lives. Well, at least two of us."

"I'm so sorry," Sharon said, starting to cry.

"*Do not apologize to them!* The only thing you should do is thank me for fixing the mess your life has become. Now take us downstairs!"

Lori aimed the gun at Sharon and she looked at her sister unsure if the woman would pull the trigger. Not wanting to risk it, Sharon instead pulled a clothes hook on the wall that suddenly turned her office into something out of a spy novel. A small portion of the wall rotated to open and revealed a secret passageway.

"*Dio mio!*" Alberta exclaimed.

"Exactly," Lori answered. "The nuns like to pray in front of their own private altar so this secret wall was built to give them access to their own mini-church where they could pray at any time of the day or when the kids raised holy hell and they needed to be reminded that there would be salvation when the class bell rang."

Sharon entered the passageway and Lori waved her gun to indicate that Jinx and Alberta should follow. They didn't need a second push to get them moving.

The room they entered looked like something out of the past and was both exquisite and eerie at the same time. It was only one room that contained a small altar, a statue of Jesus, his hands at his side, but outstretched, his hair and robe long, his expression peaceful and inviting. In front of the altar was a kneeling pew that could accommodate two people, and there was a metal pedestal, rusted in several places, holding a white porcelain bowl filled with holy water. A few unlit candles decorated the area, but otherwise it was empty. The room was for contemplation, not entertaining, so it had a serene quality about it, and Alberta felt like she was trespassing on sacred ground. Lori, however, treated the space like it was nothing more than a means to an end.

"Keep moving," she announced. "You'll have time to pray once we get downstairs."

Sharon led them down a staircase that turned once to the right and continued in the opposite direction and stopped only when she got to a steel door. She hesitated only slightly before entering the room that was clearly the sub-basement of the high school.

The room was swarming with musty smells, shadows, creaks, and sounds like metal hitting against metal. They were in the boiler room and in the distance they could hear the crackles of a fire.

"I'm guessing that you ladies are religious," Lori said.

Alberta answered for both of them, "Yes we are."

"Then welcome to your own private hell."

CHAPTER 24

Dove c'è la morte, c'è la vita.

As a child Alberta didn't believe in the concept of hell. She couldn't accept the fact that God would allow such a place to exist. As she grew older and the hardships and discomforts of life became reality, she began to realize like many others do that hell was actually right here on earth. Standing in the basement of St. Winifred's next to her frightened granddaughter and in front of a madwoman and her accomplice, she acknowledged that she was right. She had descended directly into the mouth of hell, and there was nothing that God or any angel could do to save her or Jinx. If she wanted to get herself and her granddaughter out of this predicament, she was going to have to rely on her own fortitude and strength. She could honestly say that she didn't care what happened to her, but there was no way she was going to let her granddaughter die in some disgusting high school basement.

"You may not believe me, Lori, but you are not going to get away with this," Alberta asserted. "I give you my word as a grandmother."

Hardly disturbed by Alberta's passionate declaration, Lori looked rather bored and merely smirked as her broad, thick shoulders rose up slightly. "And I give you my word as a sister who has spent her life protecting her sibling from her own bad choices and righting her wrongs since our parents were too preoccupied doing anything else instead of raising and taking care of their children that I will get away with killing you both just like I got away with killing the two fools who came before you." She waved her gun to the right and continued, "Now move over there so when I shoot you both we don't have to move you so far to throw you into the furnace."

Jinx clutched Alberta's hand and when she turned to look at her there were tears in her eyes. "Gram, I'm so sorry."

"Lovey, no . . ."

"I never imagined . . ."

"That you would get your grandmother killed?" Lori interrupted.

Ignoring the venomous comment, Alberta kissed Jinx's hand. "*Mi angelo,* do not give up, we survived a car crash, didn't we?"

"I should've just planted a bomb in the car instead of cutting your brake line," Lori commented. "But I didn't have enough time to gather all the necessary materials."

"It was you," Alberta said. "You could've killed all four of us! Four innocent lives!"

"I know!" Lori cried. "Talk about hitting the jackpot."

Stunned by Lori's apathy and loathing for human life, Alberta turned to the one person she thought could reach Lori. "Sharon, please, this isn't right and you know it. Your sister needs help."

"Don't you think I know that? But there is no way

that I'm going to help get my sister locked up in some state mental institution to live out her life on drugs and wrapped in a strait jacket," Sharon declared. "And you can't look me in the eye and say that you would allow the same thing to happen to your sister. Or your granddaughter. Or any one you loved for that matter!"

Alberta opened her mouth to protest, but her heart wouldn't let her speak. She knew that on some level Sharon was right. She hoped that if she were ever faced with such a decision that she would do the right thing and turn her sister, family member, or her friend over to the police and work diligently to make sure that justice and decency prevailed, and that she wasn't just throwing a loved one to the wolves, but she wasn't certain. If she were in Sharon's shoes she might be acting in the same way. It was a horrible thing to contemplate that she would let others suffer to allow her loved one to survive, but she would be a hypocrite to say that it was impossible.

"But think of Nola," Alberta pleaded. "Think of the damage you're doing to her."

"And when was the last time you thought of Lisa Marie?"

Lori's question slammed into Alberta's face and she felt like she had been punched. She even stepped back a few steps, stopping only when Jinx put her hand on her shoulder to stop her from moving.

"The truth hurts doesn't it?" Lori asked. "You treated your own daughter so reprehensibly that she had to move a thousand miles away to escape Mama Alberta's clutches in order to breathe easier so do not play the guilt card on Sharon, you're hardly mother of the year."

The truth like the flames flickering wildly in the furnace had a way of scalding and forcing a person to peel back layers of thickened skin that they've hidden behind for years. Alberta's heart was filled with shame, guilt, and self-loathing for all the mistakes she made in her life that caused her daughter to move so far away and disappear from her life. The only thing that filled Jinx's heart was vengeance.

"You're sick!" Jinx shouted.

She lunged forward and Alberta had to grab Jinx by the waist to pull her back. Jinx's arms reached out in front of her in a futile attempt to grab hold of Lori, but merely grabbed the empty air instead. Alberta pulled hard and was finally able to push Jinx behind her so in case Lori wanted to shoot she would hit her first.

Lori, however, had no intention of pulling the trigger just yet, she was laughing too hard. "Like I never heard that one before! In grammar school, high school, at St. Joe's, from my no-good husband, they all called me sick, crazy, insane, but that's because no one understands the bond between two sisters. Sharon likes to say that she doesn't understand or that she doesn't appreciate what I've done, but that isn't so, is it sister?"

In response, Sharon could only hang her head in shame and look away.

"Answer me!" Lori roared.

"I love you, Lori, you know I do, and I will do anything to help you, whatever you want, whatever you need, I will do, but I am begging you to stop this! This isn't right!"

"And neither is acting like a whore and cheating on your husband who has given you everything a man could!" Lori replied. "You could've been married to the piece of garbage I wound up with, but no, you had a good man! A man who gave you money, security, properties, never denied you a thing, and how do you repay him? By sleeping around with a man half your age."

"You wouldn't understand . . . David is not this saint you've made him out to be," Sharon protested.

"Has he ever cheated on you?" Lori asked.

Again, humility and shame washed over Sharon's face. "No," she whispered.

"Has he ever hit you? Does he abuse you emotionally? Do you have scars, invisible or otherwise?"

This time her voice was more defiant. "No, but—"

"There are no buts!" Lori shouted. "He's a good man and you betrayed him. Though I don't know why I expected anything less, you cheated on him before you were even married. You just couldn't help yourself, could you? You had to behave like a no-good gutter tramp and sleep with Jonas one last time so before you even said, 'I do,' to David you had to say, 'I'm pregnant,' to Jonas!"

"Jonas Harper is my father?"

The comment alone would have been shocking, but it was doubly shocking to see the person attached to the comment. A person who was supposed to be locked up in a prison cell. But before anyone could ask Nola why she was standing at the entrance of the boiler room on the steps leading up to the secret passageway that led to Sharon's office, Lori, rattled by the unexpected outburst, fired a shot in Nola's direction missing the young woman, but hitting a gas pipe instead.

An immediate hissing sound filled the small room accompanied by the smell of sulfur. With the furnace door open and flames flickering and dancing excitedly a few feet from the leaking gas pipe, the basement suddenly became an even worse place to be. Unfortunately, it was not a place that anyone was going to exit from any time soon.

"How can Jonas Harper be my father?" Nola asked.

It was the kind of question that could only be responded to by asking another question. "How did you get out of prison?"

When Jinx spoke, Nola turned her gaze away from Sharon and it was as if she was seeing her friend for the first time. Then she looked around the room and took in the scene in its entirety. "What is going on here?"

"Don't worry about that," Alberta said. "Sharon, do the right thing and let the girls go."

"No one's going anywhere," Lori said. "Not while I'm still in charge."

"Lori . . . in charge . . . with a gun?" Nola muttered. "Seriously, what's going on here?"

Before anyone could attempt to explain how the four of them ended up in a dungeon of sorts, Nola answered her own question. "I didn't realize they gave the medical examiner a gun, but that makes sense since you are part of the police force," she said. "I'm here doing police business, too . . . kind of."

"Kind of?" Jinx said. "I think you're going to have to explain yourself a little further."

Nola took a few more steps into the room, and if she was scared by what she was seeing she didn't show it. Alberta thought she looked more confident than she had in weeks. Unfortunately, she didn't think this was the most opportune time to recapture lost bravado.

"Sharon, I know who you are, I know that you're my mother," Nola confessed. "I've known all along and that's why I moved here to Tranquility in the first place after my parents died so I could be near you and get to know my real mother. And that's the reason I agreed to keep your secret about Kichiro. It wasn't because you're my boss and you knew I was short some college credits, it's because you're my mother. But this all has to stop now, it's gone too far. I don't know the details, but you've killed twice and even though you're my mother, I can't let you kill again."

Dumbfounded, Sharon didn't know what to say or which comment to address first, but Alberta didn't want Nola to hear the full truth just yet. She needed to stall for time.

"Nola, honey," Alberta said. "How did you break out of jail? Vinny couldn't have just let you out."

"Actually, he did."

"A *stunod* and incompetent!" Lori hissed. "I never liked that man."

After the commotion and individual outbursts died down, Nola explained how she acquired her freedom.

"Your sister and Joyce have been trying to reach the two of you for the past hour, and when you didn't respond to their calls and texts they got worried so they finally went to Vinny and told him everything that they know," Nola said.

"And what exactly does the rest of the Ferrara clan know?" Lori asked.

"That Sharon is my mother and she killed both Jonas and Kichiro," Nola explained. "They know Kichiro was your secret lover and figure you killed him in a sort of crime of passion. They don't know why you killed Jonas, but now I do. He was my father and you were afraid he was going to reveal that piece of information and ruin your life. That's why you convinced me to reverse the restraining order I had against him."

"So Sharon did make you do that," Alberta said.

"She told me Jonas was harmless," Nola replied. "But he was actually the opposite, he was the most dangerous man you knew. You were afraid he would get angry and reveal the truth."

"You're half right," Sharon corrected. "Jonas didn't know you were his daughter. I couldn't risk him finding out so I wanted to keep the relationship between the two of you civil and not raise any red flags."

"I'm sorry you're so ashamed of me."

"Oh Nola—" Sharon started.

"But I convinced Vinny to let me out so I could get you to confess," Nola said. "I know that you didn't mean to kill them and that they were accidents or something so let me help you. Bruno is willing to be your lawyer, between the two of us we can get you off and you can put all of this behind you."

"Poor sweet . . . *stupid* Nola," Lori interrupted. "I guess I shouldn't have expected you to have a smart kid since you were so screwed up your entire life."

"What . . . what is she talking about?" Nola asked, confused by the vitriol and familiarity of Lori's tone.

"Nola, listen to me," Alberta said. "Sharon didn't kill anyone, your aunt did."

"My aunt?" Nola said, now even more confused. "I don't have an aunt."

"Yes you do," Lori said. "You've got the baddest aunt of them all."

The shock of Lori's comment hit Nola so hard, she actually stumbled, and Alberta and Jinx had to grab her arms to steady her and keep her upright.

"Jonas was my father and you're . . . you're my aunt?" Nola asked. "And you killed my father and Kichiro?"

"Yes, yes, yes . . . and yes," Lori replied.

Slowly, Alberta and Jinx noticed a change come over Nola. Her spine lengthened and her shoulders dropped. Her expression lost its look of surprise and fear and was replaced with steely determination. "You killed both of them? You deliberately killed Jonas . . . my *father* and Kichiro, my friend? Did you know this, Sharon?"

Sharon tried to back away from Nola, but there was nowhere for her to go unless she wanted to try and break through the cement blocks that formed the basement walls. "There was nothing I could do. You don't know Lori. Once she makes up her mind, there's no stopping her."

"You're right, I don't know Lori and clearly I don't know you either," Nola said. "All this time I thought you were protecting yourself, at least that I could understand, but you were protecting your sister and letting your daughter take the blame for it all. How could you do that to me?"

Like a sudden inferno, Nola was engulfed with rage and without thinking backed up and pounded her fist against the wall. Instead of writhing in the pain she must have felt when her fist slammed against the metal gas pipe, she was gripped with inspiration. She yanked the loose pipe off the wall and swung it at Sharon. Her swing was wild and she missed, but in order to avoid the impact, Sharon leaped to her right and landed less than a foot from the furnace.

"Knock it off, Nola, I'm warning you!" Lori shouted.

With the bulk of the pipe torn off, gassy smoke started to fill up the small room making it difficult to see and breathe. Worse, the hissing seemed to increase in volume so it was becoming difficult to hear anything quieter than a shout.

"Listen to her, Nola, please!" Alberta cried.

"I'm done listening!" Nola screamed. "That's all I've ever done my entire life and look where it's gotten me!"

Still looking at Alberta, Nola swung the pipe and

this time connected with Lori. The woman went flying in one direction while her gun went flying into the other.

As if psychically linked, Lori and Sharon sprang into action at the same time, both leaping up to grab the gun. But Alberta and Jinx were just as connected and while Alberta lunged to tackle Lori, Jinx leaped forward and landed on top of Sharon. In the middle of them both stood Nola, not entirely sure which group to join.

Just as Sharon was about to grab the gun, Jinx slammed her forearm onto her wrist and the woman cried out in pain. She managed to throw Jinx off of her body by raising her arm and thrusting her entire body backward so Jinx slid away from her until she rammed into the furnace door.

Nola was about to run toward Jinx to help her friend, but saw that Sharon was crawling on her hands and knees to get the gun so she spun on her heels and moved in Sharon's direction. She grabbed her elbow and yanked it away a split second before she was about to reach the gun and pulled her arm back. Nola lost her footing and fell backward, but didn't let go of Sharon so the woman fell on top of Nola, the both of them careening into the cement wall.

On the other side of the room, Alberta was doing her best to keep Lori on the ground, but the woman's larger, sturdier frame was proving difficult to manage. Alberta surprised herself and used every tactic she could think of: she pulled Lori's hair, she dug her fingernails into her arm, she pressed the heel of her shoe into her shin, but each action only seemed to fuel Lori's fury and give her greater strength. Finally, she let out a guttural cry and flexed her back, and Alberta found herself airborne and didn't stop until she crashed into a

large metal cabinet. She felt the handles of the draw-
ers ram into her back and bolts of pain rushed up and
down her spine. The only thing that made the pain go
away was the fear that replaced it when she saw Lori
aim her gun at Nola.

"If you think I'm going to let you betray your
mother, think again!"

Alberta wasn't sure if it was primal or maternal instinct, but she didn't care, all that mattered was that
when Lori pulled the trigger, Sharon jumped up to
shield Nola's body taking the bullet to her chest that
was meant to kill her daughter.

"Noooo!"

Lori's scream echoed through the small room and
along with the incessant hissing of the gas pipe made
the sound of the second gunshot almost silent. Alberta
and Jinx weren't truly certain that a second shot was
fired until they saw Lori's body slump to the ground
and blood slowly ooze through her blouse.

"Vinny!" Alberta screamed. "You don't know how
happy we are to see you."

"I'm not even going to ask what you're all doing
down here," Vinny said. "But luckily that secret door
was left open or else we would've never found you."

"We?" Jinx asked.

Scurrying into the room was Helen closely followed
by Joyce.

"Do you think we were going to let the two of you
have all the fun?" Helen quipped.

"Oh, Aunt Helen."

Jinx ran into her aunt's arms and embraced her
tightly. "It's okay, it's all going to be okay," Helen said.

As Vinny called for an ambulance, Joyce helped Alberta up off the floor. "Looks like you're going to be in
a little bit of pain tomorrow morning."

"At least there's going to be a tomorrow morning," Alberta said.

"That's my Alfie, always looking on the bright side."

As they looked around the room they saw that, unfortunately, not everyone was going to have a bright, happy ending.

"Mom . . . Mom . . . stay with me . . . please."

Nola cradled Sharon's bloodstained body in her arms and was trying to will her mother to hold on and keep fighting. The sounds from the pipes, the distant whir of the ambulance, and the tears made it difficult to hear exactly what Nola and Sharon were saying to each other, and Alberta thought that was appropriate since some things that are shared between a mother and daughter were meant to be private. The same could be said for what was shared between two sisters, and as much as everyone wanted to turn away they couldn't.

Lying in Nola's arms, Sharon reached out her hand to Lori, who tried desperately to grab hold of her sister. Refusing to let her sister leave this earth without connecting with her one last time, Lori used every ounce of strength she had to crawl closer to Sharon. She grabbed her hand just as Sharon took her last breath.

Jinx fought the urge to wrap her arms around Nola, knowing that she needed these few moments to say goodbye to her mother so instead she and Helen joined Alberta and Joyce, who were standing next to Vinny. Without realizing it or agreeing, they all bowed their heads and started to pray silently. For the woman who just died and the two she left behind, both devastated in their own way by her death. Their relationships in life were incredibly complicated and not easily understandable or reconciled, but death brought with it a simplicity and finality that sometimes made things clearer. It stripped away everything that was unnecessary and left only what was important.

Alberta knelt down and placed Lori's hand on top of Sharon's, they were together again, their bond unbroken. "*Dove c'è la morte, c'è la vita,*" Alberta whispered while making the sign of the cross.

And she was right, where there's death, there's always life.

EPILOGUE

La famiglia e tutto.

The crisp autumn air seemed to have a cleansing effect on everything it touched. The sky was cloudless, a light azure color, so perfect it was almost fake. Even though most of the trees were stripped of their leaves, Tranquility Park radiated energy, filled with the sounds of crackling leaves stirred by the wind, the chirps and coos of defiant or lazy birds who had yet to fly south for the coming winter, and the smells of roses and daisies and lilies combined with the faint smell of burning chimneys to create a fragrance that straddled all seasons. Although the park had been witness to two recent deaths, life emerged from every nook and cranny.

Underneath the tree house was a blanket of flowers placed there by residents in memory of their fallen brothers, Jonas and Kichiro. It didn't matter if people didn't know them personally, the need to honor their lives and acknowledge their deaths was universal, visceral, and the sight the bevy of flowers created was beautiful to behold, it made the tree house look as if it were floating in the air. When Alberta and Jinx saw the memorial it took their breath away.

"*Dio mio,*" Alberta gasped. "*È bellissimo.*"

"Jonas and Kichiro touched a lot of lives."

"Yes they did . . . I hope that they knew that."

Alberta and Jinx added their own flowers to the overflowing display and knelt side by side on the grass to offer silent prayers.

"Do you believe in heaven, Gram?"

"I do." When Jinx didn't comment, Alberta knew she was struggling with the concept. "You have doubts?"

"I don't want to, but yes, I do. I just don't know."

Alberta wrapped her arm around Jinx's shoulder. "I did too, but they've gone away. And at least you're not adamant that there's nothing after this life here on earth, so there's hope for you yet, lovey."

Jinx laughed in her grandmother's arms and almost felt guilty for feeling so happy when she was kneeling at the threshold of such a solemn ceremonial landscape. But she couldn't feel guilty because she was part of the reason that the real murderer had been caught. She just wished there hadn't been so much collateral damage.

"How's Nola?" Alberta asked.

"As well as can be expected," Jinx replied. "I mean her entire world has literally been turned upside down. She found out her biological father was a man she'd known for years and never really gave the time of day, and then she finds out he and her friend died at the hands of an aunt she never knew she had."

"Poor thing, she must feel all alone," Alberta mused.

"She does," Jinx admitted. "I told her that she has all of us and she said she's very grateful, but all she really wanted was to get to know her mother, and now she's never going to get the chance."

"At least she knows that her mother loved her."

"Are we sure about that?" Jinx questioned.

"You saw what Sharon did," Alberta said. "When push came to shove, Sharon made the ultimate sacrifice for Nola. It's what any mother would do for her child."

"Would you do that for my mother, Gram?"

Alberta was surprised by the question. It had almost become an unspoken rule that neither one of them would ever mention Lisa Marie, keep the elephant in the room silent. But even though she was surprised, she didn't hesitate in her response. "Without question," Alberta replied. "Your mother and I, we have our differences, but we love each other, don't you ever forget that. And I would give my life to save hers. Same way I'd give my life to save yours, you're my family, and *la famiglia e tutto.*"

Smiling, Jinx replied, "It is everything, isn't it?"

"What else do you have in this world, truly, except your family?" Alberta said. "We're lucky to be friends with our family, to want to be with the people whose blood we share, not everybody has that."

In the distance they saw the figure of a man walking toward them.

"And then there are some people who don't share your blood," Alberta observed. "Who are as close to you as any family member could be."

Without saying a word, Vinny knelt down next to them and laid a beautiful bouquet of red roses, white lilies, and blue carnations, a fitting tribute to a policeman who spent his life upholding truth, justice, and the American way.

"How are you doing, Vinny?"

"Not so good, Alfie," Vinny admitted and had to swallow hard to continue speaking. "He really was like the son I never had."

"Did you ever tell him that?"

Laughing, Vinny shook his head, "No, I never said those exact words, but I think he knew. One time after we got called in to stop an armed robbery, one of the perps got nervous and started firing his gun, willy-nilly, it was a miracle that no one got shot. When we were riding back to the police station we were both pretty quiet until Kichiro said, "We got lucky today, Pops." He never called me that before or after that, but it was nice to hear it at least once in my life. If only he had confided in me about the whole Sharon thing, maybe none of this would've happened."

Alberta had never heard her friend speak so vulnerably, and she knew that he might never do it again so she didn't add her own words. Anything she said would have just been clutter so she patted his hand for a moment and hoped he understood that he was not alone in this world. And neither was Alberta, nor would she ever be. Helen and Joyce entered the park from the opposite side and knelt down next to Jinx. Joyce placed a small bouquet of tiny red roses on the ground, while Helen began to rummage through her pocketbook.

"Are you going to pull a bunch of flowers out of your purse?" Alberta asked.

"I don't like flowers," Helen replied, still searching. "They attract bugs, they smell, and they get all dry and crumbling when they die."

"Also too, they're expensive."

"Shut up, Joyce," Helen said. "I'd rather offer something that might bring Jonas and Kichiro some peace."

Helen pushed some flowers out of the way in order

to make a little clearing in the grass. When she was done, she placed a beautiful string of white rosary beads on the grass, then bent over and kissed the medallion of the Blessed Mother in the center of the beads. Alberta shook her head and thought to herself, *my sister will never cease to amaze me.* When Helen spoke, Alberta knew she was right.

"I feel sorry for Lori."

"Really, Aunt Helen?"

"You can visit her in the state pen where she'll be for the rest of her life once she gets out of ICU," Vinny said.

"Don't you think she belongs in a mental institution?" Alberta asked.

"She might wind up there after they get through with the evaluation," Vinny said. "But first she'll be sent to prison; after all, she did kill three people including her sister."

Dismissing Vinny's comment with a wave of her hand, Helen explained, "That was an accident, she was trying to kill Nola."

"Helen! I know you don't like the girl very much, but that's harsh even for you," Joyce said.

"I don't want to see the kid dead," Helen said. "Banned from the theater maybe . . . What I mean is that in her own delusional way Lori was protecting her sister, that's why she shot at Nola and that's why she killed Jonas and Kichiro. I'm not saying it's right, but I'm saying I feel sorry for her because it's what every one of us would do. There's nothing we wouldn't do in order to protect our family."

No one could dispute Helen's logic because everyone knew she was right. They knew that what Lori did was wrong and reprehensible and punishable, but it was also understandable. However, there was one person gathered on the grass who was still a little confused as to how Lori turned out to be the Tree House Killer.

"Alfie?"

"Yes, Vin."

"I'm a little fuzzy on the specifics as to why Lori was pointing a gun at Sharon. Do you mind filling me in on all the details maybe over a plate of your lasagna?"

"Don't worry," Alberta said, wrapping an arm around Vinny's waist. "I'll tell you everything you need to know to make it look like you solved the crime all by yourself. But we both know the truth."

"And what exactly would that be?" Vinny asked cautiously.

"That this mystery wouldn't have been solved without the Ferrara Family Detective Agency," Alberta said.

She smiled impishly at Vinny, who couldn't help but return a friendly hug. She then looked over at Jinx, Helen, and Joyce, and her heart was filled with pride, joy, and promise. This was her family. It wasn't perfect, but it was hers.

And like Alberta always said, family was everything.

Please turn the page for recipes
from Alberta's kitchen!

Recipes from the
Ferrara Family Kitchen

JINX'S VEGAN STUFFED PEPPERS

For the Sauce
2 28-ounce cans of fire-roasted diced tomatoes
4 cloves garlic, minced—or 2 if you're like Freddy,
    who says, "I like garlic, but garlic doesn't like me!"
2 tablespoons olive oil
¼ teaspoon chili flakes—or disregard this entirely if
    you're like Freddy, who says chili likes him even
    less than garlic.
1 teaspoon salt
According to Gram, you need "a realla gooda pincha"
    black pepper, whatever that means!
1 teaspoon dried oregano

For the Peppers
6 peppers, cut in half and seeded to make 12 halves
2 cups cooked brown rice—never, ever use white rice!
2 tablespoons olive oil
2 cloves garlic, minced (see above if you want to cut
    this in half)
1 large shallot, 2 celery stalks, 3 zucchini—all diced
1½ cups finely chopped broccoli and kale
1 cup of walnuts and black olives, chopped
As much parsley and basil as you want for the garnish

For the Sauce
1. Heat the olive oil in a medium sauce pot and when
    hot add the garlic and sauté. When the smell makes

Freddy leave the kitchen, I add the tomatoes, salt, pepper, chili flakes, and oregano letting it all simmer and thicken for about 40 minutes. Once hot, add the garlic and sauté until softened and fragrant. Add the canned tomatoes, salt, pepper, chili flakes, bay leaf, and oregano. Bring to a simmer and simmer for about 40–45 minutes, until thickened.

2. Once it's done, puree about ¾ of the sauce in a blender and then return it to the pot to mix with the rest of the sauce.

For the Peppers

You should start this while the sauce is cooking. Gram says, "One of the keys to good cooking is all in the timing." And she should know!

1. Preheat the oven to 400 degrees.
2. Cook the brown rice and set aside 2 cups.
3. Cut peppers in half from top to bottom, seed them, and brush them with oil, salt, and pepper. Lay them cut side down on a greased baking sheet and cook in the oven for 15 minutes.
4. Heat 2 tablespoons of olive oil in a sauté pan and when hot add the shallot, celery, and garlic, and cook until it's soft, but not brown. Add, the broccoli and cook for an additional 3–5 minutes. Add the zucchini and kale and cook for 5 more minutes. Everything should be super tender by now.
5. Finally, add in the walnuts and olives and heat it a little bit longer.

Now the Fun Part: Stuffing the Peppers!

1. Spread a layer of sauce on the bottom of a large baking dish and place the peppers cut side up.

2. Mix the vegetables and rice, ½ of the sauce, and some chopped parsley and basil in a large bowl and then stuff those peppers!
3. Cover the peppers with some sauce, then cover the dish with foil and bake for 20–25 minutes.

ALBERTA'S ITALIAN STUFFED SHELLS— ENOUGH FOR THE WHOLE FAMILY

2 tablespoons olive oil
1 teaspoon tomato paste
1 teaspoon dried basil
1 small diced onion
3 minced garlic cloves—and do not listen to Jinx, you can never, ever have enough garlic!
1 32-ounce can whole, peeled tomatoes
1 pound ground beef
1 cup cottage cheese/1 cup ricotta/2 cups shredded mozzarella/½ cup shredded Parmesan—if you need to use dairy-free cheese, do not make this recipe, it'll be terrible so just go make something else.
18–24 jumbo shell noodles, cooked and drained— they're easy to cook, just read the instructions on the box or ask your grandmother.

1. Preheat the oven to 350.
2. Heat olive oil in a pot, add onion and cook for 10 minutes. Then add garlic and chili flakes and cook for another minute. Add tomato paste and fry for 1 minute. Add tomatoes and basil and simmer for 20 minutes.
3. While this is simmering, cook the beef in a skillet in the rest of the olive oil and set it aside to cool.
4. Puree the tomato sauce and combine the beef, cot-

tage cheese, ricotta, and half of the mozzarella and Parmesan.

5. Spread a thin layer of tomato sauce in a casserole dish, stuff the shells with the beef mixture, and line them up in the dish, topping with lots and lots of sauce and the leftover mozzarella and Parmesan.

6. Cover with foil, bake for 15 minutes, remove the foil, and continue baking until the top is slightly browned.
   Mangia!

JINX AND JOYCE'S NO-BAKE VEGAN TIRAMISU

1 13.5-ounce can of coconut milk—not skim and it has to be cold

2 teaspoons of stevia powder or whatever sugar substitute you like to use

½ cup walnuts, soaked in water

10 teaspoons of water

3 shots coffee liqueur—Kahlúa's our fave

1 package of ladyfingers—Schär's are gluten-free!

1 cup of your favorite flavored vodka—pick whichever one you want, it's vodka so there's no way you can go wrong.

10 tablespoons coffee

Cocoa powder

1. Scoop out the hardened coconut cream from the top of the can. Don't do like Aunt Joyce did the first time and shake the can because then the cream mixes with the coconut water and you have to go out and buy another can of coconut milk.

2. Whip the coconut cream with the stevia powder and put it in the fridge.

3. Blend the walnuts, water, and Kahlúa until it's creamy.
4. Soak the ladyfingers in the Kahlúa or the vodka or both! Then scoop the ladyfingers, which will have broken up, into the bottom of six glasses.
5. Mix half of the coconut whipped cream with the walnut mixture and scoop into the glasses, add some more ladyfingers if you have any left over, and top with the rest of the whipped cream and dust the cocoa powder on top of it.
6. Leave it in the fridge overnight and enjoy a very decadent breakfast!

HELEN'S FAVORITE DESSERT—SICILIAN CASSATA CAKE (WITH A LITTLE HELP FROM ENTENMANN'S)

⅓ cup dried currants
5 tablespoons Marsala wine
1 16½-ounce can pitted cherries—do not get rid of the cherry syrup!
1 pint ricotta cheese
¼ cup white sugar
2 tablespoons heavy cream
1 12-ounce Entenmann's pound cake
12 1-ounce semisweet chocolate squares
1 cup unsalted butter

1. Combine currants and 2 tablespoons of wine in a small bowl and soak for 15 minutes. Drain the cherries, cutting them up, and then drain the currants.
2. Puree ricotta cheese, sugar, the rest of the wine, and the heavy cream until smooth. Mix in currants and cherries in a larger bowl.
3. Cut the pound cake lengthwise into 3 horizontal layers, placing one layer on a platter. Spread half of

the filling over it, place a second layer, and spread the rest of the filling over that. Then, you guessed it, top with the third layer of pound cake.

4. Refrigerate for about 2 hours so it can get firm.
5. Make the chocolate frosting by combining the cherry syrup, semisweet chocolate, and ¼ cup of wine in a saucepan. Stir over low heat until the chocolate melts, then remove the heat. Add unsalted butter and let it melt. Put the frosting in the fridge so it can thicken.
6. Put 1 cup of chocolate frosting into a pastry bag— do not let Alberta do this, she's terrible at it—and spread the rest over the sides and the top of the cassata. Use the pastry bag to decorate the top of the cake with swirls and rosettes.
7. Refrigerate the whole shebang for a few more hours.

Grab These Cozy Mysteries
from
Kensington Books